AFTER THE *storm*

written by Dianna Hardy

After the Storm
Four Eye of the Storm Novelettes

Published by Satin Smoke Press, February, 2026
First Edition | ISBN 978-1-916840-14-0

Written in British English.

Designed by Bitten Fruit Books

A CIP catalogue record for this book is available from the British Library.

Satin Smoke Press
(an imprint of Bitten Fruit Books)
South Hampshire, UK

www.satinsmoke.com

Reviews for After the Storm

"... packed full of emotion and story line ... Blanket of Snow has the feel of a full length novel wrapped up into about an hour long read." – *Rhonda McGuire (for Blanket of Snow)*

"...it was a joy to read it. I'm really looking forward to more from the Surrey pack in the future!"
– *Clare's Little Book Obsession (for Blanket of Snow)*

"This is a beautiful novelette that explores themes of trauma, change and healing, of facing your shadow self and learning to let go. The relationship between Lydia, Taylor, Ryan and Lawrence is still so strong and nuanced; the way they communicate with each other, love and trust one another, even when they don't completely understand everything that goes on in one of their minds, how they are still fully present in their relationship, is such a wonderful portrayal of a polyamorous relationship." – *Ninfa Hayes (for Twisted Roots)*

"This ... is about healing. It is a personal glimpse into how Ryan has been dealing with life after the traumatic events of the series, and ultimately how hard healing can be. How it can't be done alone, and shouldn't be." – *Elizabeth Morgan, author of the Blood series (for Sins of the Father)*

"My affection for this series grows deeper with each revisit. I can't seem to get enough of it. I could happily reside in this world alongside Lydia, Lawrence, Ryan, and Taylor for eternity."
– *Nancy Allen at The Avid Reader*
(Review for Jewels of the Crown)

After the Storm collates all four novelettes in the After the Storm mini-series and should be read after *Reign of the Wolf*, the last book in the *Eye of the Storm* series. For a full understanding of the layers to the stories, it is recommended you also read *Blood Shadow* and *Aftershock*.

BLANKET OF SNOW

CHAPTER ONE

The skin of her feet had toughened over the past few months. Even in human form she couldn't feel the prickles of the twigs and stones that lay on the forest floor under the few remaining orange leaves that had hung onto autumn.

She'd wanted to shift and run as her wolf – her wolf and her were truly one now – but, such were the way of dreams, this comfort had been denied to her for reasons that would only ever be known to the ether.

So, as a woman and on two legs, she sped through her home – her home; it was hers *– every tree for the next half a mile, one she would be familiar with; know off by heart, by scent, by look, by feel... And more than that, she was becoming attuned to the earth beneath her. She was beginning to sense the coming of new growth – flowers; saplings – like the snowdrops that would be the first to bloom any day now. They stirred inches beneath the soil that squelched through her toes as she sprinted; the slight change in scent that heralded their birth was in the air.*

Yet, a sense of doom clenched her heart. She knew what she was looking for today, and only half of her wanted to find it. The other half of her wanted to stop running; freeze the scene. Her wolf would never let that happen, and so she sped on, letting her wolf lead the way. She owed her that. Her wolf had saved her life more than once.

Far too soon, the trees she knew so well ended. She slowed her pace to a jog, wondering if she should stop entirely, then found herself doing just that, though for reasons other than confusion. It was horror that arrested her.

Although much more used to running naked than she had been since her first change over six months ago, nudity was never a suit best worn amid the dead. And that's where she stood.

Tears filled her eyes as she took in headstone after headstone protruding from the grass and ferns that protected the trees. Hendrickson was the first name to fill her vision, and then, next to it, Amelia.

The tears fell. It was all too fresh. She could still remember how her gut had turned – could still hear Ryan's wretched cry – the moment they'd discovered the siblings' frozen bodies and realised their fate.

Lydia turned away, her breath hitching, only to find Brendan's name glaring at her from the headstone she now faced. Grief washed over her, anew. Only six months ago...

She'd pondered, too often, whether he'd been tortured before brutally murdered; whether he'd screamed; whether he'd passed out from pain. Guilt gnawed her every time the image of his dismembered limbs flashed through her mind.

Stepping away from his grave, she walked, backwards, unable to completely pull her eyes away from the etched date of his death. Only when she stumbled, did she look away to see what had tripped her.

A cry she failed to muffle left her lips: Richard's right hand lay next to her foot. Bile rose, and she quickly turned before she lost control of her stomach, only to come face to face with...

Sarah Harper, beloved wife of—

"No." She spun around, reaching out for the nearest tree trunk to hold her up as she closed her eyes against the grave she now faced: Sarah's. And Taylor's name was one she could not bear to see on a gravestone, no matter that he was very much alive and very much hers.

He felt Sarah's passing greatly, she knew that. But he was her husband now, right along with Ryan and Lawrence, and while her marriage to Lawrence was the only one that human law acknowledged, it made her stated commitment to Ryan and Taylor no less so. In some ways, it made it more solid. Even without words and gestures, they were mated, and that went beyond any marriage on paper.

She could not *see his name on a grave.*

She needed to leave; get the hell away from this burial ground.

"It's just a dream," she muttered, as if that ever worked. "Only a dream. Sarah isn't buried here; Brendan isn't buried here..." Even Hendrickson and Amelia were not buried here. They had been laid in the earth with the rest of their family in Sussex, where their grandparents had remained with their original pack, and where their parents had also been buried many years ago.

Lydia staggered forward, giving up her tree trunk crutch, but almost tumbled into a sturdy oak. One foot in front of the other would eventually get her out – that's all she had to do. One step ... two steps...

But try as hard as she might, she couldn't escape the next marker. Nor could she do anything other than sink to her knees before the grey cenotaph – because he was *buried here: her father.*

James Philip Martin

And she suddenly remembered why she'd gone running through the woods in the first place; what she'd been looking for. "Dad..."

She reached out and touched the cold stone. Someone replied, but it was not her dad.

"Sweetheart?"

God ... *a thousand memories flooded her at the sound of the voice she'd not heard in over ten years. With fresh tears streaming, she looked over her dad's gravestone to find her mother standing, staring at her with unmatched affection and a smile on her face. A little shorter than Lydia, her blonde hair framed her face in soft waves that fell just as she remembered.*

Lydia looked far more like her father, but her violet eyes, she'd inherited from her mother. Right now, they mirrored hers in all ways but for the fact her mother's were dry.

"Mum." With difficulty, she pulled herself to standing, and then the steps came easily. One, two, three, four... She fell into her mother's outstretched arms, her warming scent as it had always been – lavender and cookies. "I've missed you," she mumbled into her neck, and the words became a wail and a sob, and then many sobs she couldn't hold back.

Her mum just held her, unperturbed by her messy, embarrassing display. "I've missed you, too."

"This ... isn't real," she squeezed out between gulps.

"It's real enough."

She wanted the moment to last – certainly for longer than the minute she was afforded – but a sudden chill befell her, causing the skin on her arms to pimple. Still nestled into the crook of her mother's neck, she looked up at the darkening sky. It wasn't night, but it might as well have been. Urgency rose. "You're why I came here. You and Dad."

"I know."

"I need you."

"You're going to be fine, Lydia."

"No, you don't understand."

"I do, sweetheart."

"I can't do this."

"You can."

"It's too big."

"You're bigger."

"No." She shook her head vigorously, aware she sounded like a defiant child. Her eyes moved from the sky to the woodland floor she stood on. So much blood had been spilled. "There's so much death."

Her mum pulled back.

Cold seeped in, replacing the heat of her hug.

"To make room for so much life to come."

"I can't do it again."

Hard metal pressed into her hand.

Lydia looked down at the object her mum had placed there.

"Why haven't you danced?"

Blinking her tears away, she held up the key to the dance studio that Lawrence had given her. It seemed like a lifetime ago – so much had happened since then – but it had only been half a year.

"You were so very good at it. You were such a natural."

"I lost..." She didn't finish the sentence. What she'd lost couldn't be put into words. "I tried. I couldn't."

Her mother smiled, then let out a small sigh. "You should try again."

"It's too late."

"Never. And you've watched him dance, I know you have."

Yes. She had watched Lawrence dance. With a smile on her lips and a longing in her heart. What a simply beautiful sight it was; the regain of his legs, a miracle he was grateful for every single day.

He'd asked her to dance, too, but had been patient with her mysterious refusal and had never pushed the issue.

"It wasn't too late for him," said her mother.

"He's planning shows."

Her mum laughed. "Wastes no time, does he? You shouldn't either."

Again, she shook her head. "You don't understand."

"Oh, I do. I understand what it is you don't want to see, but you must. Over there."

Here? *Alarmed, Lydia searched her mother's gaze and followed it.* No ... no, no, no.

Sarah's house stood to her left, appearing as if by magic. It hadn't been there before. It wasn't Sarah she saw in her mind's eye, though, but Taylor, choking up blood as his body trembled in convulsions; his veins – dark blue with poison – bulging. "No."

"You need to go in."

Every sound seemed to fade as she looked at the house: birds, wind, and the rustle of leaves; the scurrying animals and the small twigs that snapped under their meanderings... all gone. The silence was like a tomb of its own. "I don't. I won't."

Her mother sighed again, but reached out and tenderly brushed a strand of her red hair from her face.

Lydia felt it unglue from the drying tears staining her cheeks. "I'm sorry, but I'm not strong enough."

"What a lie, my darling, after everything you've achieved; after everything you've done. Nobody would be here at all if it weren't for you and your strength."

"You're not here."

Her mum placed a hand on her bare chest over her heart. "I'm always here. But..." Her mum moved both hands to the tops of her shoulders and turned her firmly towards the house she didn't want to see. "You have got *to go in."*

It was cold. Really cold. Something fell on her collarbone and made her flinch.

Snow.

That's why the sky was so dark – snow clouds had been forming.

She took a tentative step towards the house.

"That's it, sweetheart."

Fuck this – no. *She couldn't do it. "Mum..." She turned and froze, her entire being cramping in pain at the emptiness she encountered. "Mum?"*

She was gone, and she might never see her again. "Don't leave me!"

Silence.

She'd left her with nothing but the key. "I can't do this alone."

"We're all alone in the end."

Startled, Lydia looked towards this new, harsh voice that cut through the air.

Gladys stood in front of the door to Sarah's house. She leaned on her cane. "If you want my advice, I'd turn around and walk home. Go back to your males. There's nothing but death here."

Anger fluttered in her belly. "I don't want your advice."

"You should. I also see what you don't want to see, and I see it bloody clearly – you know I do. Me, of all people."

The snow fell harder. Ice flooded her veins.

"Go home to your family, child."

She couldn't speak; fear held her tongue. Family.

The curtain behind the bottom left window twitched.

Lydia started. "What was that?"

"Nothing that can be fixed. Go home."

She had to go in. She knew she did. Defeat matched her fear. Yet, she couldn't move her feet; she couldn't move anything apart from her fingers which were starting to go numb as the snow blanketed the ground. They gripped the key like a lifeline.

A movement and a thump made her jump.

A small hand fell flat against the glass pane, and then another, and then another. Very small hands. Children's hands.

Terror noosed her, and she almost fled.

Their fingernails looked dirty and bloody, smudging the glass black and red. How long had they been in there for?

Suddenly, a girl's face pressed up against the glass, mouth open in a silent scream that was no longer silent when it burst from Lydia's lungs.

And finally, she moved.

She thought she'd screamed herself awake, but the scream was in her mind.

Tears still sheened her eyes. Her muscles bunched in fear,

but before the cold of the nightmare could settle into her bones, heat from her right seeped into her instead – heat from Lawrence's large frame as he lay on her breast, breathing deeply in slumber.

Relief raced through her, and Lydia let out her own shuddering breath, silently, careful not to wake any of her mates.

The room was grey with the dawn still to come, and it always came late on January mornings, the sun as sleepy as the rest of the world.

Greedily – and somewhat guiltily, for she should not need her mates to make her feel safe – she soaked in Lawrence's warmth like a sponge.

Not just *his* warmth.

She turned her head to the other side of her pillow, and there lay Ryan on his left side, snoring gently, his back to her, but radiating just as much warmth as Lawrence did.

As always, she felt the briefest second of panic when she couldn't immediately see Taylor, perhaps pronounced by the lingering presence of her nightmare. She found him quickly enough, though, curled up by the ajar bedroom door in the form of his wolf.

Finally, she allowed herself to relax – as much as the nightmare allowed, anyway. She'd not had it before, and her sleep had been dreamless for weeks if not months. In fact, she was sure she hadn't dreamt since that wretched night.

And what a bloody awful dream to welcome them all back. *Well done, brain.*

Lawrence moved. Eyes still closed and mumbling something in his sleep which she could not decipher, he rubbed his cheek into her chest, then sighed, and settled once more. But his grip around her remained a little tighter than before.

She smiled a sad smile. She may not have had a single dream for months, but he had had many – a brutal consequence of placing a gun under his chin and pulling the trigger (or forcing Richard to). He always played it down – just dreams; not real; he'd suffered worse at the hands of Tridents – but she saw the haunting of his eyes and knew the truth. New tortures replaced old ones.

Yet, he laughed now. He laughed a lot. And he danced. No matter what the new torture, he rose above it all.

No sweat marked his brow; his breathing had returned to its methodical rhythm. She could look at him all day – this male was stunning – although...

She let her gaze roam down the defined muscles of his unclothed torso, past his abdomen and hips, until they fell upon his legs.

Nothing was more stunning than the sight of his legs and the awe they provoked in her – still. Always.

Currently entwined with her own, his thighs were as defined as the rest of him. Fine, flaxen-blond hairs stippled his limbs from top to bottom. When the sun shone on them at the right angle, he almost glowed a white-gold, and his wolf ... well. His white wolf, running, was a majesty to behold.

Without meaning to, she next found herself staring at the pale blond nest of curls at the juncture of those limbs. His cock – another magnificent sight – was half-erect and languishing across the top of his inner-thigh, this erection without a doubt the result of his body's morning needs and nothing more, though that didn't stop her own body responding to where her mind inevitably took her.

They'd all made love last night, and every night before that. Last night, though, had been the full moon, and the love-making had been long and slow; unhurried in every sense, for no enemies existed to bash down their door, and no mating pains festered to torment them with stabbing aches so agonising that it crippled them.

Love was free.

It made their coming together a *real* choice, and simply beautiful.

Lost in thought, she didn't hear the soft moan at first, and it took even longer for her to realise it came from her own lips.

Refocusing her gaze, she found herself staring into Lawrence's open eyes as his fingers lazily brushed across the top of her left nipple. *Ah*... the cause of her little exclamation. But it was more affection than lust that coloured his ice-blue eyes in the darkness of the room.

When he spoke, his voice was a husky shadow of itself so as not to wake the others. "I can smell your want."

She raised an eyebrow, enjoying the feel of him, and happy to jest after escaping the clutches of the nightmare. "I can *see* yours."

His grin became wide, sleep still holding on to every curve of his face, and they both looked down at his growing cock. "It's more awake than me."

A frown crept across her brow. "Were you dreaming? You were making noises in your sleep."

He breathed out, long and slow, and let his head fall back onto her chest. "I was. But it's fine. Just dreams."

She bit her tongue – didn't want to get into it with him at the crack of dawn, but also ... she didn't want to be reminded of her own dark dream. *That's not the only thing you don't want to be reminded of though, is it?*

Lydia banished her inner voice – damn thing never knew good timing. "You can try and sleep some more. We don't have to be up yet."

With a kiss to the left side of her ribs, Lawrence levered himself across her, and turned so he was lying fully on her, his nose brushing hers. His next kiss fell on her lips. "It's got to be seven o'clock. Richard will be leaving soon. I want to say goodbye."

Lydia reached for the back of his head, and brought his lips back down to hers, not wanting the kiss to end just yet. And she could have done without the visual of Richard's hand lying next to her foot. It wasn't true that they were 'just' dreams. They were small pockets in the fabric of their souls, where grief became stuck in a continual loop. She wished she could lighten his burden.

And your burden?

"Hey, hey..." Lawrence nipped her bottom lip with his teeth, then pulled back, looking concerned.

"What is it?" she asked.

"You. That was a very intense kiss. Are you all right?"

Damn him and his perceptiveness. At least, telepathically, they all stayed out of each other's minds – mostly. "Yes. I just love you."

He stared at her as if he could see right through her, and, indeed, the matter of Richard and everything he'd lost hung, unspoken, between them – because what could they say? There were no words to make it better. And Lawrence, Lydia knew, felt particularly for the old wolf, for with the return of Lawrence's legs came the loss of Richard's hand. Lawrence couldn't convince him to see his prosthetist. The man wandered around with his stump like it was some kind of trophy, and maybe it was in a way. Lydia didn't know – Richard hadn't spoken much of that night. None of them had.

But Ryan, Taylor, Lawrence, and herself had all been inseparable every night since then, as if the closeness of each other could heal every fracture. Maybe it would with time.

They had been loving and affectionate, and passionate when passion was needed. Last week's wedding between all four of them had been the unneeded (but wanted) seal on their already committed union. On a more superficial level, it had finally chased hungry media journalists away from the hottest story of the year: thousands of lost persons found, lost and disoriented, on the Gunvald Estate. One good thing came out of all that: Russell Maddox had been scared away by the scandal.

In addition, her marriage on paper to Lawrence assured Russell Maddox would not be getting a penny of the Gunvald legacy. At least not without one hell of an acrobatic attempt at diving through loopholes, which Lawrence suspected would cost Maddox more than he was willing to pay. The news of Gladys' death had also dimmed the fires of his interest in Lawrence, and Maddox had retreated back to Hollywood. They hadn't heard from him in months now.

"I love you, too, Mrs Gunvald." Heat lit his eyes.

She didn't much like people referring to her as 'Mrs' – it made her feel bloody ancient. But when Lawrence said it like that, possessively and – damn it – *with complete ownership*, it turned her insides to puddle.

Very non-PC of you, Lydia.

Yet, she couldn't seem to care. He bloody knew she wasn't his physical possession, but his stated claim of her heart and soul was a fucking sexy thing and no mistake – because he held them aloft and unconstrained. His claim was a promise to protect her freedom for as long as they both shall live, and that protection extended to all four of them. To be Mrs Gunvald was to be loved in every sense.

His next kiss was almost bruising, his need to demonstrate said ownership one hundred percent clear. Lydia gasped as the searing kiss trailed down her neck and to her breasts. His hands followed the curve of her legs, then one delved between them, testing her readiness.

Lawrence groaned as he pushed his fingers inside her, the sound of his pleasure vibrating around the nipple devoured by his mouth.

Ryan mumbled loudly in his sleep where he lay next to

them, and flung out a hand behind him which met Lawrence's thigh. "Fu-mm...mb-king stop it!"

They both froze. Lawrence stifled a snigger, and that set Lydia off. She clamped her hand around her mouth to muffle her giggles.

Since the moon no longer fuelled them with an insatiable yearning for sex, they had all discovered what Ryan now yearned for instead was sleep. The male slept a *lot*. He loved sleep, and he was *not* a morning wolf – if anyone interrupted his dreamtime, woe betide them. And their jostling the bed was clearly bringing out his morning grump.

Both of them still shaking with laughter, Lawrence crawled up her frame until he was lying on top of her, his weight holding her down. "Keep very, very still," he whispered.

"What are you doing?"

But it was obvious. His fingers slipped back inside her, and he wasted no time.

Lydia sucked in a breath as he pushed in deep.

"Sshhh ... no sound." With his free hand he stroked her lips, then he pushed his thumb into her mouth.

Ownership. *God, yes.*

She flicked it with her tongue, but protested all the same, the mention of Richard, and Ryan's unconscious disgruntlement, bringing the reality of the day's tasks and chores too near to the fore. "We don't have time."

"Sshhh," he repeated. "Do as I say. Don't move the bed." He was using *that* voice. His tone grew darker. "Keep still."

His commands had her reeling in both ire and submission, as he knew they would. He bloody fed off it. So did she if she cared to admit it.

With his thumb back in her mouth, he turned her head to the right, not hard enough to hurt her, but hard enough to ensure she obeyed and kept still.

Her body already trembled beneath his, his entire being bearing down on her all she could feel, see, and smell – he consumed her. His fingers delved deeper, finding her core, every stroke as sure and masterful as the next words he growled against her ear...

"I'll make you come fast."

Oh, hell.

However skilled a lover he was, it was those words that did it. Who was she kidding – for a few seconds, every time they made love, he *did* own her body and always had. In those moments, she craved his ownership of her, just like she did now.

With his thumb suppressing her moan and his body subduing her movements, she gave in to it all, sinking down to meet her furious, rising orgasm.

Lawrence sighed into her ear as she came, the sound one of pure contentment. "You're so fucking beautiful." He sighed again. "There's no better way to wake up."

She had to concur. "Your turn," she mumbled, still floating on ecstasy.

He shook his head. "No"—kissed her lips—"I don't want to."

She opened her lazy eyes, stared at him, and smiled. Wasn't that a thing to hear.

"I want to carry this ache all day, knowing I can; knowing you gave it to me."

Perhaps it would sound odd to anyone else, but she smiled in understanding. Being able to carry sexual arousal without pain, without needing to release it, was a gift to them – to all wolves – and Lawrence out of all of them, had found a new, carnal energy to try and master. Something the Dominant in him relished.

He dropped a final kiss on her lips, and with a last stroke between her legs, he pulled himself out and away, eliciting a grunt from a still-asleep Ryan as he jiggled the bed stepping off it.

Lydia remembered Taylor, but turned towards the door to find him gone. A hint of that familiar panic stole over her at his absence, but it was no match for the aftermath of her orgasm. She hadn't noticed him leaving the room.

"What are you doing this morning?" asked Lawrence in a hushed tone as he pulled on his trousers.

It was Saturday. They didn't need to be anywhere.

"Thought I'd go for a run." She loved running as her wolf now. She wasn't quite as comfortable as Taylor with the animal change – she doubted any wolf was as comfortable as Taylor with it – but it was a huge step up from her old self-conscious self.

Lawrence frowned. "Where are you going?"

"I want to explore the back of the lake – that patch of forest north of it."

His frown deepened. "I haven't been there yet." He'd only just started to explore parts of the land he owned – he simply hadn't been able to venture into some places with no legs. But now that he was a fully able wolf, he'd relished in some recent discoveries, like an old, defunct mine hidden in a mound under the earth, a quarter of a mile east of the lake. He'd not ventured north of it yet, though.

"I'll let you know if I find anything exciting."

"Be careful."

"I will be."

"I mean it." He pulled his shirt down. "Some of the terrain hasn't been used in decades or longer. Be mindful of loose soil and surfaces."

"I'll be fine."

"Reach me with your mind if you encounter trouble."

"I'll be *fine*."

He didn't seem convinced, but he let it go. He wasn't going

to forbid her from her own land. "I wish I could come with you, but I really do need to speak to Richard."

"I know. Please wish him the best of luck from me."

He nodded.

"Do you think he'll find her?"

'Her' was Selena.

Lawrence stared at her, the look in his eyes hinting at his sorrow. "He has to try."

"He might still find her. They never found her body."

He shook his head. "They found Gabriel's. There was evidence of Selena's blood and skin on him, and on the abandoned car by the cliff. The chances of her surviving his death..."

They left the rest unspoken. Gabriel had died before Himet and Yemet had worked their magic and ended the Trident's existence. As Gabriel's mate, Selena would have suffered his death greatly, and most likely died soon after. Richard was going to spend some time at the place Gabriel's body had been found. The old male carried some hope. It was clear to her Lawrence didn't want to dash it, even as it was equally clear to her that Lawrence thought the search futile.

"And he won't let you go with him?"

"He wants to do this alone. I respect that." Finally dressed, he walked over to the side of the bed and leaned in for a kiss, which she gave. "I'll see you later," he said.

"Probably not 'til dinner. I want to explore properly."

That crease across his brow was back, but he hid it with a smile and said nothing about his concerns. "If Ryan wakes before you leave tell him the Christmas tree needs taking down."

She grinned. "I will."

Three weeks ago, Lawrence, Ryan, and Taylor, had brought her down the stairs, hands over her eyes, leading her every step of the way so she didn't fall. They'd positioned her in the entrance hallway; then had revealed the most stunning, large tree, felled from the land, decorated to the brim and fully lit, with a star on the top.

She'd cried.

She'd cried wishing her dad could have shared the moment, and cried, grateful for the three males that loved her enough to indulge her wish, even though two of them had never put up a Christmas tree in their lives. It was a little piece of 'family' that had made this house truly a home, not least after all the repairs they'd needed to do after Himet and Yemet's storm. Taylor had fully understood the significance of the tree, of course.

"It was the best gift."

Lawrence smiled from ear to ear. "I'm glad. I'll see you later."

"'Bye."

He left, and she found herself wondering where Taylor had gone.

It was much lighter outside now, though still the grey of winter.

Ryan still snored.

The clock across the room told her it was twenty minutes to eight. If she wanted to get a full day of exploration in, she could do with leaving soon.

The wolf inside her trotted around happily at the thought of a day running.

She remembered her nightmare as she got out of bed; pushed it away again.

Can't push it away forever – you know what you dreamt.

She didn't want to hear it. Panic trembled beneath her surface; queasiness washed over her.

Breakfast first. Then run.

CHAPTER TWO

Despite needing no clothes for her run as a wolf, she found herself dressing for breakfast.

Taylor reappeared just as she was finishing her toast with not a word about why he'd left the bedroom, but a big smile to greet her nonetheless. "I just ran into Lawrence. He told me you're going on a run."

"I am. Did you want to come?"

"I'd love to, but if I don't get the tree down today, I don't know when I can fit it in next week. Figured Ryan could help me once he's shaken the moondust out of his eyes."

She laughed. "I feel bad you doing all the work. Maybe I should stay and help."

"No. Go running. I love that your wolf's out and about so much. And it won't take long with two of us." His gaze wandered up and down her dress, his expression unreadable.

"What?" Was there something wrong with it? She'd kept it simple – she wore a black, mid-length wool dress with long sleeves.

"You'll freeze. Forecast says snow's coming in."

"Snow?"

"That's what it says. Lawrence reckons it will miss us as the wind's blowing east, but ... I don't know. Everything's so silent outside, and the sky's turning that colour it does just before the snow falls. I reckon it might hit us."

She tried not to dwell on the images of the nightmare her mind threw at her. "I won't freeze – I have fur," she teased.

"You know what I mean."

"I do," she smiled. "But really, I'm going to slip the dress off as soon as I reach the woodland so I can shift – I wanted clothing I could take off easily and was light to carry."

There it was again on his face – that unreadable expression. She decided to let it go, but the quiet fell just a little too thickly.

"How are you doing?" Taylor asked, his voice soft.

Her heart skipped a beat. She knew what he meant – he meant everything. He meant *all* of it. But how did one quantify everything that had happened? "I'm fine." And that's all she said.

The next pause stretched out a good thirty seconds, and then… "You've worn that dress a lot the past few weeks."

She had? She looked back down at it, confused as to why that might be a problem.

Then, Taylor was there, right in front of her, circling an arm around her waist as he turned her to face him.

She stared at him, surprised, though not at all minding the kiss he placed on her lips.

Her arms went around his neck, slipping under the ends of his brown hair – his second arm joined the first around her waist – and she deepened the kiss. His kisses always bathed her in gentle familiarity; a subtle, but no less fundamental sense of security. It wasn't the heavy kind of security that came from Lawrence and Ryan's uncompromising ways – it was more of a 'hope' that came from his humanity. It weaved its way into her senses promising that everything would be all right, even long after the kiss had ended.

"Wow," she whispered, her eyes closed, her lips still tingling. And then she caught herself, and blinked her eyes open, a bit embarrassed. She felt her cheeks redden at her clumsy dash of honesty.

His green eyes crinkled at the corners. "Well, I really do enjoy making you wow."

She rolled her eyes, going redder.

His smile became a grin. "I love you. Be careful out there with the weather turning. Come home straight away if it gets bad."

"I will. I love you, too."

"I'll leave you to it. I'm going to wake the big guy up."

"Good luck with that."

"Yeah, I'll need it." He squeezed her arm, then left the kitchen.

She found herself smiling after him, then her eyes teared up without warning. They'd nearly lost him twice – by silver poisoning, and by her own damned lightning altering his DNA. *What if...*

No. It didn't bear thinking about. *Don't think. Run.*

Yes.

Run.

Straight through the bluebell wood, due south, until the hollow oak appears, surrounded by three yew trees. Turn left and carry on until the tall hedge looms; go through the hedge. There'll be a field with a path – take the path until it comes out above the lake...

Yes. Half a year since first setting foot here, and she knew the way like the back of her hand.

The Gunvald Estate in winter was a domineering stretch of land that looked unruly and wild under the darker, cold skies. It shrieked its impassableness to anyone unfamiliar with the terrain. Lydia, though, knew of many of its bounties now; natural treasures like the canopies that would shield the rain, and the hollows in the earth that would keep the cold at bay. She knew where the deer made their home, and where the rabbits burrowed; which trees the few barn owls liked to inhabit, and where the badgers tunnelled their setts.

The lake, however, was one area which remained half

unexplored. Lawrence had come here often and made the areas he could traverse his sanctuary. But there were areas he had never been able to reach at all until recently; until four wolf legs made it possible. Two human legs had still posed some problems for the inclines and dips of the quarry walls surrounding the lake; no legs at all had made exploration impossible.

Ryan and Taylor had never ventured here alone – this was Lawrence's refuge.

Lawrence, himself, had only just begun to explore the areas surrounding the lake now reachable to him. A month ago, he'd discovered the defunct mine built into the side of a rock wall, east of the lake. It wasn't listed anywhere, not even on the deeds of the land. He suspected it had been used to mine chalk, but also for shelter during the second world war given the trinkets he'd found stored within – that had been over two decades before his family had bought the land and made a home here. The fact it wasn't listed on the deeds (had been removed from the deeds?) suggested it might have been used by British Intelligence at that time. He was looking into it, like an excited school boy, but had found no information to give up its secrets yet.

Lydia wasn't interested in the mine. She was drawn to the dense forest that clung to the north side of the lake. The climb from the lake to the forest was steep, and there was no way around the lake to get to it, but the last time she'd come here, she'd spotted a very narrow pathway, hidden and overgrown, that led up to the forest from the bottom of the lake. It looked like it might offer a less hazardous way to reach those trees.

Still in wolf form, with her bunched-up dress between her teeth, she trotted over to the path, enjoying the feel of the chilly air on her fur. She wasn't cold at all, but knew she would be when she shifted back to human form.

And soon, you won't be able to shift at all.

Annoyed, she pushed that thought far, far away and focused

on the task ahead: following the narrow path up the quarry and into the north forest.

The sky did look daunting. She hoped she had enough time to fully explore before the snow came. It would be good to be able to bring some news of her adventures back to Lawrence – it would make her feel useful. And she loved seeing his eyes light up when he became excited about something. For him, being able to venture on his own land again was akin to winning the lottery. Or *all* the lotteries.

Half an hour later saw her nearing the top of the path. It had been quite a climb – more than a scramble – but her paws hadn't suffered too much, and some of the mud on the ground, not yet hardened, helped to soften any friction. She dropped her dress on a grassy bit of earth, doing her best to avoid getting mud on it, and took a moment to take in her surroundings and scent the area.

She stood at the very edge of the north forest. Holly trees guarded the way into the woods – very tall ones, never once pruned by man. They were such beautiful trees when allowed to grow unhindered.

She'd done it. *I made it to the top!*

But falling flakes from the sky ruined the triumphant moment somewhat. It had started to snow, and the flakes seemed to be getting bigger. Sense told her she should turn around and go home; come back another day now she knew her way up. Her more stubborn self didn't want to give up when she'd just achieved the win. And there was the matter of the forest yet to be explored.

She looked up at the sky, sniffing the air. A snowflake fell on her muzzle. The clouds were dense – the snowfall would last a while.

Five minutes. Just five minutes tracking along the edge of the woods so you can imprint its scent into your memory ... then go home.

She could spare five minutes – she hadn't come here for nothing.

Mind made up, she left her dress where it was and trotted onwards, every new aroma promising potential and adventure – on *her* land. It still blew her away sometimes. She *owned* this terrain.

She'd go no more than a few metres in. The natural canopy also offered some reprieve from the fast falling snow, although the ground surrounding the woods was already turning white. Without a doubt the snow would settle.

Her right paw landed on something hard. She jumped back with a growl, hoping all the adders were deep underground by now. Something caked in mud and rust bulged under the dirt.

Letting out a small whine, she bent down and sniffed it – definitely rusty, whatever it was. And not alive. This was an inanimate object.

Getting to work, she dug around it until she was able to move it a little, and then she attacked it directly with her paws in a bid to push it out of the ground. It worked.

It was a key. A big, old key.

She needed to inspect it more closely.

Lydia shifted into her human form, gritting her teeth against the sudden blast of cold to her skin. Fur was such an awesome design of nature.

She picked up the key and did her best to rub the rest of the mud off it; some of the rust came off, too. Hell, this looked like one of those keys to castles or dungeons, or something. Maybe it opened a gate.

If she cocooned it carefully in her dress, she'd be able to carry both items back in her mouth.

Satisfied with that thought, she hurried back to where she'd dropped her dress and did her best to wrap the key in it and tie three or four knots in the cloth to hold the key in place.

She had to wipe snow from her eyelids a couple of times – it was speeding down now. She was glad at the thought of taking the key back – Lawrence would undoubtedly find it intriguing. She just had to be careful going back down the steep path.

Ignoring the bite of the icy air she called her she-wolf to the fore and focused on making the physical change.

Nothing happened.

Fighting her rising panic, she tried again, closing her eyes this time in a bid to strengthen her concentration.

Nothing.

"Shit ... no."

You knew this would happen. You knew it was coming.

But not now. *Not now.*

With a sinking heart, she tried one last time to shift, and failed. "No! Damn it!"

A shiver racked her body. Hurriedly, she undid all the knots in her dress, placed the key on the ground, and slipped the dress on over her head. Taylor was right – she'd bloody freeze in this, but it was all she had. Gathering the key, she put it in the small front pocket of her dress; so small, the key poked out the top. It would have to do.

She jogged back to the path she'd climbed up, and looked down it, exhaling a sharp breath at the incline. She couldn't do it. Not with the snow hiding any tripping hazards and her bare, human feet slipping all over the place.

And it was far too steep.

She looked around her, at nothing at all but trees, and then back at the path and the lake right at the bottom. *At least three hundred metres down.*

Should she attempt the descent anyway?

God, it was getting hard to see properly for the heavy snow. And she was getting very wet right along with cold. The chances of her getting hurt, or worse, attempting to climb down were too great.

Too great for the consequences ... so much death.

"Fuck."

Closing her eyes once more, and feeling sick at the thought of everything that could go wrong, she tried the only other tool she had at her disposal, even though she already knew it wouldn't work – not any more; not now. She tried to reach her mates with her mind.

Her mind hit an invisible wall, as she knew it would. *They can't hear you any more.*

All options were gone.

A gust of wind blasted her cheek. She had to get out of the heavy snowfall.

Cursing to no one, she turned and ran back towards the woods, alarmed at the numbness starting to make itself known in her toes. Her fingers would be the next to go numb. She had to protect herself. The woods offered some dryness. Where she was going to find warmth, though, she had no idea.

CHAPTER THREE

Lydia wasn't sure how far she'd walked. In the dark of the forest, and fighting the cold, time had done that thing where it bent out of shape. All she knew was that she was warmer if she kept moving, and if she tried her best to stick to a straight line, she might just be able to find her way back.

Tracking by scent was proving tricky now – it was too cold. Smells were getting lost amid the snow which was fast turning into a small blizzard with the wind picking up the way it was. But forests had to end sometime. There *had* to be an exit, and beyond the exit, a village or a town she could go to for help. She could phone Lawrence from a pub, or someone's house.

Her teeth chattered.

She scrunched up her dress at either side of her waist and brought the material across her, keeping it tucked under her arms as she folded them over her abdomen, trying to hold the heat in; trying to generate more.

What have you done? It's going to happen again. Because of you – again.

Tears could wait. This wasn't the right time for wailing her woes.

A shape, darker than the trees, appeared on her left.

Slowing down, her heart rate increased when she saw what it was: a house. Old and derelict – hopefully empty (no one should be living here without Lawrence's permission) – half brick and half wood. This was probably a good thing, but it made her stop nonetheless, fear gripping her harder than it should because all she saw in her mind was Sarah's house from her dream; Gladys standing in front of it.

Get a grip.

She swallowed hard and shook her head. *That wasn't real; this is.*

Yet, she didn't want to go in. Not one bit.

It's shelter. You have to. You have no choice.

Forcing her legs to move her numb feet forwards, she approached the house, her eyes scanning everything around it; her nose searching for any aroma it could find that might give away what lay inside.

Her ears picked up no sound. She half expected to hear Gladys' voice – if any ghost would come back to haunt her, it would be that old hag.

Nothing stirred.

Gathering all the courage she could muster, she climbed up the wooden porch to the front door. The planks of wood creaked under her feet, revealing their age and lack of use. "Hello?" she called out. Better to be safe than sorry.

There was no reply. That was a good thing, but it left her feeling oddly bereft.

With a shaking hand – from cold or fear, she couldn't tell – she placed her fingers around the door handle and turned it. Or tried. It was stiff and rusty, but the wood and iron held together just fine and didn't give way. It was locked.

Stepping back, she studied the front of the house. She could probably break her way in, but wasn't sure how stable the structure was. It had clearly been here a long time.

A sudden thought hit her. She looked down at her dress and pulled the key out of the pocket. It seemed too coincidental, but it was worth a shot. The door's keyhole certainly looked big enough to accommodate this type of key.

Hurry. You're shivering badly now.

Shit, she was.

Without thinking on it further, she pushed the key into the

lock. It slid in like magic – loud magic with a clunk.

She turned it hard – another clunk – and the door opened.

The darkness of the house seemed to soak up all sound. Gloomy was an understatement. So was daunting. This house reeked of secrets ... terrible secrets. She was somehow reminded of the outhouse that Lawrence and Ryan had smashed down; the one his family had been massacred in.

Great. That's great. You think about that as you make yourself at home.

She wouldn't be making herself at home, but she did need to make herself dry and warm. She shut the door behind her, shutting out the snow, and sort of wished she hadn't. Sealing herself in here seemed ... wrong.

Lawrence would be beside himself with this new discovery on his turf (after he'd verbally flayed her for being so careless while on her little outing). The secret house. It probably went hand in hand with the secret mine. But...

Something really wrong happened here.

It was an instinct she couldn't shake.

Another floorboard creaked as it strained under her weight. "How long have you been empty for?" she asked the dank air.

The window pane rattled in reply.

Outside, the snow whipped. The blizzard was here. *Let's hope it ends quickly.*

Her gaze refocused from outside to inside, and she gasped in horror when she understood what the stained patterns this side of the pane were showing her.

Black and brown-red streaks of dirt and ... handprints.

She shook her head and stepped back, dread rising.

Small handprints. *Children's handprints.*

This IS your nightmare.

"It can't be – that was just a dream."

Dream or not, it was another visual that now tore through her mind – one that wasn't a dream at all, though she wished with all her being that it had been: Taylor writhing, dying, in Sarah's garden; lightning tearing through him; then, blood between her legs.

With a cry of despair she turned away from the glass, clutching her stomach. *There's no blood now ... you're okay.*

She couldn't stay in here, she just couldn't.

You can't go back out.

She realised she was crying when a teardrop fell on the floor, the dark spot on the wood a strange sight in this dilapidated house ... it was as if her tear brought history to life. Her breathing became ragged; air non-existent.

I can't do it again! She paced the room in a panic, needing to find a way out, but not through that door – not that door near the window smudged with children's blood. Had they found their way out?

There was a deafening CRACK and she screamed as pain tore through her right leg. She was falling before she knew it, but caught herself with her arms stretched out along the wooden boards now level with her chest.

The floor had given way.

Riding on terror alone, still screaming, she kicked with her legs and levered herself up with her arms, needing to go faster; praying the floor under her arms would hold. Jagged wood poked into her ribs. *No, no, no...*

With a cry, she made it up, throwing herself onto the floor, pushing herself away from the hole that had almost swallowed her.

She had to lie there for a moment to catch her breath, but the sinister presence of this house wouldn't allow her to stay there long. She pulled herself to sitting, inspecting her damaged leg. It was bleeding, but not broken. The wood had sliced her when she'd gone through it.

She wiggled her foot and winced. It hurt, but she was sure she could walk.

Carefully, she pulled herself up, her right leg the last thing she put her weight on. When she finally did, she had to grit her teeth. It hurt a lot, but it was bearable.

Taking in a breath, she patted the rest of herself down, making sure she wasn't injured. Her hand found its way to her belly.

Her eyes landed on the hole in the floor and ... something else. *Something in the hole.*

Feeling faint, she leaned forward to get a better look, her mind screaming at her not to.

It was dark down there, but there was still enough light for her to make out what she needed to. Another cry left her – this one bordering on hysteria. Bones were scattered on the ground in the hole – skeletons. She saw skulls – one, two, three ... small skulls. *Three children.*

She was looking at a fucking tomb.

Without warning, she heaved; doubled over, clenching her stomach, but nothing came out. All that existed was the pressing need to *get the fuck out.*

She ran. Stumbled and ran. Straight out the front door into the torrent of snow. Giant flakes smacked into her eyes, ears, and nose; the wind whipped her hair around her face and neck. Disoriented, she sprinted back towards the woods, eyes streaming with tears and the imagery of death.

She couldn't find the small break in the trees she'd come out of. Was she even facing the right way?

Never mind. She just had to get back amid the protection of the trees.

Pulling apart branches and twigs, she ignored their scraping of her skin – she ignored the blood from her leg painting the snow red – and finally succeeded in propelling herself into the woods. The snow fell a little less here, but it still fell. She just wanted to get back to the lake; somewhere familiar.

Numb and wet, she ran blindly, her need speeding her through the trees. She didn't fully understand why she suddenly found herself in mid-air, flying ... shit, no – *falling*.

She must have tripped.

Arms up to protect her head, the last thing she remembered doing was curling up tight into a ball, shielding her stomach, as she hit the ground, and passed out.

CHAPTER FOUR

She was holding the key to the dance studio.

Lydia stared at the front door to Sarah's house.

Gladys was gone.

She couldn't remember making her way to the front door, but here she was. And she knew it was locked – knew it before even trying to open the door. She also knew the key would unlock the door, which was odd, of course. Why would the key to a dance studio open the door to Sarah's house?

But dreams were weird, and she knew this was a dream because her leg wasn't bleeding, and the snow had become light again.

She looked at the left-hand window – at the glass of the pane. The smudges made by the children's hands were still there, but instead of angry, panicked streaks, they'd drawn a picture with their blood: bolts of lightning raining down from the sky. And underneath all the bolts, they'd drawn a heart.

Her head spun back to the door when she heard a sound from inside. Laughter. One of the kids was laughing?

"Hello?" she called out.

More laughter was the reply she got.

Taking in a deep breath, she lined the key up with the lock and pushed it in. She didn't even need to turn it – the door just opened, easily and silently.

The house was decorated and clean, lived in and warm. It wasn't Sarah's house after all, but her own – the one she'd lived in when she'd been a child. There were the mauve curtains of the living room, and the sofas that matched their colour. Excitement rose, along with the warmth of nostalgic familiarity. "Mum?" Was she here? She'd been there in her last dream, hadn't she? Not for long enough. It would be good to see her again, especially here, in this odd reconstruction of where she'd grown up.

Her eyes widening as so many memories returned, she raced to the stairs, then up them two at a time like she used to do. Her bedroom was where it had always been. She walked into it and smiled. It was furnished the way it had been when she'd been twelve. Her parents had redecorated that year, and her bedroom had had a makeover. She'd been weeks away from becoming a teenager – she'd needed more room, a desk, a bigger wardrobe and drawers.

She'd asked for her walls to be painted a pale sky blue; she'd asked for yellow curtains and a yellow bed-set. It had reminded her of spring and summer, and hope for whatever future awaited her.

When her mother had committed suicide three years later, she'd stripped it all. The walls had become a plain white, and the curtains black.

She wiped away a tear as she took in her childhood bedroom. She'd had so many good things. And so much hope.

A movement by the door made her glance that way. Big eyes, framed by a mop of red hair, peeked around the frame of the doorway.

"Erm ... hello?" she greeted.

The child's face – a boy – came fully into view. His freckles across his nose and cheeks looked just like hers when she had been his age, which she guessed was around five. "Hello," he replied, shyly.

"Do you live here?" she asked, not really knowing where 'here' was. Sarah's house? Her own house? Somewhere else?

He giggled as if knowing a secret she wasn't privy to.

More footsteps thudded up the stairs, and then two more faces appeared in the doorway in front of her: two more boys, one with shockingly pale blond hair and eyes; the other with slightly darker hair. But they looked almost identical. Twins? They all smiled at her and giggled. Oh, they caused some mischief, she was sure!

They raced into the bedroom and dragged her out by her arms. "Come on," they said, their voices bubbling over with joy.

She couldn't help but laugh. "Where are we going?"

"We've been waiting for you."

That didn't answer her question.

They led her back down the stairs and into the kitchen, then towards the back door.

"Wait..." Dread coursed through her. "No."

It was all wrong. It was ... different. This was not her own kitchen, this was Sarah's kitchen, which meant...

She looked in horror at the back door she was being pulled towards. "No."

But the children were behind her now, pushing. One of the blond kids darted in front and opened the door.

"No!"

They were bloody strong. They pushed her out, and when she spun around to run back in, they'd already shut the door. "Wait!"

And locked it.

"Damn!" She rattled the handle, but it was no use.

Thunder cracked overhead and she jumped with a gasp. In trepidation, she turned, staring up at the sky. Lightning streaked the expanse of it in luminous silver.

"Oh, god." She pressed herself against the door. The last time she'd wielded was the night of the Trident attack. She'd lost the ability since Yemet's possession of her body.

This was Sarah's garden. This was where...

Terrified, she look down to where Taylor's body had once lain, cradled in Ryan's arms. He wasn't there now. The garden was empty.

But this is where...

She looked over to the right where she, herself, had fallen, bleeding from between her legs. "I'm sorry," she forced out, her voice a husk of itself. "I'm so sorry. I can't do it again."

"Lydia?"

She jerked her head left towards the sound of her name. "Dad?"

It was. It really was her dad. As real as dreams got, anyway.

"What are you doing here, sweetheart?"

She felt glued to the spot. Seeing him was ... wonderful. She wanted to hug him the way she had her mother, but the estrangement between them felt all too real. She shook her head at him, not able to answer the question. Instead, another "I'm sorry" left her lips.

He waved her apology away with a smile. "It's past. It's done. I made mistakes. I'm sorry, too."

"Some mistakes are too big."

"And some you can't undo – I know. But, Liddy..."

Her heart skipped at his pet name for her. He hadn't called her that in so, so long.

"It's not about undoing the mistakes. It's about transforming them. The man becomes the wolf – that's not a mistake. Nothing that happens is really a mistake if you can change the outcome for the better."

"But..." How did she explain? "The whole world is gone, and I'm standing at its edge. It's the whole world, Dad."

"And the whole world lives in you. It's only ever as big as you."

"I'm so scared."

"I know." He put his hands in his pockets, and then he smiled at her, wide. It reached his eyes, and his heart, and her *heart ... there was so much love. "But you won't make my mistakes. Oh, you'll make your own, sure, but not mine. And not your mother's. Those have been transformed. You're going to be just fine." He brought his left hand up and held it out to her. "Hug?"*

Yes. Yes, she wanted that.

She pushed herself away from the door, and reached for his hand with her right. Their fingers met, his clasped hers, and then he pulled her towards him and she fell into his embrace. Her tears wet his shirt. "I love you."

"I love you, too, Liddy. But you need to go now."

"Already?"

"Yes. You need to look after yourself. Wake up."

She gasped as pain shot through her right leg.

"Wake up, Liddy."

Her injury ... she'd hurt herself, hadn't she?

"Wake up."

She pulled away from her dad and looked down at herself. Her eyes widened in alarm. She'd expected to see blood on her leg, not... "No."

"Wake up."

Blood ran down her thighs like a river bursting its dam. Her dress was drenched in it. "NO!"

She jerked awake, eyes flying open. *FUCK.* She couldn't breathe ... couldn't ... the cold. It was...

Without warning, Hendrickson and Amelia filled her vision, their bodies nothing but ice on the floor of the walk-in freezer. *MOVE.*

She was face-down. Unable to feel anything but an unearthly pain at her movements, she did her best to lever herself up. That's when she realised she was covered in snow – blanketed under a duvet of deathly white. She couldn't properly feel her body apart from pin pricks that darted throughout, stabbing her veins. She looked down at herself.

No blood.

There was no blood soaking her dress or gushing down her thighs, and it seemed the blood around her right leg had stopped seeping. However, there was a patch of red on the snow where her head had been.

Gingerly, she reached up, unable to completely feel the point on her head she touched; then brought her fingers back down. Red. Yeah, she'd cut her head with her fall. Hopefully not badly – she couldn't tell.

She had no idea how long she'd been unconscious for, but the snow had stopped falling, and the wind had died down a fraction.

A howl echoed, bouncing off trees as it rushed through the forest as if seeking her, and only her. She recognised it straight away – how could she not. *"Lawrence!"*

She couldn't howl back. Screaming would have to do, but she was even failing at that, her vocal chords tight from the cold; her voice hoarse. *"Lawrence!"* Desperation took hold. He was too far away to hear her, and she couldn't shout any louder.

But there was another bark, much, much nearer, from behind her.

Hope reared, and she turned, to see Ryan's black wolf galloping towards her from only metres away.

Everything in her sagged. The relief was so strong, blackness filled her vision once more, but only for a second. She stayed in the realm of the living.

Ryan's massive, black wolf came to a sudden halt, fell onto his haunches, flung his head back and howled a howl that tore through the whole wood and beyond. Birds fled from their perches high up in the trees. Alpha to alpha, it was a reply to Lawrence's call.

Ryan shifted into his human form, then all but threw himself to her side, his fear for her evident in his eyes. "Lydia!"

"Ryan..."

He looked at her head, and then her leg, back to her head; reached out and touched it. His face reflected his alarm. "Jesus

Christ, you're cold as ice and turning blue."

Before she could say a word, he was gathering her into his arms and lifting her up.

"I can walk," she said, weakly.

"Like hell you can."

That's not what she'd meant. "I mean ... my leg. It's not broken." But there was other stuff – stuff she needed to say, though her voice was strained and her lungs seemed frozen in place, denying her enough oxygen. "I found ... old house."

"We saw it. We tracked you there – saw your prints in the snow after chainsawing a new fucking path through the trees to get to you. I don't know how the fuck you got up here."

"Children died. In the house."

He paused. His voice darkened. "We saw that, too. Don't worry about it now. Lawrence will deal with it."

"Ryan..." She wished she could feel the heat of his body, but she couldn't feel a damned thing.

"Hush, now. Lawrence is here, I can see him. He's coming now. We brought our bikes – parked fifteen minutes away on foot. We came to find you as soon as the blizzard set in. Taylor's there with blankets and body warmers. Just hold on."

"Ryan..." Sleep was claiming her.

"Stay awake, babe." She heard the catch to his words. She must look in a bad way.

"Can't."

Ryan belted out profanities under his breath. "You can. Lawrence is here. We're getting you straight home."

Sleep was also here, and it was an overbearing sensation. But she had to get this one last thing out. They were going to be so damned mad she'd said nothing. It had been too much, too soon. She'd try to explain later. This wasn't how she'd wanted to tell them, but right now, they had to know. "Ryan ... I'm..."

She hoped she'd actually *said* the words and not dreamt

she'd said them, because everything got fuzzy just before the soothing blackness took over. "I'm ... pregnant."

CHAPTER FIVE

Waking up to the humming of a jaunty tune, no matter how odd and unfamiliar, was far, far better than jerking awake on the tails of a nightmare.

Wherever Lydia's subconscious had taken her, her sleep had been dreamless, and that was her first thought, accompanied by a feeling of gratitude, as she was pulled back into the comfort of the smells she knew so well.

She was home.

With a moan of contentment, she turned her head to the right, eyes still closed, fearing she might feel pain. She'd been freezing cold, hadn't she?

But there was no pain, just beautiful warmth.

She tried to open her eyes, but her eyelids felt heavy.

"Aahhh ... My Lady," called a gentle, aged voice – one she didn't think she knew. "Welcome back."

Finally, she prised her eyes open. It took a few seconds for everything to come into focus.

"You're home, in your bedroom, in your bed."

She blinked, then turned her head back around. An older man, who smelled human and wore a weird looking stethoscope around his neck, smiled down at her. And yes, she was in the master bedroom that used to be Lawrence's bedroom. It now belonged to them both, and Ryan and Taylor were welcome in here, too, although they had each decided to keep their own rooms – completely necessary for the space and privacy they all needed. She'd thought about keeping her own bedroom, but the need to step into her 'queenship' had been a prominent urge she couldn't ignore. Lawrence had felt the same. They'd needed to nurture their roles as the leaders of a species. A species she'd soon be expanding.

Everything rushed back, panic lunging to the fore. A whimper escaped her and she reached for her baby, her hand grasping her belly.

"Now, now," said the man. "Try to relax. Your baby's just fine."

He meant it. She could tell. It wasn't a lie. She closed her eyes, thanking one and all gods. She briefly wondered if it was Himet and Yemet she was supposed to thank.

"Or should I say, babies. Plural." Another smile.

She looked down at where her hand rested. She'd been changed out of her dress – she now wore one of Ryan's T-shirts. It came down past her hips. She finally managed to find her voice. "I suspected as much."

The man nodded. "I don't believe we've met. I'm Dr Ernest Matheson. Mr Gunvald called me as soon as they found you in the snow."

"How long ago was that?"

"Twenty hours or so. Don't be alarmed – your body needed to heal. It's done a fantastic job of protecting those babies."

Tears sprung to her eyes. It was the first time anyone had said that to her.

"The cut on your head is little more than a graze, and the skin on your leg has mostly repaired – there was no infection. It was your body temperature I was concerned with – you were found just in time. A little longer, and you may have slipped into hypothermia. Most of your healing's done now. It's always a pleasure treating wolves, I have to say. Your ability to regenerate never ceases to amaze me."

"How ... how many weeks pregnant am I?"

"You don't know?" he asked, surprised.

Guiltily, she shook her head. She said nothing more.

He respected her silence. "You're halfway through. One month gone, one left to go. And there are three heartbeats, all of them loud and strong."

She looked at him, bewildered. "You can hear them?"

"I can. So can you, if you like," He gave his stethoscope a tap. It had something that looked like a funnel attached to its end. "I can show you how."

God. She'd been in avoidance mode for weeks; this now seemed a little overwhelming. She shook her head. "Maybe later."

He frowned, briefly, and then it was gone. "As you wish."

She licked the dryness from her lips. "I didn't tell them. About the pregnancy."

Dr Matheson nodded. "That's a woman's prerogative. You reveal the news when you feel safe and ready."

She hadn't expected that answer at all. She stared at him. Her surprise must have been evident.

"I'm human, My Lady. I live among human rights and laws, and women have rights. But even among wild mammals, the female will only announce her vulnerability when she's ready. It's a matter of survival."

"Oh ... I don't think my mates will see it that way."

"You'd be surprised."

"I would, yes. We agreed no more secrets between us, and I've kept this huge one ... and another."

"Another?"

She tried to smile, but it fell straight off her. "I'd better tell them first."

"Of course."

"I didn't mean to be so careless."

He raised an eyebrow, but said nothing. On his countenance, he wore a wealth of understanding. This wasn't Hendrickson or Amelia, but she liked this man a lot.

"I just wanted you to know that. I didn't expect the snow to come down like that, and I didn't know today would be the day I failed to shift."

"Of course you didn't – many people didn't expect the snow to come in the way it did yesterday, not even your husband. The traffic outside Guildford was held up for miles. And I know full well you'd never endanger your baby. You'll be able to shift again about two weeks after the birth."

She nodded. She'd read the same information, although it was nice to hear it confirmed. "Do you know about the telepathic connection I have with my mates?"

He grinned, and his eyes lit up. "Ah, yes. I read about this unique storm-wielder's ability in the documents Hendrickson and Amelia sent me when they also sent me Sarah Harper's file. But I had heard of the telepathy before, although not as anything other than a myth. Quite exciting to see it in a real, live person, I have to say."

Lydia did manage a smile this time. He got excited in the same way Lawrence did about new discoveries. "Well, the same time I stopped being able to shift was the same time I lost the telepathic ability, too. That's when I knew for sure that I was carrying more than one. Before, I just suspected it, because Lawrence, Ryan, and Taylor – they didn't seem able to smell the hormonal changes in me. That happened before with us because of the 'three mates' thing, but I wasn't sure if it would be the same now that I can't wield. I mean, I'm not exactly a storm-wielder any more."

"But you still have three mates."

"True." She sighed. "Yes." She shook her head, feeling both angry and disappointed in herself. "I should have told them."

Dr Matheson raised his stethoscope and placed the ear pieces in his ears. "Again, I say your reaction was a natural one. I suspect that if all male wolves weren't able to smell when their females were pregnant, they would be told about it roundabout now at mid-term."

"Really?"

"Really. Now is when you'll start to show. Now is when the baby's growth speeds up. Now is when you'll begin to feel like a mother, and now – or very soon – is when you're going to start needing your males to do things for you, because you'll be carrying quite a load."

She pulled a face.

He laughed. "If I may, I'd like to do a final check of the three heartbeats – and yours – before I leave you in your mates' capable hands. Is that all right?"

"Yes. Thank you."

He gently pulled down her duvet past her waist.

"I'm surprised they're not breaking down the door to get in."

He laughed. "Well, my dear, that's because I put the fear of god in them when I told them in no uncertain terms that any sense of panic, or emotional intensity of any kind, would be stressful for both you and the babies given what you've just been through, and may put you all at risk. I said they would do well to not set foot in this room until you are ready for them and permit it. The last time I saw them, they had almost paced the downstairs rug to its bare threads, but they appear to be obeying my instructions."

Lydia grinned so wide her cheeks actually hurt, then she found herself giggling at the thought of her three poor alphas. This must be killing them. But she was so damned grateful for the time and space. "Thank you."

"You're very welcome. Now, if you could take a deep breath in, then out, and then lie still just for a few seconds..."

She did as instructed.

Dr Matheson moved his hand across her abdomen,

stretching the skin out a bit and pressing perhaps a little harder than was completely comfortable, and then he placed the stethoscope – funnel end down – onto her belly.

She watched. It all seemed quite surreal. *I'm pregnant*.

That still made her feel all sorts of panic, though. Everything that had happened... She wanted these children, but...

The doctor smiled, nodded; then, without moving the funnel from where he pressed it into her, removed the ear tips from his ears and handed the headset to her. "Go ahead and listen."

Trying to steady her hands, she took it from him, and placed the tips in her own ears.

She audibly gasped, her eyes widening. It was like a small drum orchestra in there. *Three heartbeats*. She could hear them. Strange, chaotic, and full of life – *she could hear them*.

Blinking away tears, she handed the stethoscope back.

"I've never heard healthier hearts in the womb, My Lady. Those babies survived quite a bit yesterday; they'll survive anything now."

She wanted to hug him. To hear those words... She daren't hope, though; experience clouded her joy just a little. "Dr Matheson, I'm ready to see my mates now. If they want to come in, they can."

"I shall let them know." He packed up his stethoscope and pulled out a bottle of pills from his bag which sat on the chair to the left. "These are multi-vits. Essential nutrients. You don't need much else, thankfully, but please take one a day for the next week."

"I will. Thank you so much for coming."

"Oh, I'm around until the birth now, so you'll be seeing me again."

"Lawrence insisted, didn't he?"

He bellowed out a laugh. "Let's just say that when the king

uses a certain tone, you don't refuse him."

Lydia rolled her eyes. "Please don't let him bully you into staying here. I'm sure you have a life and things to attend to. You can't just—"

"My Lady, it's a pleasure to tend to a pregnancy such as yours. Superfecundation is rare, and I'm rather excited to see the results. I suspect it will be heteropaternal, too – possibly three children from the three different fathers. Time will tell. But you'll need speciality help with the birth, and I can offer it. Mr Gunvald only saw the sense in that."

"Well ... thank you again."

He had his coat on now. He picked up his bag and nodded. "You're very welcome. And there's no need to stay in bed, by the way. As soon as you feel able, a bit of exercise will help rather than hinder, but do take it easy, and be mindful of your body's changes over the next four weeks before the birth. I'll pop in to see you tomorrow, and I'll let your mates know you're ready to receive them."

She waved the doctor out, grateful for all his help. But her apprehension was rising. She'd have to talk about everything she didn't want to talk about. And she owed her males one hell of an apology, no matter what the doctor had said. She'd put their children in danger.

With a long exhale, she looked out the bedroom window. She couldn't quite see the ground from this angle on her bed, but she could see the tree tops spanning miles. Snow sat thickly atop them. It looked as if five or six inches had fallen in that short space of time she was out in the blizzard.

Lydia smelled Taylor before she saw him, and she found herself relieved it was he who would venture in to see her first. If anyone had hope of understanding her mind, it was him.

He knocked gently on the door.

"Come in."

Kind, green eyes and a huge smile filled the room as he stepped in. Tears filled her eyes anew because that was everything she needed right now.

He carried a bowl of grapes in his hands. "Hey, you," he said.

"Hi." She reached for him, needing his embrace, and he didn't hesitate, but delved into her arms, bringing her in tightly to his chest.

The quiver in his voice belied his steadfast manner. "Jesus, Lydia..."

"I'm so sorry," she cried.

"Sshhh, don't be sorry. You're here, that's all that matters." He popped the bowl of grapes down on her bedside table. "I thought you might be a little hungry."

"I am a little. Thanks."

"When I saw you in Ryan's arms when he carried you back to the bikes ... I was so scared we'd lost you. Your skin was blue."

She sighed into his shoulder, feeling suddenly exhausted.

"And, Lydia ... you're pregnant?" He pulled back enough to look at her.

She attempted a smile, but guilt pounded her chest. Her tears fell. "I am."

Taylor beamed. It was the best reaction possible, but...

"I'm so sorry I didn't tell you. I have things – other things – I need to tell all three of you."

"Hey, come on. It's your body. You tell us when you're ready."

She was the luckiest wolf alive, she really was. After everything they'd been through, to have him say that... "I love you for saying that, but I should have told you. I was scared and avoiding it."

"But, honey, why?"

"It might be better if you're all here together for me to explain."

He looked at the door, and then looked back at her. "Ryan's here, but Lawrence has gone. He wanted to scour the area around the house you stumbled upon before it got dark. He might not be back for a couple of hours.

Oh.

She didn't know why, but that skewered her a little. He wasn't there with the others waiting for her to wake up.

And she knew. She knew out of all of them, she'd have upset him the most with her silence about her pregnancy.

Hurt, she looked away.

Taylor pulled her back into his chest. "Don't worry about Lawrence. Dr Matheson has kept us all in the loop. We know the babies are doing well. Lawrence knows, too."

That didn't help. His family had all been slaughtered. She needed his forgiveness for putting his future family in danger, even if that hadn't been her intention. "You all trusted me, and I've dented that trust."

Taylor kissed her on the forehead. "Please don't stress about it. I mean it. It's no good for you or the babies. And we can talk about it whenever you're ready, there's no rush."

Oh, sweet man. "I love you so much, Taylor."

"Ditto."

Footsteps pounded on the stairs. Taylor stated the obvious. "Here comes Ryan."

The door swung open, and Ryan's huge frame filled the doorway, his dark brown hair and eyes, and those two scars across his face, making him look much more intimidating than he really was. His gaze landed on Lydia and he grinned. He held up a small bunch of white flowers as he bounded towards her. "The first snowdrops of the season came up this morning. I picked them for you and the babies." He seemed quite delighted with himself.

She laughed. "They're gorgeous. Thank you." She took

them from him. They were very cute and so fresh, she could still smell the outside dew on them. "I'm not sure where to put them."

Ryan looked around, scratched his head, and then reached for the glass of water on the bedside table to her left. "Here." He held the glass, half full, towards her.

"All right, then." She placed the small flowers into it, then Ryan put the glass back on her bedside table.

The way he simplified everything had always made her feel buoyant. She wondered if he could find it in himself to simplify the things she needed to say.

"Lawrence is up at that abandoned house. I've just called him to tell him you're awake. I told him Dr Matheson said you and the babies are fit as a fiddle. He's going to head back when he's done."

Lydia blinked and tried to hide her crushing disappointment. *When he's done.* Not straight away then. "I've really hurt him, haven't I?"

Ryan met her eyes, then looked away before meeting them again. "Don't worry. He just needs a bit of time."

"You're all telling me not to worry because Dr Matheson said I needed to feel calm, not because there's nothing to worry about."

Taylor stroked the top of her hand with his thumb.

Ryan sighed. "Ah ... you know what he's like, Lydia. He's a moody arse when he's been wounded. He's like a bloody woman."

"Oi!"

"Sorry. You know what I mean, though; you know what he's like. Look, when he saw you passed out in my arms, he went all 'His Majesty' on us. We got you back here, he barked out orders at us, phoned the doctor first, then everyone he needed to about that old house to keep himself busy, and barked out even more orders at us... But he did this all from your side. He wouldn't leave you until he had the doctor's fucking blood oath that you and the babies were healthy."

A metaphorical blood oath, she hoped.

"When the poor doctor had managed to convince him you weren't going to die on your next breath, he took off up into the woods and that's where he's been since ten o'clock this morning."

She looked at the clock on the wall. It was three in the afternoon now.

"He just needs a bit of time. He'll be back when he's ready."

She couldn't ask for more. She hadn't been willing to divulge her pregnancy until she was ready – she couldn't ask him to speak to her until he was ready, too.

"Hey, now." Ryan reached across and wiped a tear from her cheek. "No stress. Doctor's orders."

"I *am* sorry I didn't tell you all. I just couldn't. I need to explain why."

"There's no rush, okay?" said Taylor. "Let's just focus on getting you back to one hundred percent. You and the babies come first, and in that order, Lydia. Ryan and I will speak to Lawrence when he's back."

After a moment of hesitation, she nodded. "Okay."

"Good. Can we get you anything?"

"Maybe another glass of water, please."

"I'll bring it straight up."

She found herself yawning.

Ryan mussed her hair and kissed her. "Get some sleep."

She felt annoyed she needed it, but she could feel the fatigue in her bones – she still had some recovery left to make.

"And eat your grapes," smiled Taylor.

She smiled back. "I will."

"We'll be downstairs if you need us. Shout, and we'll hear

you."

She nodded. "Thanks."

After a bit more fussing, Taylor and Ryan both left. Taylor had placed the bowl of grapes on her lap, directly in front of her, before walking out the door. She picked a few and ate them. But her stomach was in knots over the pain she'd caused Lawrence.

She forced herself to eat a few more grapes – for the babies more than for her – then moved the bowl, and shuffled down the bed, bringing the edge of the duvet higher up her chin.

Her mind turned. She wished she could speak to Lawrence telepathically, but that was selfish. If he needed time to himself, she had to let him be, no matter how she felt about it.

Amid the turmoil of her thoughts, her eyelids closed, and she fell asleep.

She was back at Sarah's house, but the dark sky, and the lightning above it had gone. She was alone in the garden. This wasn't a place she wanted to be, but there was something she had to say. She couldn't remember what it was right now, but it was on the tip of her tongue – the urgency of it had brought her here.

A humming floated towards her through the air. It was coming from inside the house. It sounded like a lullaby.

Strange how she didn't feel panicked or scared – not this time. Perhaps it was because she knew her babies were safe. Or perhaps it was because she was finally facing the truth of it.

I'm pregnant.

She looked down at her belly. She'd start to show soon – within a week – and then they'd grow really fast until their due date. Just yesterday, she hadn't felt ready. She almost felt ready now. Almost. There was just this one last thing to put right...

Lydia walked into the house through the back door that led into the kitchen. She followed the humming into the hallway and up the stairs. It was coming from the second door on the right.

The door was ajar.

Quietly, she pushed it open.

A woman in a long dress stood over a crib, a loving smile on her face as she hummed her lullaby for her baby. At least, Lydia assumed there was a baby in the crib – she couldn't see inside it from where she stood.

She stepped into the room, and a floorboard creaked.

The woman stopped humming. She straightened her back, and then turned to face Lydia.

It took a moment. Lydia didn't see it straight away, although the familiarity did press against her mind – the woman's mid-brown hair, held up in a loose bun, and her mid-blue eyes...

She was of average height – everything about her looked average, actually, apart from the love she had for her child. That wasn't average, that was huge. It was very clear to see.

It was only when Lydia cottoned on to the vintage style of this woman's outfit, that everything fell into place. "Gladys."

"Hello, Lydia," Gladys replied – a young Gladys of no more than thirty years. "I knew you'd come even though I asked you to stay away. You always were stubborn."

"I have to put things right. I can't live in the past any more."

"The past is always there waiting to take you back."

"No. I'm done now. I'm not going back."

Gladys tutted, then turned around and looked back down at the crib. She smiled at the baby, and Lydia heard it coo at her from its bed. "The past will always find you."

"Then it can come and find me in the future. I'm not staying here."

"Then why did you come in the first place? Why are you here at all?" Gladys reached down for her baby. She was now talking to the child and not Lydia. "Come to Mama, my love. That's it. Mama loves you so much." She brought the baby up to her chest.

Lydia gasped. Her eyes welled at the horror before her, but she refused to look away. She had to stop turning away.

Made of nothing but bloody muscles and tendons hanging loosely from its skeleton, the baby gurgled in reply to its mother. It turned its head, empty sockets staring at Lydia.

"I..." There was her fear, right there. It was more than fear. It was an overwhelming terror that wanted to eat her whole. It was the destruction she was capable of causing; had already caused. "I came to say goodbye."

Gladys' gaze didn't waver.

"Some say, in some ways, your enemies mean more to you than your friends. And you've always haunted me. As a child, I feared you. I despise you for your role in the disintegration of my family – what you did to my father, I can never forgive. But what I feel when I look at you standing there with your baby in your arms ... what I feel is my own terror at what I could become.

"I came to say goodbye to you because you're not me – you're not. Your mistakes aren't mine." Lydia's eyes fell back to the child Gladys held. "I came to say goodbye to death. Your death isn't mine, and your baby's death has no place among the life I carry. You're right. I have been holding onto the past, because the past is familiar no matter how painful. The pain *is familiar. But I don't need it any more." She walked towards the woman and her child until she was standing inches from her. She looked her right in the eye. "Goodbye, Gladys."*

"You won't escape it, Lydia. The past is too big. Look what you've already done – endangered lives; so much death... Every mistake you make will build your children's pasts; they will suffer for your mistakes as my daughter suffered for mine."

"Mistakes cease to be mistakes once they're transformed. The past is big. But I'm bigger, and the future I carry, is even bigger than me."

That was it. No more words. Lydia turned around and walked out, down the stairs, through the kitchen and back into the garden.

It had snowed. She stepped onto its white blanket; a blank canvas; a new chapter. Snowdrops peppered the scene as the sun broke through the clouds and shone its bright, winter rays.

She continued on, and Sarah's house faded into the distance behind her. Before her, Lawrence's mansion came into view, and she smiled, her step feeling more and more weightless as she made her way home.

The future was already here.

CHAPTER SIX

Lawrence's presence was a thing no one ever ignored, and Lydia felt it now as her eyes drifted open.

The bedroom was dark. She must have slept until night.

Her gaze fell to where she felt her mate and husband to be, and he was, although all she could make out was his silhouette on the chair he sat in about ten metres from the end of the bed. "Lawrence?"

There was a pause, and then… "Congratulations."

Shit. But she'd expected no less. Her heart sank, but she refused to be defeated at the familiar and unwelcome icy tone to his voice. They'd been here before, but she wasn't going to join him in his frozen chamber. She'd had enough of the cold for one day.

She glanced at the snowdrops sitting in her glass of water. *You can do this*.

She looked back at Lawrence. He hadn't moved a muscle from what she could tell, so she began. "When I gave my life to save our species, I wasn't expecting to come back. You know how that feels because it was the same with you."

Silence.

Okay, good. She didn't want any interruptions. "I remember the Trident tearing me apart, at least until I passed out. And then, just as with you, what was left of my body was possessed by a god who put the pieces back together and brought me back to life. I'm so glad Yemet did what she did, but I didn't ask for it either, and it's taken a while to accept that I *am* really back.

"When Yemet took over my body, I heard her thoughts –

things she said to Himet. She said I was carrying a seed – a child. She and Himet did something to it – some kind of protection – and they said no harm would come to it. Yes – I was pregnant then, but I forgot straight after. When I came to and Yemet had gone, I didn't remember her words, or that I was pregnant. I didn't remember anything until days later, and even then, it was fuzzy." She could sense the wheels turning in his head. If she'd been pregnant ... that had been four months ago.

She sighed. Here came the hard bit. "It was the day of Hendrickson and Amelia's funeral. We were there, burying them, do you remember? It was two weeks after the storm, and I asked to be excused from the ceremony. I said I needed to go home. You all thought I was grieving. I wasn't grieving ... I didn't know what was happening at first. I felt pain, and then..." Fuck, she'd told herself she wouldn't cry, but it was hard. "There was blood. I was bleeding, and ... I miscarried. I lost the baby. I ... lost it. It was at that point Yemet's words came back to me and I realised – remembered, I guess – that I'd been pregnant all that time.

"It wasn't that I never intended to tell you about the miscarriage, it's that we were at a funeral and it seemed *so* wrong to say ... I just couldn't. I couldn't bring more sorrow to the table, and in the days and weeks after the funeral, things got a bit better. We started to laugh more, and the house was being repaired ... I didn't want to bring the darkness of my second miscarriage into our lives – we'd gone through enough. And I was fine – I was *fine*. I'd cleaned myself up after it happened and took care of myself; I never once thought I needed a doctor. Everything was okay. Except ... physically I was good, but my heart was a bit ruined. When Yemet's words that night came back to me, it cut me. They'd protected the baby, and I'd *still* miscarried. I felt ashamed. I didn't know what to say or how to explain that to you. I'm supposed to be bringing a species to life, not killing it all over again, and I thought maybe ... maybe it was *because* of me. All the lightning and the death ... maybe I'm not *supposed* to be the one carrying your..." She bit back a sob. She had to get it all out. "So I said nothing, and did my best to forget about it completely.

"Then, about two weeks ago, I realised I was pregnant again. It was just before Christmas, and I so wanted to tell you, but I ... froze. I froze and I got scared because what if I miscarried again? What if I *always* miscarry? What if it happened over and over again? And I guess, without really thinking it through, I told myself I'd wait. I'd wait until I knew for sure I wouldn't lose the baby before saying anything because I didn't want to put you through that, and I didn't want to go through it again either.

"But what happened instead was I pushed it away. I ignored it and pretended it wasn't there. I think in my head, I was just waiting for it to go wrong. I was waiting to miscarry, because I couldn't even hold onto a seed protected by gods." She laughed, though it wasn't funny at all. Her laugh faded into silence. She picked at the hem of her duvet. "What I did yesterday was careless, and a result of me avoiding my fears, and I am so, so sorry. If I could rewind time, I wouldn't have gone for a run, and I would have told you I was pregnant when I first found out. Instead, I put my fear before our children and our future, and it was unforgivable. I will never make the same mistake again, I swear it."

A whole minute must have passed. The silence in the blackness of the room was beginning to feel unbearable. Lydia exhaled, and looked up at Lawrence's silhouette, trying to see his face, or gauge his reaction, or anything. But she didn't ask him to speak. She wouldn't – he'd speak in his own time.

Which is exactly what he did. His tone carried all his weight. And his anger.

Her heart flipped and sank. She hung her head.

"Lydia Gunvald, I've given you many things: my blood, my

lineage, my fucking kingdom ... and I've forgiven you many things. I forgave you for running to Brendan when I advised you not to; I forgave you for experimenting your wielding on Amelia in secret when it could have hurt her; I forgave you for visiting Gladys behind my back putting both you and Richard in danger; and I've forgiven you"—his voice cracked, then darkened—"for walking into a horde of Tridents and getting yourself – the woman I gave every damned thing to – killed for a species hanging on by nothing but a thread from a tainted bloodline." He stood from his chair. "But god help me, Lydia, I will not forgive you if I *ever again* hear you say you're not supposed to carry my children."

She was a stupid, crying mess as she looked up at him, bewildered.

He came into view under the beam of moonlight through the window, his eyes streaked with tears and rimmed red, expressing the depth of his love for her, and before she knew it, she was under him, pressed back into the mattress as his mouth crushed hers in a fierce kiss she returned with both relief and abandon.

Her hands reached for his hair, her fingers twining through it.

"You should have fucking told me," he whispered, his voice thick.

"Lawrence, I—"

"I understand why you didn't. But, Lydia, after every single thing we've been through, after what you sacrificed, do you really think I'd hold you responsible if anything had happened to those babies inside you? Jesus Christ, I want to have children with you, but not at the expense of *you*. You mean the goddamned world to me, and it's *not* because you can bear my children, it's because you bear my heart. If anything had happened to you out there today... I've been angry with myself. I should have known the wind would turn and bring the snow in. Even Taylor thought it would, but I was distracted after speaking to Richard. Lydia…" He stared right into her eyes. "You are *not* the mother to a species, do you understand? I can't believe you thought that; that you've been putting yourself under that pressure. That's insane. You're the mother to my children – *our* children. The species comes second. We've never spoken about this properly – something else I'm angry at myself for. Six months ago, you came into this pack blindly and without your consent. A hell of a lot has changed since then, but I need to ask you – I need to know … do you want these children?"

"Do I *want* them?"

"Half a year ago, you bought ten packs of condoms and stated, unequivocally, you were too young to even think about it; that your life wasn't even sorted."

"Lawrence." She brushed his falling hair behind his ears. "I didn't tell you about my pregnancy because I was afraid of all the mistakes our parents made; that I might make. But having these children at all, that's not one of them. I've been terrified of heralding death instead of life, but these kids in here – they survived a blizzard. So, I think, maybe they're bigger than my fears, and stronger than I'll ever be."

"Lydia, you're not responsible for life or death."

"But it kind of feels like I am, what with Himet and Yemet and what we went through. I felt like I had to be responsible for everything that came next – to make sure it was right."

"You don't."

"I know that now."

"I mean it. You come *before* the species. We're not repopulating it, Lydia. All we're doing is living our lives. We have children *if* you want to, and we stop when you want to."

She smiled. "The condoms will be out of date by then."

He let a grin slip through.

"I want these babies, Lawrence. I think I want them more than I've ever wanted anything." She reached up and kissed him.

He sighed into the kiss, and deepened it; then pulled back and studied her.

"What is it?"

"I don't want you to take this the wrong way. I feel terrible you miscarried again, and I wish that hadn't happened – I really wish you hadn't suffered that alone – but..." He reached down between them and gently touched her belly. "I'm glad these babies were conceived *after* it all happened; after the storm. It makes it..."

"Ours," she finished, and smiled. "It makes it ours. *Our* story, and our children's stories – not a story that belongs to gods and our ancestors' mistakes."

"Exactly."

"I hadn't thought of it that way, but you're right. They deserve an untainted beginning."

"And this is it."

"Lawrence, what about the children in that house?"

He frowned, and shook his head. "There are no records of that house on this land that I can find – my parents never spoke of it; they might not even have known about it. I have no idea who lived there, but I'm going to see if I can deal with this off-record as much as possible. Legally, I have to report the bodies, but I know a guy who knows about us – about wolves – he used to be in the police force. I'm hoping he can sort this out quietly because we've been through enough for one lifetime."

"I found a key."

"The one in the pocket of your dress?"

"Yes – you saw it, then. It's the key to the house. Lawrence, those kids were locked in from the outside. Someone *did* that to them."

"Try and put it out of your mind. That house, and those

skeletons, look to be a hundred years old at least – probably older. What happened, happened an age ago, and it's also not our story. I'll speak to the guy I know, and make sure they receive a proper burial wherever that may be."

She nodded.

"Try not to let it bother you. What happened in that house happened a century ago – that's not part of our new beginning."

"I know." But she wondered if someone needed an ending. Her dreams, that house, those children, and her own pregnancy...

Lawrence kissed her once more, and all her thoughts faded. A burden had been lifted; she did feel like they had a clean slate before them, and no, she didn't feel like she was connected to those children in that house in any way – more that she'd been living out her own fears in her dreams, and her mind had placed that house and its occupants into her last two dreams because they'd made such an impact on her.

Whoever they were, she hoped they'd found peace, or at the very least that her finding them yesterday would offer them the peace they needed once they were laid to rest. Everyone needed an ending.

And Lawrence, Taylor, Ryan, herself – and the future she carried for all of them – finally had their new beginning.

"Lawrence," she whispered into his kiss.

He pulled back and stared at her, waiting.

"There's something I'd love you to help me do."

"Name it."

"The last time I danced was the day of Brendan's funeral, and the day I miscarried at Sarah's house when we nearly lost Taylor. I want you to help me dance again."

The slow smile that spread across his face was a small piece of heaven. And fuck it, his eyes welled up. "I thought you'd never ask."

"It's hurt me to think about it."

"I know, although I didn't know the full reason why until now. Did you realise you've been wearing that black dress of yours a lot?"

"The dress?" The one she'd worn yesterday? She had four black dresses, but this one had the longer sleeves. Because of the cold weather, she'd thought—

It hit her like a ton of bricks. "Oh, Lawrence." She hadn't realised. "It was *the* dress. The one I wore to Brendan's funeral."

"And the one you miscarried in."

That's what Taylor had meant. They'd all seen it, except her. "I've been so blind."

"No. You've been hurting."

"No more hurting. I don't want my dancing to remind me of death. It has to stop. My dancing used to be for joy."

"It will be again, I promise."

She smiled, brushed his wet cheek; then laced her fingers through his right hand, and brought it down her length until it rested over her womb. "I believe you."

* * *

THIRTY-NINE-YEAR-OLD WOMAN ATTACKED AND MURDERED IN KENT WOODLAND

Even though he'd shoved this morning's newspaper to the far end of his work desk, Taylor's eyes fell on the headline for the third time.

It's got nothing to do with you.

It really didn't. Nothing at all. Except he knew that stretch of woodland the article referenced. That was where he and Sarah had been attacked by a rogue wolf, a year and a half ago now.

That was where he'd been turned. His attraction to the headline had little to do with what it said, and everything to do with history.

"Taylor?"

He snapped his head around at Ryan's call, then rose from his desk and switched off his lamp. Work was done for the day, and Lydia was fine. The babies were fine. And they were going to be dads.

He smiled as he walked out of his room. "Yep. I'm here."

Ryan stared up from the bottom of the stairs. "Dinner's done. Can you sort the drinks?"

"No problem. I've got elderberry cordial stored from the autumn."

"Sounds perfect."

"Is Lydia coming down?"

"Yeah, Lawrence said she'll be joining us."

"That's good news." He reached the bottom step and followed Ryan into the kitchen.

"Certainly is. And Lawrence's mood has improved, thank fuck."

Taylor laughed. "Thank the gods."

Ryan snorted. "Nope. Had enough of gods for a lifetime."

And he wasn't joking. Taylor decided to change the subject. "How do you feel about becoming a dad?"

Ryan turned to him with a grin to light fuses. "I've been ready for it a long time. You?"

"Yeah ... I'm good." But he'd stalled with his answer, and he didn't fully know why.

Ryan's grin faded a fraction, a hint of concern replacing it. "Are you sure?"

"Yeah." But that sounded ... not quite right to his own ears. He couldn't pinpoint the seat of his discomfort because he truly was more than happy about the pregnancy. It was quickly forgotten when Lydia and Lawrence entered the kitchen. She was carrying the glass of snowdrops.

"Hey!" Taylor greeted her with a hug and a kiss, as did Ryan. "Table's laid – take a seat."

She held up the small, white flowers, their petals now closed for the night. "I thought it would be nice to have these on the table."

"They make the perfect finish," he agreed.

She placed them in the centre. "Dinner smells amazing."

"It's roast beef. Ryan made it, so it is, in fact, amazing." Ryan was a damn fine cook, not that it was a talent the large male really nourished.

Lawrence and Lydia took their seats as Taylor poured the elderberry.

Ryan brought all the food out of the oven and served it up, then finally took his seat among everyone else. "Dig in and help yourselves to more," he said. "There's enough food for seven."

There was an awed silence as they all took in what that really meant; then Lydia let out a small laugh, her face red, but full of joy, and, more importantly, full of life. She'd scared the crap out of them all with her escapade in the snow. Ryan was right – enough with the gods and their dramatics.

The newspaper headline flashed through his mind, briefly, and then Lawrence held up his glass, obliterating those words with his own. "Here's to the seven of us."

"The seven of us!" They all cheered, and Lydia went redder. But her smile got bigger, even as her eyes shimmered with unshed tears.

She raised her own glass and smiled at him, then at Ryan, and finally at Lawrence. Her hand fell to her abdomen, where a whole new world resided. "And here's to new beginnings."

TWISTED ROOTS

CHAPTER ONE

The setting sun strew its rays into his bedroom, setting the tips of Lydia's hair on fire, or so it seemed, its red lustre redder than ever.

Taylor kissed her right shoulder and then turned into her side, pressing himself against the curve of her extremely pregnant body, relishing in the feel of both their nudity and their togetherness. He saw her belly ripple with the babies' movements. "Are you all right lying on your back like that?"

"Not for long," she mumbled, drowsy from this little nap they'd accidentally fallen into after dinner. She'd wanted to spend the night with him before his trip out to Kent with Lawrence in the early hours. A trip no one was overly enthusiastic about him taking, but they had conceded, because they all understood the hidden needs of the other after the events of the last seven months or so – the craziest seven months of their lives that began with Lydia's arrival and ended five months ago with nothing short of carnage on this very land they called home.

Rebuilding it was never going to be grief-free. Healing was needed; was taking place every second of every day. The sweetest victory always came at the highest price.

Lydia groaned, lightly, as she turned onto her side, supporting her giant mound with her hand as she did so, finally relaxing into a more agreeable position on her left.

Taylor spooned her from behind and she sighed her contentment. He kissed her again on the nape of her neck, then trailed a few more kisses down her spine.

She sighed again, this one carrying a small moan with it. "Are you sure you wouldn't rather just stay here with me *all* night?"

"Of course I would. But I need to know."

She turned her head – just her head – to look at him, not quite willing to change her better position now she'd found it. She said nothing for a couple of seconds and then, "Sarah's death was an accident. A nonsensical, badly timed accident. The suddenness of it, though, while we were going through every crazy thing we went through that night ... it makes it *seem* like there needs to be a reason."

"I've run all of that through my mind. I really have."

"But you still feel there's more?"

"That's the thing – I don't know for sure and won't until I do this. I can't shake the feeling there's something missing. I was in shock, and it all happened so fast, and then there was the whole change from human to wolf... I might easily have forgotten something important."

She sighed for the third time, turned her head back, but took his hand in her right and brought it across her belly, clasping it tightly. "I can't stand the thought of that thing in your system, especially after seeing it work on Nikolai."

"It's benign with no instruction – Lawrence is certain of its safety."

"He doesn't like you doing this either, you know."

"I know. He's going through with it for me."

"And because he knows I'll feel better if he's there to guide you and watch over you." She squeezed his hand. "You know I understand. The way my father died ... I get it. I *had* to go see Gladys about it. I had to know what she knew; I had to know if she had anything to do with it. But Taylor—" She pressed his palm into her side. The kick under it was astounding in its *life*. It flooded his heart with warmth. "Don't forget this – the future. *Our* future. It's right here waiting for you, and it needs you."

A pause held the night between them before his voice broke it, tears springing to his eyes. "I need it, too. More than you know. It's why I need to do this now."

"I know, Taylor."

He laid his forehead against the top of her back, settling himself into her frame and all the love he felt for her. "I know you do. I love you."

"I love you, too."

The sound the car's tyres made on the barely tarmacked country lane sounded far too loud for the eerie black of night.

The moon was nearly full overhead, not that it mattered anymore. No werewolf was ruled by the wax and wane of the moon – not for five months now. Leaving Lydia lying under its luminescence had been hard as hell.

Taylor took a deep breath in as Lawrence pulled to the side of the lane and brought the car to a stop. Gnarled trees with twisted roots rose up either side of them for a good mile in either direction – yew trees, mostly, with some birches, holly, and the occasional oak. The wood was thick here. And he didn't need to see Lawrence's stiff movements as he switched the engine off to know he was apprehensive about this revisit to the past.

Ryan had wanted to come, too, upset Taylor was attempting this at all, but he'd finally relented to what they had all insisted: that Ryan stay near Lydia's side so close to the birth of their first child. Their first *three* children to be exact. Triplets.

Dr Matheson was certain Lydia still had a few days left – the babies had not dropped in her uterus yet – so as far as Taylor was concerned, it was now or never. He wanted this clean slate; every dark thing behind him, once and for all, before the new and pure entered their world.

Lawrence reached across him to open the glove box and pulled out the small black bag inside it. Unzipping it, he brought out an ampoule of Amnesthipine and a syringe and needle, still in its sterile wrapping. "The liquid in here"—he waved the sealed ampoule in his hand—"I'm loathe to put this in you. *None* of us are happy about this."

Yeah, he knew. But he'd seen the weight Richard carried having arrived back from his travels in search of Selena ten days ago, none the wiser and defeated, and it had sealed the deal in Taylor's own mind. "I can't shake this feeling and I don't want to hold these brand new lives in my arms for the first time with this shadow cloaking my mind." He glanced down at the little bottle in Lawrence's hand. "I trust you implicitly. And I know you wouldn't have driven me all the way here if you were in any doubt about your skills using this stuff."

Lawrence let out a long breath. He was no stranger to ghosts that plagued the mind and soul. "Amnesthipine works deeply when using hypnosis techniques. Not everyone in their natural state can be hypnotised – but Amnesthipine ensures everyone can. It obliterates the autonomy you have over yourself and you'll be completely under my suggestion. That's the sole reason we're able to erase memories – and reprogramme them to an extent – so easily and thoroughly. And permanently. Taylor." Lawrence waited for him to face him; to look him in the eye before continuing. "I've *never* tried using this to bring memories back before."

"But you're sure that on its own – without the hypnosis – it wouldn't do a thing?"

"It would make you drowsy, but that's all. Without anything to instruct you, without the words to take you to the recesses of your mind, you would simply stay as you are – no change – until the drowsiness wore off."

"So, all you have to do is take me on that journey."

Lawrence's jaw clenched. "I won't be saying a single thing to wipe away anything you remember. This is all about finding what's lost and bringing it back. And I know you know I'd never abuse your will. But Taylor"—his eyes searched him out amid the shadows of the car—"I'm concerned you'll bring back your trauma. You all but died that night."

"I've all but died three times and I remember them all – mostly."

"*Not* in the detail this drug can muster."

"I need to know." He felt Lawrence's stare bore into the side of his face. "I was swimming in and out of consciousness for at least an hour before you and Ryan arrived, and much of it was spent *out* of consciousness. But even in a comatose state people can hear and sense – I know it's possible. I need to know what I missed. Because I can't shake the feeling something *is* missing. A word; a scent; I'm not sure what, but—"

"But you think Sarah's death might not have been a run-of-the-mill accident."

Taylor turned to look directly at Lawrence. "What are the chances, eh? On that night of all nights?"

"Accidents *do* happen. And what if you do find a clue to give some indication it was premeditated – that it was all part of Bab's great master plan for some reason or other – what then? Bab's dead. The Trident are dead. Who pays? Why bring it all up within you all over again when there's nothing to be done about it?"

Taylor fell silent. He'd asked himself this same question over and over again. "I can't give you any logical answer to that. I just... A woman was murdered here a few weeks ago according to the local paper. While I'm certain that's nothing to do with Tridents, Bab, or us, I've been wondering why *here*. Ryan said the energy of places ... when bad things happen, it can attract other bad things to the same spot, like some kind of vacuum. Maybe ... I dunno. Maybe I can cleanse it somehow. Get rid of the bad stuff. What if it's still a part of me. What if I..." He left that sentence unfinished.

"What if you what?" asked Lawrence, softly.

Taylor gulped past the tightness in his throat. "Bring the bad stuff to our children's door."

His mate's left hand fell onto his right and squeezed it. "Out of all of us, you are the *least* likely to do that, *believe* me."

He knew Lawrence was thinking about his own past. He returned the affection with his own squeeze. "I just have to know there was nothing I missed; that nothing's going to leap out of the shadows and come for our new family because of something I did – or didn't do."

After a moment of silence, Lawrence nodded and placed the syringe and ampoule back in the black bag. He reached for his mobile phone. "Let me check in with Ryan that all's okay at their end and then we'll start."

Taylor voiced his thanks and braced himself for the familiar scent of these woods as Lawrence sent his message; he knew it would be ten times stronger the minute he stepped out of the car, along with it, stark memories of the night he'd been turned, changing his life irrevocably. He'd made peace with the turning, having *chosen* to return as a werewolf after his last spate at death's door five months ago. He would never walk away from his wolf again – he knew that. But he hadn't made peace with everything that had happened to Sarah, nor her unexpected (and apparently accidental) death. The love he'd held for her had eventually changed along with his DNA and Lydia's arrival. Sure, it was always there in some form, but that form was no longer one of marital union. He had happily – in the end – released it, finding a new and perfect union, and love, in the unusual four-way mating he'd been thrust into instead. He was where he was *meant* to be. He knew that completely.

But he wasn't sure Sarah was where she was meant to be.

"Lydia's fine," said Lawrence, bringing him back to the present. "Just irritable, according to Ryan."

"Hardly surprising. Have you *seen* the size of those pups?"

The phone sounded another incoming text message. Lawrence smirked, bemused, as he read the words on the screen. "My ears are ringing. The dogs of Hades wouldn't cross her."

Taylor laughed. "Sounds like our Lydia."

Lawrence grunted and pocketed the phone. "On a good day, too." But his pride in her feistiness was evident; his obvious love for her like a beacon in the dark. "You ready?"

"As I'll ever be."

"Good. Let's get this over with."

CHAPTER TWO

This was the spot. Right down to the tree itself – the one he'd slumped against, shredded to pieces and bleeding to death. The hawthorn, a few metres to its right, was where Sarah had huddled, catatonic, apart from the odd whimper and scream. He'd known the memories would rush in; nevertheless, they came at him like a ball from a cannon, far more brutal than he'd prepared for. He swayed on his feet and closed his eyes.

Lawrence clearly saw his reaction. "We can leave right now."

"No." He breathed in deep and opened his eyes. "It's the past – it's not now. I won't lose sight of that throughout this."

One blond eyebrow arched upwards. Lawrence looked utterly unconvinced. "The hypnosis will pull you into the past as if it's happening now. I'm not sure how prepared you are for that." Not a leaf stirred as he studied him. It was a still night – no breeze; barely enough light from the silver moon and her sister stars. Their werewolf sight saw enough, though.

"I've relived it enough times in my mind over the past year and a half." Taylor turned and sat down in the dip of the yew's roots – the exact same dip where he'd lost his human life. Six seasons had passed since that night, and yet, he swore he could still smell the blood he'd shed and Sarah's fear. Maybe the tree had soaked it all in. With concerted effort, he allowed himself to slump until he was lying in what he felt was the same position he'd been in.

Lawrence swore under his breath.

Taylor could tell he was battling with memories, too. But for him, at least, that had been just another day. He hadn't known

Taylor, then. At all. He'd just been one more unfortunate human to deal with.

"That's not fucking true," came the retort.

"You're in my mind?" Each of the four mates could read each other's minds if they really wanted or needed to. They had agreed not to out of courtesy and privacy.

"I'm going to be *leading* your mind in a damned minute, so hell, yes, I'm staying in it so I can see which way I'm going."

Taylor's breath hitched and he silently cursed. He hadn't considered, in full, how painful this might be for Lawrence – especially now they were mated.

"I'll be fine," he stated, clearly still inside his head. "Lydia can cope with my memories in her system; I can cope with yours."

"Thank you," said Taylor, sincerely. He meant it. He needed this before the babies were born. He'd carried too much guilt for too long – new beginnings shouldn't start with any guilt.

Lawrence nodded as he studied their near-black surroundings, nostrils flaring, his wandering gaze precise – undoubtedly in hunter mode – and then, when satisfied they were on their own, he knelt beside him. He unzipped the black pouch again and got everything ready. "Do you remember what I told you? You'll feel a bit cold at first, but that will wear off as your body regulates its temperature. And then you'll get drowsy – that's when I'll start speaking. This will all happen within the first minute, and you need to *listen* to my voice when I speak – *only* my voice. The Amnesthipine will ensure that's the case in some ways – the way the drug shuts you down chemically, it forces the brain to home in on whatever it deems to be security and safety to ease the stress. Your mind should latch onto my voice. But if you also focus consciously on it, it makes the whole thing go more smoothly."

Taylor nodded, nerves rising for the first time over what was to come.

"Hey." Lawrence placed his left hand on his shoulder, holding the ampoule and needle in his right. "I'll never risk your safety. I'll be with you to some extent in your mind, but not completely – I need to be in control out here to guide you through and to make sure no one comes upon us. But I'll know if you're in too far. I'll feel what you feel. I'll see what you see."

Taylor nodded again. "Okay." There was some comfort in that. "I'm ready."

"Take your coat off and roll up your sleeve."

They'd agreed to do this in the middle of the night for two reasons. The first: it would recreate the same scene from the past and make it easier to place themselves in it, and the second: the chances of running into anyone out here at 1:00 a.m. was close to zero. No dog walkers; no hikers.

Lawrence pierced the ampoule's seal and filled the syringe with the drug as Taylor hitched his sleeve up past his elbow. "I don't want this lasting more than two hours," he said. "Ideally not even that long, but the drug tends to wear off around the two-hour mark."

"The attack couldn't have taken more than three minutes; and then one hour for you to arrive. So that shouldn't be a problem."

"I'll be leading into the attack from what took place the hour before. Hold steady." He straightened Taylor's left arm and felt for the vein.

Before the attack? It dawned on Taylor he'd only ever had flashbacks and thoughts about the attack itself since it had happened. He'd never really focused on what had happened earlier that night – had never really wanted to because the inevitable destination of his train of thoughts would always bring him right here and *here* was not a place he ever wanted to be. Ice cold shot through his entire system. He exhaled, sharply.

"It's all right. It's taking effect. Try to relax into it."

He tried. It wasn't easy. The cold went straight to his head like when eating ice cream as a kid. It hurt his nose. It was as if he could feel the icy tendrils mushroom into every groove that made up his brain matter – grey and then white – infiltrating his very core. He thought he groaned in protest, but he wasn't sure because everything was ... everywhere. And also not there at all. He could no longer feel his body. But there was a sound. Familiar. Very familiar. He needed it. It was like coming home, even though he couldn't form words for it. It ... it ... a voice...

"Listen to my voice. Taylor, follow my voice."

Yes. He wanted to. It wrapped around him like it owned him.

"Taylor, can you hear my voice?"

He heard himself say yes and that was the freakiest thing ever because there was no *thought* behind his reply. No decision. No intent.

"Can you hear my voice?"

"Yes." He'd done it again. The 'yes' had been immediate as if it was prised out of him. God, he had no control at all – none.

Until the voice gave it to him. *"It's the 1st of November – only just turned midnight – eighteen months ago. Where are you, Taylor?"*

His mind took him there straight away and it wasn't a memory or a thought, but a facet of something *very* real. He was *there.* Walls loomed around him, forming into shape; music blared; laughter permeated his senses ... *his senses.* The smell of beer and perfume ... a soft touch on his arm.

He looked down at it. *Sarah.*

He *landed* in his body right in that chapter of midnight, on the cusp of All Hallow's Eve and All Saints Day. The house party they were at was a civilised, but lively one.

Somewhere incredibly distant, he heard himself reply to the

voice, telling it exactly where he was – he had no control over his replies, but he had control over *this.* This was *real.*

"Well, I think Zoe won't be going home alone tonight," laughed Sarah, her eyes twinkling as she gestured at her old friend from university. "I'm so glad – she's usually so shy and she's been on her own for the best part of four years. Taylor..."

"Hm?" he replied, loving the way her hand felt as it fluttered across his chest and rested there.

"Let's leave soon. I want to go home." Her eyes shone with a subtle passion, and he wondered if Zoe's flirtatious laughter was lighting a particular fire. She reached up, rose on her toes, and brought her lips to his, an incredibly sexy smile on her face.

A strange and out-of-place twinge at his navel seemed to distort everything around him for a second.

"Stay with the scene, it's all right."

Taylor relaxed. The twinge disappeared, the walls of the house grew solid once more and so did Sarah – very much so when that kiss deepened, and her tongue twined with his.

He sighed into her mouth. "Mrs Harper, you are divine." Seriously – he was the luckiest man alive.

"The costume helps, huh?"

He glanced at the white Ancient Egyptian-style dress she'd designed and sewn herself for this fancy-dress party. Actually, that was a total lie – he was looking at the way the tops of her breasts swelled before dipping into the most glorious cleavage. "Cleopatra's got nothing on you."

The twinge at this navel announced itself more painfully this time. He swooned, or maybe everything around him did instead – he couldn't tell. It was like he was a part of his surroundings. He grimaced in pain, but that familiar voice alleviated it. Mumbled something he couldn't catch, but he knew a part of him heard it and obeyed it.

His mind, following instructions he couldn't quite fathom,

reconstructed the scene before him. An hour had passed. They were still at the party, but now outside in the garden, despite the chill in the air. Sarah was no longer beside him, but he caught sight of her just a few yards away speaking to a guy he vaguely recognised. Well-dressed; good-looking; he looked like he worked out under that shirt – he clearly hadn't bothered with the fancy dress theme; half the people here hadn't. Taylor was glad he'd donned his more simple Woodcutter's costume rather than the Big Bad Wolf one he'd worn last year. Most of the people here were Sarah's friends from university or previous jobs. He wasn't sure he'd met this guy – he was sure he'd have remembered. Maybe he'd seen him in photographs.

It looked like he was offering her wine. She refused, waving the bottle away and holding her glass of lemonade up as she spoke. He guessed she was telling him she was driving home – she'd insisted she was happy to since Taylor was giving up the evening for her and her friends.

He made his way to her. She'd wanted to leave a while ago but had gotten caught up talking to people she hadn't seen for years.

She spied him before he reached her. "Hey, Taylor." Her grin was wide. She reached for him, and he placed an arm around her waist. "This is Scott. I knew him from my first job placement – god, was it six or seven years ago?"

"Eight, actually, I think."

"Can you believe it? I can't remember if you've met my husband, Taylor."

They exchanged greetings and shook hands.

Something weird happened. He couldn't stop it. Time seemed to shift, or perhaps he did, like he was on a train and couldn't stop the movement (was that the voice he heard again?) and suddenly they were out the front and he was holding Sarah's coat out for her.

She put it on. "I hope there's no traffic."

"Unlikely this late. We'll take the short cut through that stretch of wood before the motorway – there won't be anything along that lane at all."

She yawned.

Taylor smiled. "And I'll drive."

"No," she started to protest. "I'm not tired. I promised I would."

"Really, it's fine – I didn't drink anything anyway. Have a snooze in the car if you need to."

"What time is it?"

He looked at his watch. "Nearly quarter to one."

She groaned.

"We're only half an hour or so from home."

"I know, but I wanted to ... you know."

"I do?"

"Spend some *time* with you when we get home. Rather than fall face first into a pillow." That was said on the tail of another yawn.

Taylor laughed. "We can spend *time* with each other tomorrow. We have the rest of our lives."

She threw him a loving look. "I'll *try* to stay awake. There's something, um ... there's something I want to talk to you about."

They made their way to their car having checked they had everything they arrived with. "What is it?"

"No, not here. At home. I don't want to tell you here."

"Sounds ... serious?"

"No. Nothing to worry about at all, I just ... just not here, okay?"

He creased his brow, wondering what it was. He knew she had been worrying a bit about the bridal shop she'd bought last year. Overheads were expensive. Had she decided to get another job? Or perhaps go into partnership? She *had* spoken to quite a lot of people tonight – many were her old contacts; her network.

They got in the car.

"Have you got a new job?"

She laughed.

"Sorry. I'm intrigued now. You've stirred the pot."

"It's not about work. Really, we'll talk when we get home."

"Oh, wait – it's Beth, isn't it? What's she done now?"

"Taylor," she admonished.

"All right, all right."

"I'll tell you at home, I promise."

"What if you fall asleep?" Curiosity ate away at him as he turned the ignition, wincing at the way the engine spluttered before it whirred. He wasn't sure this rust-bucket would pass its MOT in two weeks.

"Then we have tomorrow and the rest of our lives, just like you said."

There was a strange lilt to her tone he'd not heard before. He looked at her as he pulled away from the curb where they had parked.

She flashed him a secretive smile he couldn't for the life of him decipher and then her attention was drawn elsewhere, conveniently bringing a change of subject. "Oh, look, Taylor," she gasped. "Look at that moon!" It hung large and bright and low in the sky. "Isn't that just beautiful?"

"It really is," he agreed, but it was her he was looking at, not the moon.

She laughed and probably blushed, and they both fell into an easy silence as he turned right at the next junction.

CHAPTER THREE

"Taylor, can you hear my voice?"

"Yes."

"Where are you?"

"Driving up the country lane, through the big patch of thick wood, before turning onto the A-road that takes us towards Westerham."

"What do you see around you?"

"Trees. The moon. Darkness. Sarah's in the car to my left."

"Taylor, I want you to freeze the scene. Bring everything to a standstill in front of you as if you've paused a film."

His mind had already begun the process, doing what the voice asked because it couldn't do anything else.

"You can still move in this scene. You are the only thing that can move in this scene. Do you understand?"

"Yes."

"Good. Has everything stopped now?"

"Yes."

"Is everything as it was that night? Is the scene a moment from the past?"

"Yes."

"Look around you. Take your time. Is there anything that appears unusual or different?"

Taylor turned to Sarah first. She was, indeed, frozen in place. In her attire, she looked like a statue of some ancient goddess under the hue of the moon's light.

"She's all right. This is a moment in the past. It's already happened, and nothing can hurt you now. Do you understand?"

"Yes."

"Tell me what you see around you."

"There's the car – the dashboard – Sarah's coat is in the back. She took it off after we got in because it kept pulling up her costume at the back. There are just trees outside. Lots of trees."

"Can you hear anything?"

He listened. "No."

"Do you remember why you wanted to come back to this memory, Taylor?"

"To find something."

"What is it you're looking for?"

"Something I missed. Or something I forgot. Something that's mine."

"Yours?"

"Yes."

"Do you know what it is? Is it to do with Sarah?"

"I don't know."

"See if you can find it now."

He turned to Sarah again; took in the frame of her face under her hair. Warmth flooded him. She was everything to him and she looked stunning in the stillness of his mind, more so because he knew she was beautiful on the inside, too. Out of nowhere, panic snared him. Something bad was about to happen.

"You're safe. Taylor, you're safe."

He calmed. Yes – he was.

"Nothing can hurt you – this is a memory. It's not happening to you. Do you understand?"

"Yes."

"All right. See if you can find what you're looking for now. I'm going to briefly join with your mind so I can see through your eyes. But I can't stay there long."

He studied his wife; looked down at her dress, taking in

what he could – a white, robe-like garment she'd designed herself, decorated with jewellery. Her earrings were large and glimmered with gemstones; her necklace had a regal quality; her copper bracelet looked rustic and a little less grand than everything else. He glanced at the coat flung on the backseat of the car, and then he looked at the tiny clutch bag by her feet. The straps of her Roman sandals reached all the way to her knees.

"Taylor, look at her bracelet again."

He did.

"Describe it. I can't see it as clearly as you."

"It looks like copper. It looks heavy. It looks simple compared to her other jewellery. I think it's designed to be a snake or a serpent. I can't see the other side of it at this angle."

"Can you move yourself to see it better?"

He tried. But even when he leaned right over, the position of her arm obscured the bracelet.

"Have you seen this bracelet before?"

"I don't think so. I didn't even know she was wearing it until this moment. I mean, I must have known, but didn't notice."

"I can't stay with your vision too much longer. Can you go back to the party in your mind? You were in the garden and Sarah was holding up a glass as she was talking to that man. Can you see the bracelet on her arm?"

"Yes."

"As if you're in a photograph, I want you to freeze that image and try to zoom in on it. Can you see the detail of the bracelet now?"

It took a moment – his mind trying to piece together everything he had seen at that party out of the corner of his eye. "It is a serpent. The head of the serpent is different, though. It's ... I think a lion. With a big circle behind its head and ... something carved on the circle, but I can't make it out."

"That's all right. I think we left this scene too early last time. Can you stay here for a bit longer and let it continue playing? We'll return to the car scene we've paused in a while."

The scene was already in motion before him...

"This is Scott. I knew him from my first job placement – god, was it six or seven years ago?"

"Eight, actually, I think."

"Can you believe it? I can't remember if you've met my husband, Taylor."

They exchanged greetings and shook hands. "So," began Taylor, never quite knowing what to say since he knew nothing about fashion or clothes design, "are you in the fashion industry, too?"

Scott threw him a pleasant smile. "Indirectly, yes, but I've veered towards archaeology."

"Didn't you take a second degree?" asked Sarah.

"Yes – that was the archaeology. I became rather besotted with the fashion, art, and pottery of ancient civilisations around the world. You start discovering the richness of their mythologies and the links between them all, and I wanted to explore that in much more detail."

"Wow, that sounds fascinating," replied Taylor.

"What about yourself?"

"Nothing anywhere near as interesting I'm afraid: computing and graphic design."

"But you could create the software I might need for all manner of historic reconstruction."

"Yes, that I could probably do with enough time."

"There you go – that's pretty fascinating, too."

"Taylor," cut in Sarah. She stroked the bracelet on her arm. "Scott was the one who pointed me towards this—"

"Scott!" It was Steve who shouted his name – he and Amy were hosting this party at their house. "Fireworks!"

"Ah, that's me. I'll be right there!" he hollered back. "I'm pyrotechnics guy."

"Can't wait to see it."

"Catch you later." Scott excused himself and left just as Amy bounded up to them, grinning from ear to ear.

"Sarah!" she exclaimed, engulfing her in a bear hug and then treating him to the same. "I've barely had the chance to speak to you all night. This costume is *amazing*. Taylor, can I grab your lovely wife for five minutes."

"Of course you can." Although she was already dragging Sarah towards the nearly empty buffet table for whatever she wanted to talk to her about.

Taylor stuffed his hands into his pockets and wondered if standing still was better than wandering aimlessly about.

All right, Taylor, bring yourself back to the car now. I'm not seeing through your eyes any more for the moment, but you will still hear my voice."

Almost instantaneously, his surroundings changed, one reality morphing into another, and he was back in the car, the scene paused in the exact place he'd left it.

"I want you to remember that at any time, you can freeze the scene, just like this. If you feel scared, or need a moment, just freeze the scene in front of you, okay?"

"Okay."

"When you're ready, start the film up again, like you're pressing play, and carry on with your drive."

Everything came to life again as the car started to move. He stared at his hands on the wheel. It all felt completely normal, but also surreal, because he had a faint awareness this was the past – a moment out of time being relived. Yet, when fully in the moment and reliving it, it was like he *was there* without knowing it was the past. He felt split in two. The part of him that knew it was the past could not reach the part of him that was living it like it was the present. He had no control. His breath hitched, anxiety surfacing.

"I'm here. I'm with you. I'll bring you out if you go too far."

The anxiety faded. He knew that voice. It was familiar and safe – very – and his memory, whether it belonged to the past or present, whispered a name for the voice: *Lawrence.* It was a name – a person – he trusted completely, although he couldn't remember why.

Releasing his worry, he relaxed into his seat and allowed himself to come fully into the scene; allowed the past to become the present; allowed himself to forget there was anything else.

"What about this? I think it's Ella." Sarah's hand rested on the volume knob of the radio as she turned it up a bit. The radio was as old and battered as the car, so it seemed fitting that Ella Fitzgerald filled the space with her soulful melody.

"Sounds good to me." He flicked his full beam on. The lane ahead lit up making it easier to see any potholes and roadkill they were best avoiding, but it made the tree trunks look even more eerie.

Sarah seemed to follow the direction of his thoughts. "These are yew trees, aren't they?"

"I think so – most of them. Hundreds of years old judging by the size of some of these trunks."

"It's so amazing the way their roots twist like that. You know there are fashion designers that try to get their dresses looking like that."

Taylor laughed.

"It's true." Sarah smiled. "Everything we try to recreate is based on nature somehow or another. Rockets and aeroplanes have aerodynamics like birds and insects; submarines and boats have fins like fish."

"Nature rules," concluded Taylor.

Something that sounded like a gunshot fired and Sarah

shrieked.

Taylor jumped and slammed the brakes, although he really didn't need to because the 'gunshot' was the final exclamation from a fatigued exhaust and the car died of its own accord. Ella shut up, abruptly. The engine whirred into silence. And all the lights went out.

CHAPTER FOUR

Taylor opened the door.

"Where are you going?"

"Pop the bonnet – take a look."

"Do you know what you're looking for?"

"If it's nothing to do with the engine oil, the fan belt, or the screen wash, nope."

"It sounded like something to do with the exhaust pipe or engine. We need to call breakdown."

"Try them on my phone while I take a look under the bonnet." He'd tried the ignition damn near ten times. The car was deader than dead. He didn't know why he was bothering to even look under the bonnet – he was sure the problem would be nothing he could fix, even if he could figure out what it was.

"Taylor, you've got no signal."

Shit. "Use your phone," he called back from the front of the car.

"I didn't bring it. No pockets, remember?"

He drowned out the rest of Sarah's words to focus on what was in front of him as he made some quip about woodcutters being on Facebook – he was talking nonsense because he was starting to feel anxious. And he couldn't see a damn thing anyway in the dark. He mentally kicked himself for never having got around to putting a new battery in the torch he kept in the boot. Using his phone's torch would kill most of its battery and he might need that to make a call.

He needed to get to a house – to someone with a phone. He dropped the car's lid. "It's futile. I can't figure out what's wrong, and the lighting's not helping. I'm going to walk up the lane until I find a house. I'll take my phone with me – there might be better signal just a little further along."

She handed him his phone.

He held back a grimace when he spotted its battery at just 25 percent and then pocketed it.

"I'll come with you." Sarah opened her door.

"Sarah, you'll freeze. Especially in those sandals."

He was suddenly above the scene watching himself and Sarah discuss what to do. Dread crept up on him.

"Taylor?"

"I don't want to go, I don't want to go," he whispered. "I can't stop it."

"Taylor, why did you come here?"

To find something. He'd wanted to do this to find something.

"You're not going to find anything if you don't go through the events of the night. But we can stop now if you want to."

"No. Wait." He just needed a moment.

But the characters below him were not waiting. He saw himself kiss Sarah through the open window and tell her he loved her before walking away from the car. "No, no, no."

"You can freeze the scene."

He did just that, on that reminder. It happened in an instant, before he'd barely even intended it. He looked down at himself, mid-stride, hands in pockets, completely unaware of how everything was about to change.

"This is the past."

"I know. It just *feels* like it's the present and happening when I put myself there."

"You knew it would."

"But when I'm there, I forget who I am *now*. And it's like it happens all over again."

There was a pause, then the voice – *Lawrence* – spoke. *"Try and stay up here then, as it all unfolds."*

He already felt himself settling into his out-of-body state at that suggestion. "Will that work?" When he was up here, he could tell the difference more easily between the past and the present; who he had been then and who he was now, even if he couldn't recall all the details of his life.

"It's worth trying, and maybe you'll see something from this angle that you missed while down there."

Yes. He was here to find something – that was the point. Somewhat relieved to be up here – whether by choice or suggestion – he looked down at himself and then at Sarah in the car, though he could only make out her arm resting on the open window.

Oh ... he did remember this bit now. He was going to have to watch himself get mauled to death.

"We can stop. I can wake you up."

"No. I want to do this ... I need to." Although he couldn't quite remember why he had needed to find whatever he thought was missing. Something big was happening in his present day, wasn't it? Something important. The start of something new. But he couldn't remember the present day – there was only a faint remnant of it in his mind.

"All right, then, when you're ready, press play."

He knew what he meant. He steadied himself, steadied his breathing, and then with his mind, started to move the scene below him like he had in the car.

"You can stay up here," reminded Lawrence. *"You don't have to feel the pain."*

He could still hear the thoughts he was having down there, but couldn't so much feel what 'past Taylor' he was feeling. Thank god.

His fear dissipated and he took this moment to look around

'down there' at what he could see from this aerial point of view. Not a lot at the moment. He could tell that down there he was thinking about where the nearest house might be – calculating the time to get there – and thinking of Sarah's safety. He *really* didn't want to leave her alone in the car.

A movement caught his eye. From his bird's eye view, he saw the werewolf close in and his heart sped up. "Run!" he shouted – *at himself* – which was stupid, of course, but his primal instinct to survive had kicked in. The Taylor down there didn't hear him at all, as he knew he wouldn't. Nothing could stop what was about to happen. Interestingly, from this angle, up here, Taylor could see – clearly – how he'd been prey; how the wolf had closed in slowly until the time was right; how it made little to no noise.

There was nothing I could have done. That revelation hit him like a bolt of lightning and lifted a cloud – one he hadn't known was hanging above his head. All this time he'd wondered ... had they been too loud in the car; what if they'd just left the party earlier; what if he'd gotten the car serviced even just two days before...

This wolf had been living in the wood a while. It looked dishevelled – was likely sleeping rough – and seemed to know its way through all the trees. *He – not 'it'. A werewolf. A sentient being with intelligence – not an animal.*

Yes. With Taylor's own werewolf senses, he even thought he could make out the male's scent, the smell of this wood thick on him. He'd been here for weeks if not months. Unmated and on a full moon, he would have hunted anyone down no matter how quiet or loud; no matter what vehicle they might drive.

And there was nothing you could have done.

The wolf howled. It was one of pain and desperation and the imminent conquest that would quench both. And it was a monstrous sound if one didn't know werewolves existed. (And even if one did.) He howled because he knew there was no escape now for his prey – even if Taylor ran, the wolf would catch him with his speed and strength. It was over.

Taylor saw his own body stiffen and still; heard his own thoughts from the past, his mind racing in every direction, a hundred questions with no answers.

Sarah, clearly frightened, briefly sounded the horn and waved Taylor back.

Taylor's thoughts shifted completely to Sarah and how much danger she was in, especially if she was pregnant.

WHAT?

The sheer *shock* of hearing that thought from his own mind knocked him right out of his aerial view and sent him hurtling back into his own body.

"Taylor!" That was Lawrence's voice, but it was really far away – too far away. The bombshell of what 'past Taylor' was thinking drowned out all else because he could *not* remember thinking that the night this all happened.

Sensation hit him like a freight train and it was *loud*. Past-Taylor's panic was painful, and it was now his own, too, realities merging and becoming one – *that* one. He felt the link to his present self leave his grasp completely, and then there was only the here and now. He was running back to the car, his fear at its peak, the conversation with Sarah, from earlier, playing on his mind: *"No, not here. At home. I don't want to tell you here."*

God, could it be? So soon? They'd only just started trying – casually, even – without taking it too seriously.

The way she'd smiled at whatever secret she was going to tell him...

Every last thought fled his mind when something barrelled into him from his left – he barely glimpsed it before it was on him – and then there was just pain. And his scream. And Sarah's scream. He wasn't sure which came first. He felt a muscle pop inside him near his right shoulder. He screamed again and he couldn't tell if it was the sensation of ripping, or the sound of it, that had him understanding what was happening to him.

He registered hearing the car door open. *God, no! Sarah, don't!*

"Taylor!"

"No! Sarah, no! Get back!" he yelled. She was right *here,* running towards them – it would kill her!

"Freeze it, Taylor!"

What? That ... wasn't Sarah ... what?

"Stop fighting me."

The pain was astronomical, but confusion pushed through everything else ... the scene in front of him swam.

"Freeze. The. Scene." Came the command.

And finally, it all stopped. He made it stop. But he was still clamped between teeth and—

"Rise above yourself."

He was taken up out of his body, or perhaps he made that happen, too – he was too dazed to figure it out. All he knew was that Sarah had been—

"What happened?" Lawrence sounded not overly happy despite trying to keep his voice level. *"I lost you. I couldn't see you or feel you or anything. It was like you were torn from me."*

He *had* been torn – in more than one way.

Silence. And then, *"You're safe. You're safe, Taylor."* Lawrence had recomposed himself and his voice carried the surety it had had before.

While it calmed Taylor – as intended – he also had more awareness than before of Lawrence's presence, and he wondered if that meant the drug was wearing off. Were those two hours almost up? Or had the shock of what he'd realised—*how* could he have forgotten he'd thought Sarah might be pregnant?—done something to the drug? He didn't know the answer, but he knew he wasn't ready to go just yet, not after *that* revelation. "I'm going back down." And nothing had stopped him from saying that. He had his own function back – to what extent, he wasn't sure.

"What? No."

"Yes. I can do it." He needed to get to the bottom of it.

"Taylor, I lost *you."*

"But I have myself back – a bit, anyway. I can feel you, too, Lawrence. I couldn't before."

There was a pause. *"The Amnesthipine must be wearing off – sooner than I'd thought, too. This isn't how it's suppose to work."*

"That's the story of our lives, right?"

"Taylor—"

But he was spurred on by the memory he'd forgotten. "Just bring me back at the very end. You did it before, you can do it again. And it's not even really happening this time. There'll be no death tonight. No three-day sleep. I'll be right here." He sounded so lucid, even to his own ears.

"Fine. I don't think I'll be able to stop you now, anyway, if that's what you really want. I'll try to call you back if you take too long. You'll arouse once the drug wears off in any case."

More confident in every way, he 'pressed play' on the scene below. Terror-filled screams split the night. It was horrific. God, Sarah had just *thrown* herself on the beast. He hadn't seen it properly from down there. From up here she looked... How the *hell* had she found the courage to do that?

He hesitated, now not sure descending back into his body would be the best move. He might be able to see more from up here after all. It was hard, though. He was lying in agony on the ground, bleeding profusely, and the wolf was on her now – had her on her back – and Taylor thanked the stars the drug was wearing off a bit. He had more of a sense of his treasured memories of now – the present, Lydia, Ryan – and his fear was less.

The wolf shifted into a man as it wrestled Sarah to the ground. It was bloody weird to watch the shift now, knowing what he knew, knowing how it felt to shift; even enjoying watching his mates go through the same process. The past was all starting to look more like the memory it was, except...

He hadn't noticed *that* eighteen months ago. Sarah appeared to say something to the man who was now on her – he couldn't make it out – and it *stopped* his attack of her. He just stared at her and she ... touched him. She touched his face with her hand, and Taylor almost thought he'd imagined the whole thing because the male suddenly resumed his onslaught and Sarah screamed. That scream was what got other Taylor moving his ruined bleeding body, an arm limp by his side, which he forced into action when he grabbed a large branch – far too large, really, but it was the nearest thing to him, and it was that or nothing.

He didn't have to be in his own body to remember that moment. The Taylor down there trained every last ounce of his strength towards the single need to save Sarah's life and didn't think. If he'd thought, he wouldn't have been able to do what he did next. With a shout – more like a war-cry – that carried all his weight, he barged into the wolf, tearing him off his wife. The male went rolling, and so did he, but separately – not tangled up with the wolf. He never lost his hold on the branch and the minute he was back on his feet he lunged at the male that still looked dazed and as if his head might have hit the trunk of the yew tree that loomed above him. With the sharpest end of that branch outstretched, Taylor charged, and plunged it into the largest part of the male to ensure he wouldn't miss. It sank into his chest, not least because Taylor lent on it with his whole body to make up for his injured arm, all of his mass pushing it down.

Everything seemed to still and that wasn't because he'd 'frozen the scene'. Shock permeated the air. God knew how many seconds passed until the dead man transformed back into his wolf before their eyes.

Sarah sounded out little whimpers and half-sobs. She'd backed into a hawthorn bush just a few metres away. Her eyes were wide and unblinking – he couldn't even tell what she was looking at.

"Sarah," whispered Taylor, needing to get to her, but he'd used up all his strength. He collapsed, no part of his body working any more. Slumped against the yew's roots where they wove into the ground, he looked at Sarah; reached for Sarah ... or he thought he did. He might not have moved at all. Everything went dark.

CHAPTER FIVE

"*Are you ready to come back?*"

He heard Lawrence's voice more clearly than ever and could even sense he was nearby. Perhaps by his side in whatever was the 'real' world.

"I don't know. I wasn't conscious for most of what happens between now and your arrival. Can you wait a bit longer?"

"Not much. You might find you bring yourself back, regardless. I don't know how longer the Amnesthipine will stay active in your system – it's wearing off faster than I'd anticipated."

"Her bracelet's gone."

There was a pause. *"What do you mean?"*

"I mean it must have fallen off in the attack – it's not on her arm anymore." Taylor studied poor Sarah, sitting with her knees huddled, mumbling nonsensicalities and staring off into nothing.

"That explains why I don't remember seeing it on her the night we brought you both in. I think it's worth looking for in case it's still here. I'll search for it before we leave – it won't be too hard to sniff out oxidising copper."

"You took note of the bracelet before me – you think it's important?"

"Not sure until I find it."

Taylor sent Sarah a mental apology for all she was going through and was about to go through in the months to come. A sense of ... *something* ... caught his eye. Something Sarah seemed to be staring at above her to her right, but... His eyes must be playing tricks on him. All he saw were shadows and they seemed to morph with the now gently swaying breeze as the leaves caught the moon's rays. The wind had picked up.

He looked back at himself, eyes closed and lying in his own pool of blood, and he caught his breath. *That* wasn't a shadow.

What *was* that? "Lawrence?"

"I'm here."

"Can you see what I see? Through my eyes, I mean."

"I see you lying on the ground."

"Can you see the ... shape?" He trained his eyes on it, but couldn't make it out properly. It looked like a person – a child? But no matter how much he tried to focus his vision, the shape was *just* out of focus as if he were wearing glasses of the wrong prescription, or had cataracts. Or as if it were a ghost.

"I only see you."

"It's standing to my left – right hand side from our angle."

"I see nothing there."

He frowned. Or his mind did, anyway, in this weird hypnosis trip they were taking. "I'm going back in my body."

"Now? You're dying. You won't be able to stay long."

"Maybe I saw whatever this is and can't remember, just like I couldn't remember Sarah was pregnant."

Silence.

Oh. He didn't know if Lawrence had actually heard his thoughts at that point in his memory.

"Taylor, Sarah wasn't—"

"It's moved! That shape's moved." It was right next to him now and he said nothing more because time was of the essence. He willed himself into his body in the past; willed himself to merge with everything he was then; ignored the pain, ignored the ragged breaths he was barely taking; ignored it all except the need to open his eyes and *see* what was hovering beside him and his *eyes wouldn't open.*

He couldn't have cursed out loud, but it bloody well sounded like it in his mind. *Open your fucking eyes!*

A whisper caressed him, and he stopped, stretching his ears to listen, his need to open his eyes halted. *"You need to live. Please. She wants to kill me. You need to live."*

The voice belonged to a child – a girl, he thought. Young.

"I'm going to live," he tried to reply, but of course it was just in his mind – his lips didn't move; his eyes wouldn't open. "I *want* to live."

He was sure he heard Sarah scream at that point. Inside, he wept because there wasn't a damn thing he could do.

Feather-light caresses soothed his brow. *"It's all right. You're going to be all right."* That was the child.

He tried again to open his eyes. He had to *see*. And then, he did.

Sort of.

Holding his breath with his efforts, he tried again. He wondered if it was blood crusting the edges of his eyelids, making this the hardest task in the world for him, but the faintest of light flickered through his lashes. And then, movement.

He gurgled some kind of noise through his throat; blinked again. Everything was blurry as hell, but ... it *was* a child. Longish dark hair was about all he could make out – likely a girl as he'd suspected – but her face was still a mystery. Her hair covered most of it; the rest looked like chalk rubbed out; smeared. He blinked again, willing his vision to clear, but it was fading instead, sucking him back into darkness and he didn't have the strength to fight it.

It felt like she kissed his forehead. Something fell on his cheek, and he wondered if she was crying. But perhaps they were tears of joy because her next words were light and sounded filled with happiness. *"Thank you. Thank you, Daddy."*

"Wake up, Taylor. It's time to wake up."

Hands grasped his face.

"Come back to the present. Come back home."

Home.

The 'present' crashed down upon him just as completely as he had entered the past. Every memory rushed back: Lydia, her pregnancy, Ryan, Lawrence and his legs, five months ago, seven months ago, eighteen months ago...

Taylor's eyes snapped open on an intake of breath; the need to *breathe* in his life.

"That's it," encouraged Lawrence, relief evident in his tone.

Taylor reached for his mate's arms, grabbing both to steady himself. He was still lying down.

He pulled himself up to sitting, using Lawrence as a crutch.

Lawrence aided in pulling him upright. "I lost you again when you decided to put yourself in your body ... at death's door no less."

That memory came hurtling back, too. "Did you hear her? Or see her?"

"Who?"

"I don't know. A young girl, but I couldn't see her properly – only hear her."

"What did she say?"

"I..." He shook his head, stilling himself as he tried to remember. "She said someone was trying to kill her and I had to live. Then, she thanked me. She called me Dad."

It took a few seconds for him to realise Lawrence wasn't moving. He looked up to find him staring straight at him with both a sadness and determination in his eyes.

"You didn't see her, then?"

"Taylor, please listen to what I'm saying. Sarah wasn't pregnant that night we found you both."

Ah, yes, there was that memory, too – the little epiphany

he'd had about what Sarah had wanted to talk to him about that night. "She was going to tell me—"

"We would have smelled it on her."

Oh.

"Ryan and I both would have. Hendrickson, too."

Bewildered, he slowly shook his head. "The way she was acting with me about this *thing* she wanted to tell me—"

"Taylor—"

"We'd been trying. Not for long; not even that seriously, but we had decided 'so what' if it happened and we stopped using protection, and—"

"You're going to be a father."

His words faded into silence.

Lawrence altered his position from crouching to sitting in front of Taylor. His hands dropped from his face to his shoulders. "You're going to be a father in *days.* You *are* a dad. Now – here – in the present and in the future. Your chance isn't gone – it's about to happen."

Lydia's face filled his mind. He welled up, his heart longing to be by her side. But—

"You made amends with Sarah in the hours before she left – in so far as you could, anyway. And then she was gone, suddenly and inexplicably and it was unfair. It *is* unfair. But you have nothing you need to find – no logic to make sense of the unfathomable; no tool to fix the error."

He blinked back tears. "What about the girl?"

"A chance regained? A wish come true? A need to make amends?"

"You think I made her up?"

"I don't know. I *do* know the mind will do what it can to protect itself in the most terrible of moments. You thought Sarah might be pregnant that night and you heard a girl who told you – on your deathbed – you *had* to stay alive; that she might be killed if you don't. Because Sarah was in danger. Because you needed to make it right."

The next breath Taylor took shuddered on a repressed sob. Everything hurt. It hurt because he wanted to be home by Lydia's side; it hurt because he didn't want to be by her side while carrying his shit in place of their new babies.

"You told me once, after I monumentally fucked up with Lydia, I couldn't close the door on my past and shut people out any more. I'm going to do the same for you now: Death is the biggest 'what if' we're given. *What if* my sister and I had sneaked out to the lake that night, like we'd wanted, because we were finding our grandmother's party so damned boring – all these relatives we'd never met before. An hour before the Trident arrived, Elana asked me to leave with her because she didn't want to sneak out alone; I was the one who said we should stay – because of duty."

Taylor stared at him, then looked down.

Lawrence pulled his hands from his shoulders and sat back a bit.

"I'm not sure I've told anyone that before. I've played that conversation so much in my mind, it became worse than a ghost – it became a branding. A scar that kept me fully there when I needed to be here. We never went to the lake because of my choice. And she *did* die. And I *did* survive. And every now and then, the scar burns a bit – usually when I'm scared, or possibly about to do something stupid. It tries to take me to a place of failure and worthlessness, but I don't let it anymore. Instead, I let it remind me of all I've overcome; of how *far* I've come, because you see, that error – that *death* – it never goes away completely. But you can become a better person *for* it; *because* of it. That's what my sister teaches me every single day and it makes her death *worth* something. I look at where I am now on the cusp of a brand new era with those I could not love more standing beside me, and I thank Elana for the most difficult lesson no one else could have taught me. She didn't die in vain. And neither did Sarah."

Silence fell; merged with the night, and became a blanket that enfolded them both in its warmth.

"There's one more thing I want to say."

Honestly, this was the most talkative the guy had ever been. Taylor looked back up at him.

"I'm sorry about what I did to you. I'm sorry I took the memory of you, from everyone who ever loved you."

Christ, that hurt. He'd *never* expected him to say that and somehow the acknowledgement made everything he'd lost more real. He shook his head and one of those tears he thought he'd successfully quelled, slipped through. "Lawrence—"

"It was your mother's birthday last week – she turned sixty."

"Jesus." He shook his head again, dropped it to hide his crumpling face, and rubbed the wetness from his cheeks.

"I know because I note the dates on all the birth certificates of everyone whose mind I have to erase. I kept these dates eighteen months ago because I wanted to look out for you – your mental health – anything rash you might want to do on those dates. I didn't know you well and you'd just turned – it happens. I'm *aware* of the patterns of the highs and lows you go through."

He had no idea what to say. He wasn't angry. He just felt kind of tired. It was a messy dichotomy to find himself frustrated at having been under Lawrence's scrutiny so completely, yet deeply touched by the very same – that he'd cared enough to ensure his well-being after he'd turned; as much as was possible, anyway.

"I know you've accepted what I did. I don't know if you've forgiven it, but I'm not asking for your forgiveness because the truth is, I knew no other way, and even now, I'm not sure there's another way for those who turn – it happens so rarely and it's so important our kind don't get found out and suffer terrible consequences at the hands of those who don't understand. But I need you to know, I'm sorry – very much so – that I had to take the actions I did."

Taylor said nothing for a while.

Lawrence changed his position on the ground to something more comfortable.

"It was on my mother's birthday when I asked if you would do this for me – tonight with the hypnosis."

Lawrence nodded.

"You're right. I thought about her a lot and"—part of him didn't want to say it, but part of him did—"it bothers me that our children will know of your parents, and Lydia's parents, and Ryan's parents, but will never know mine. It hurts a lot. I wish it didn't. It makes me feel like I have nothing to give them. I guess, tonight, I was hoping to find that thing I could give them. Something that's mine; that helps them know who I am."

"How can you think you have nothing to give?"

His throat constricted as he sought the right words. "I wasn't born in the world they'll be born into. I don't know what it's like to be a wolf pup – what their needs are going to be."

After a beat, Lawrence replied. "They'll be born in a *new* world where Tridents don't exist, and they'll never need to feel the pain of the moon. I don't even know what I'm supposed to teach them about mating, or their biology, or... *No one's* been born into that world yet and *you* helped create it. Furthermore, you can give them the one thing none of us can: a doorway to humanity. And *their* children will damn well know who Grandpa Taylor is and what he did to keep them all safe."

Dried tears pinching his skin, Taylor laughed, 'Grandpa Taylor' sounding just a little too bizarre.

Lawrence grinned.

Taylor sighed and rested his head against the yew. "Just five months ago, we said goodbye to everything, and now here we are, decades stretched out before us."

"Can't say I've gotten used to that myself, to be honest."

Silence fell on them for the second time, each lost in their own thoughts of everything the future could be. All they had to do was *enjoy* it. After Sarah's death, their own near deaths – hell Lawrence and Lydia *had* died – the loss of their friends ... *enjoying* it seemed—

"Survivor's guilt is a bitch."

Taylor met Lawrence's gaze, echoes of both torture and strength evident in its pale blue.

"But it gets easier with time. It helps when you have one hell of a pack to pull you through."

Taylor's next smile came easily and lit him up from the inside out. He felt it shine, along with a near-overwhelming love for the four of them – and right now for the male who sat opposite him. "Thank you. I mean that." *Could* Sarah have been pregnant? Even if no scent had been picked up by the wolves who had rescued them? And what did it matter anyway? If she had been, and whether anyone knew it or not, she'd obviously lost the baby. Her next pregnancy was one he'd had no part in. To lament something he wasn't sure had even existed in the first place was crazy. "Let's go home, Lawrence."

"Are you sure?"

"More than sure."

The blond male stood, holding out a hand to help Taylor up.

He took it, the feel of his feet on the ground, his body and his *presence* in it, a beautiful thing he thanked the stars for. *Home*. "Wait – you wanted to find the bracelet."

Lawrence said nothing as he brushed bits of earth off himself. He breathed out, took a moment to look around in contemplation, and then he smiled. “Leave it. We don’t need it.”

“We don’t?”

“It stays here with the past, if it’s even still here. I wondered if it might have anything to do with Himet and Yemet. You’re not the only one who needs to let go of shadows that make no sense.”

Taylor nodded, comprehending Lawrence’s need to understand everything that had taken place that night he’d given up his life; to make sense of his survival of it and his regrown legs. They’d all stumbled, bewildered, into the months that had followed, accepting and cherishing the miracle it was; perhaps too shell-shocked to question it. And none of them had wanted that miracle taken from them, so they’d turned away from seeking answers and had sought each other out instead.

“But all that really matters now is Lydia and our new family.”

As if on cue, Lawrence’s mobile phone beeped. He took it out of his back pocket. “It’s Ryan. The babies have dropped. Dr Matheson reckons her water should break in the next forty-eight hours.”

“Wow.”

“Yep, this is it.”

“You scared?”

“Fucking terrified. You?”

“Apprehensive. Not terrified.”

They strode back to the car. “I never thought I’d have this after my family were slaughtered and my legs were ... it was just an impossibility in my mind.”

“Is that scar burning again? Trying to drag you back down?”

“You bet it is.”

“We won’t let it.”

“I know.”

They got into the car.

"Do you wonder if any of them might look like your sister?" Taylor asked.

"Sometimes. Or my mother, or father. You?" Lawrence turned the engine on, and it hummed so solidly – *so* different to Taylor's memory of a spluttering engine and a dying battery. That old life wasn't this one and never would be.

He'd worried the past could touch the present; ruin the future; invite some monster in through an unclosed portal. It couldn't. The past and present were worlds apart. *He* was worlds apart from who he'd been. "I mostly just wonder if any of them will have Lydia's red hair and freckles."

"And her ire?"

"Oh, yeah, they'll all have that."

Lawrence laughed.

Taylor glanced at the door mirror, seeing the tree he'd been lying against become smaller and smaller, and it wasn't too long before they were out of the woods, taking the A-road towards Surrey, and home.

CHAPTER SIX

The lights were on in the main house when they pulled up at the top of the driveway just after four in the morning. Taylor's sensitive hearing picked up Lydia's undulating syllables, although he couldn't quite make out what was being said until they were just outside the front door.

"Promise? You know it makes no difference to me."

"Hadn't even thought about it until you brought it up," came Ryan's somewhat exasperated reply. It sounded like they were in the kitchen.

He and Lawrence walked in, and Lawrence shut the front door behind them before they headed into the hall.

"They're back," stated Ryan, still out of sight, and two pairs of feet were already making their way out of the kitchen towards them.

"You haven't thought about it at all? Not even once?" pressed Lydia.

"No."

Taylor smiled at Lydia who wore an incredulous expression and held a bagel in her hand. The babies had *definitely* dropped. She was massive in her long, blue dress. "4:00 a.m. munchies?" he asked.

"And 1:00 a.m., and 10:00 p.m." She grinned – a little – but it didn't quite reach her eyes. Those were lit with a look he wasn't sure he'd ever seen before as they roamed up and down his body. She took another bite of bagel and her nostrils flared.

A hand found his elbow and Ryan was there beside him. "You all right?"

Lawrence went to drop Lydia a hello kiss.

Taylor looked at Ryan. "I am – it's all good. And I'm glad to be home."

Seeming reassured at that, he turned to Lawrence. "Dr Matheson's on his way – I've told him to stay in what was Adam and Tiegan's barn while he's here."

"Good," nodded Lawrence.

"Nothing's happening yet – he doesn't need to come," said Lydia, her tone carrying a hint of annoyance.

"But when it does, it could happen fast. Best he's around."

She didn't bother replying to Lawrence, but turned back towards Taylor with that stare again, something weird and a little wild behind her violet eyes.

Taylor cleared his throat, not sure if he'd upset her. She'd seemed okay when he'd left her side earlier.

"I doubt I'll get back to sleep now," stated Ryan. "I reckon I'll go for a run, see if I can wear myself out. You're not planning on disappearing again, are you?" That was directed at him.

Taylor shook his head. "No. I'm done."

Ryan made some kind of grunting noise, his fractiousness at Lydia's fractiousness, palpable. The babies were due, and everyone was on edge.

"What were you talking about when we came in?" asked Taylor.

Lydia was the one to reply. "Whether you're all okay if any of the babies *aren't* yours – biologically, I mean." She'd said that with a bit of snipe as if she was itching for a fight.

Really? "Do you honestly think we wouldn't be?"

He saw Lawrence raise his eyebrows in amusement. *Glad someone's finding her 'due state' entertaining.*

The last of the bagel went into her mouth and she shrugged, her arms held out, looking pointedly at Lawrence. "Well, what if two of them look like Taylor, and one of them looks like Ryan? *Your* royal sperm's, like, missed out."

Lawrence's smirk showed he wasn't rising to the bait. He dropped another kiss on Lydia's forehead. "I don't give a fuck, darling – we're *all* bringing these pups up; each one is as much Taylor's and Ryan's as it's mine. And we'll all know soon enough, anyway."

"When?" she pleaded. Her hand rubbed her bulging dome, a slight grimace on her face. Her expression suddenly changed and her gaze landed on Taylor once more, violet irises gleaming, and he distinctly wondered if he was unwittingly caught in some strange game in which only she knew the rules. "Taylor?"

"Hmmn?"

"Can you help me upstairs back to your room?"

He guessed she wanted a rundown of what had taken place in the woods. He hoped it would calm her when she realised he really had nothing to tell – no great discovery other than the want and need to be back home.

Lawrence kissed her one last time and gave Taylor a nod. "I'm heading for a shower, then might try and get a couple of hours sleep if I can. Ryan, has Dr Matheson got the key to the barn?"

"I've told him where it is – it's all sorted. He'll let himself in."

"Thank you."

"No problem. I'm heading for that run."

"Hey." Lydia grabbed Ryan's hand before he left. "Come see me when you're back?"

He threw her a lop-sided smile and a wink. "'Course I will."

He made his leave and then it was Taylor's hand in Lydia's as she led him towards the stairs, Lawrence already at the top and heading to his own room.

"Are you sure you don't want to be in Lawrence's bed? It's bigger."

"Like hell am I going up that many stairs just to come down

them again when I need breakfast." She moaned a little and actually did look in a bit of pain.

"Here." He placed his left arm around her waist and took her weight a bit as he offered her his right arm to lean on.

She clutched it with her right hand and let out a sigh as they ascended the stairs. "I thought the babies 'dropping' was like a metaphor or something, but Jesus Christ, it's actually literal and it's like they're squashing everything. I swear they're going to come out holding all my internal organs like trophies."

Taylor laughed and quickly stifled it when she shot him the mother of all glares. "Sorry." He cleared his throat. "You'll be fine, I'm certain."

"Because I'm a wolf with fast healing abilities. How *human* women do this – with *three* babies for *nine* months – I have no idea."

"I think painkillers are involved. Sometimes anaesthesia."

"Yeah, well, none of that for me because of the super-sensitiveness of the pups – same reason for the lack of ultrasound."

They reached his bedroom, and he led them in, closing the door behind him. As Lydia rested against the door, he rushed to the bed to fluff up the pillow and pull the sheets straight for her. "Well, it's been done this way for aeons, so we let nature take its course, I guess."

"Nature's playing a wicked game. Speaking of nature..."

He looked up when she didn't finish that sentence and *that* look was back again.

"Do you know what else Dr Matheson said?" Her voice was light and almost teasing, and he suddenly wondered if that was a trick question.

"Um ... no?"

She smiled.

Yeah – he had the distinct feeling he'd just stepped into a human-sized web. She shuffled towards him, and he bit back a smile at her attempt at a sexy swagger, pretty damn certain his smile would *not* go down well.

"He said that at this stage, a good dose of werewolf sperm can get things going."

"Going? Werewolf ... sperm?"

"The sperm can induce the labour." The swagger turned into a determined stride towards some invisible finish line. And he appeared to be standing in front of it. "I want these babies *out* of me, Taylor."

She might not be able to move with the same speed and force, but she was heavy, and when her lips smacked against his, she didn't mess around with her weight, but used it to take him with her, backwards onto the mattress which bounced beneath them.

Concern stole over him. That had been quite a drop onto the bed. "Whoa, whoa, wait, are you okay?" He reached for her stretched belly where she sat astride him, but she seemed more than fine.

"Have you forgotten," she mumbled as her tongue met the crook of his neck, "how much I love the smell of the woods on you?"

He'd thought his concern for her would overshadow any concupiscence he could muster. His cock happily stirred, though, seemingly independent of his concern. "Lydia"—yep, his voice sounded a little hoarse; turned on—"I don't want to hurt you; we have to be really careful." Just a minute ago she had looked in pain. And he hadn't quite had time to process everything he'd been through earlier, not that that was more important than anything Lydia needed right now; it was more that he didn't ... well, he was a little scared his 'performance' might not be up to scratch, and he didn't want to disappoint her.

Something was also a little odd. He couldn't put his finger on it, but the 'weird' of the moment was back, just like when she'd stared at him in the hallway. This was different to a normal enactment of passion. "Lydia—"

"You're mine, Taylor," she whispered, something incredibly possessive in that whisper and ... *something else.*

His anatomy responded to her possessiveness immediately, agreeing wholeheartedly with her claim on him, but his conscious self struggled with whatever he was missing.

"Lydia, are you all right?" Hell, he'd barely been able to get that out. A soft groan escaped him when her tongue found his nipple, some part of him only now noticing she'd wrestled his T-shirt up his chest. And then it hit him. The *way* she was licking him – tongue flat, then swirling, then flat, then swirling, and ... *yes* – the *scent* on her saliva. The realisation made him almost painfully hard against her crotch, but he was also bewildered. "Lydia, are you *marking* me?"

This wasn't an area he knew much about because mated wolves didn't usually mark their mates with scent; there was no need – their mating carried their joint scent anyway. Unmated wolves sometimes did mark their chosen (and likely temporary) partners in an act of ownership, and sometimes in play and experimentation – he'd heard it usually took place among the teenagers and younger adults of the pack. He'd never grown up in one to know. His only experience of being marked was one he had been unconscious for, thankfully: he'd woken up mated to his three mates again after Selena had *unmated* them with Gladys' magic, ultimately failing in her aim to have him for herself – but he'd woken to Selena's 'mark' all over his chest. Had he not witnessed the horror of her accidental mating to Gabriel, he might have held her actions against her. It had taken a couple of showers to get rid of Selena's mark.

Lydia's mark, though – her essence, whether it was a pheromone or something similar – had him near delirious with arousal. It was a rush that felt almost dangerous. *No wonder teenagers get a kick out of this.*

Her tongue dipped into his belly button. It seemed she wasn't leaving an inch of him untouched.

"Wait, honey—" With a fair amount of effort, he angled himself up on his elbow, and then cupped Lydia under her chin and pulled her up to meet him. "I'm yours already: your mate, your bonded, your husband. You don't need to do this."

Hell, she looked feral in the best way possible. "I do."

Her lips met his ferociously and, of course, he didn't deny her, but opened his mouth and let her in, though he was quite unprepared for the affect her intoxicating taste would have on his system. His moan was a guttural, needy one, and his head swam as if he were drunk. "But why?" he managed to mumble, only half-aware he was even here anymore.

She pulled back briefly, hesitated, then her eyes softened, her gaze nothing short of loving. "Please don't get upset because it's not as bad as you'll think."

"What?" He was kinda out of it. He couldn't come down from that kiss, her scent, or the way his body thrummed, needing to be inside her.

"We knew it was all in your mind and not real, but Ryan and I could feel it – just a little – when you were with Sarah."

It suddenly came back to him – that twinge in his navel when he was reliving being with Sarah at that party. *God, no!*

"Don't do that," she interrupted before he could even sound his dismay at what she'd just told him. "It didn't hurt – not like betrayal pains. It was just an awareness and I have a feeling Lawrence probably steered you away from any scenes that might have hurt."

"Good god, Lydia, I am so sorry. I had no idea that could even happen in that way."

"Don't be sorry. Please. I said it didn't hurt. But ... what took place tonight, Taylor? Did you find what you were looking for?"

Taylor shuffled up to sitting, and Lydia altered her position so she was sitting on him – as best as she could, anyway. "Are you comfortable enough?"

"For now."

"Good. Listen to me, Lydia. Sarah wasn't the reason I went back to those woods tonight. I did find what I needed, but I only realised what I was looking for *after* I found it. I was looking for a way to be the best father I could when I know fuck all about growing up as a wolf and have no history to give my children. I was looking for history; for my roots; for a solid piece of past I could offer."

Her eyes filled with tears which she shed easily. "Oh, Taylor—"

"My whole life, I've kind of been average at everything and I've never cared before. Average has its perks – you get left alone, you can do things and get away with things no one notices, and so on. But *this*"—he caressed the side of her abdomen and was greeted with the sweetest of kicks—"I don't want to be average at this. I want to be a father they can count on for anything; I want to be *their* roots."

Her tears were streaming now.

"My aim wasn't to make you cry." He smiled.

She wiped her cheeks with the back of her hand. "My hormones are all over the place."

"That's your excuse?"

"And I'm sticking with it."

He grinned.

She leaned in and kissed him again – softly this time, but no less hungrily. "You have a beautiful soul, Taylor Harper, and our kids are going to see that clearly."

"I hope it's enough."

"*You* are enough. You *are* the roots they'll grow from. We're the beginning."

He nodded. "Lawrence said the same, pretty much. That's the truth I found in the woods tonight. That's what I was looking for."

The misty look in her eyes held all her love for him. She graced him with a gentle smile and pressed her forehead to his. "Did I ever tell you, I smelled you before I saw you for the first time?"

He grinned and suppressed his laugh. "In the human world, this would not be a compliment."

Lydia returned the laugh without suppression and sighed with contentment. "I remember it like it was yesterday. I was at the back of the biker's café and Brendan was being all mother goose because I was ill, or I thought I was – didn't realise it was mating pains leading me slowly to my death. I was heading back to the floor for my shift and there you were – your scent – before I even got to the front of the café. I had to stop and lean against the wall because it knocked me for six. It was your scent that cleared my head. It wrapped around me like the newest, freshest thing, and woke me up from the inside out and I *had* to follow it until I knew where it was coming from."

"I remember," he replied, huskily. "I *felt* you looking at me and when I turned, all I saw was this ... fire. And freckles."

She laughed. She knew he adored her freckles.

"What I really saw and felt was something alive in you that I'd lost. That I used to remember having. If I'm honest with myself, part of me wanted you from that moment."

She turned her head and brushed her cheek against his, then ran her tongue along his jawline, nibbling at this spot and that spot as she went. "And *you* woke *me* up – the wolf in me, anyway – not in dreams like Ryan could, but in the everyday, human world. Your scent still wakes me up from the inside out." The air between them was nothing short of electric. If he didn't know better, he'd expect her to wield her streaks of lightning around them both, but for better or worse, that ability of hers had returned to the skies. She traced her tongue across his shoulder and his vision swam as her mark tinged the air. "It's not just me marking you, you know." She rested a hand on his where he still held it against her side. "These babies are pretty damn clear about who their dads are." Her mouth consumed his.

He moaned into it, pretty much lost to everything except the loving eroticism of the moment and the almost painful desire now overriding his entire being, and if he'd ever wondered if a pregnant female at the height of carnality, claiming her mate for *both* her and her babies could in any way be erotic, the answer was it absolutely fucking was.

She tugged at his belt – not gently at all – releasing the buckle.

He helped her as best as he could in his lustful delirium, and sooner rather than later, his jeans and pants were around his ankles.

"Move down a bit," she mumbled.

He obliged. "Do you need help with your underwear?"

Her reply was a soft snort. "As if I can get underwear on me anymore."

He smiled against her mouth and eased her dress up instead until she could better manoeuvre into her preferred position. When her wetness met his cock, he hissed through his teeth, unprepared for just how sensitised he was bathed in this new aromatic experience.

Lydia groaned against his mouth and then covered it with her own, pressing her tongue against him hard enough for him to open wider. He was conscious of her arm supporting her overgrown belly and the way she had to bend forward to complete that kiss. This couldn't be comfortable for her even if she was on top.

Before he could offer her suggestions for relief, she raised herself up, straightening her spine.

"If you need me to—*Christ.*"

She lowered herself onto him, taking him in completely, and the fullness of her was just about all he could handle. Her irises glowed violet in the dim light.

"Lydia"—she rocked herself on him—"oh, god ... honey, I'm sorry, but your marking scent has me good for nothing – I'm going to last seconds, if that. If you want your pleasure—"

"You're mine, Taylor." Her tone was a command, even if one coloured with love and want, and he suddenly understood at a very primal level, this wasn't about her pleasure. Her pleasure was secondary to her claim on him and the need she had to see him submit to that claim, not just for her, but her family. He'd gone wandering – even if only in his mind – and she needed to know he was back for good. She rocked on him again, and then again, building a rhythm; the fact they were careful, gentle movements only adding to his love for her and the pressure in his groin.

Tears filled his eyes at the intensity of the sensation. His hips bucked under her of their own accord, but he didn't want to bloody hurt her, so he forced himself still. "Lydia—" Her name was a cry and a plea all at once.

Her tone held nothing less. "Say it, Taylor, please."

He knew what she needed to hear, and the need wasn't just hers: his own soul demanded he lay down for her; express his commitment. "I'm yours," careened out of his mouth on a moan as he was taken to the brink. "Lydia, I'm yours forever."

She made a very cute exclamation of victory, slammed a hand on his chest, moved faster and harder, and he lost all sensation as he released himself inside her. He *became* sensation – for her. For their children. For their future.

For everything to come.

EPILOGUE

"She can't have disappeared off the face of the earth."

"I-I've been v-very thorough. And the m-magic I used was good. There's n-no trace of her."

"No, I'm not blaming you, Adam – you've done a stellar job. I really appreciate your trouble and efforts." Ryan sighed and rubbed his face with the hand not holding the phone. "Do you think she could've killed herself? Taken herself somewhere quiet and hidden where she thought no one might find her..." He let his words trail off, a sick feeling in the pit of his stomach at the visual they created in his mind.

"I-If she truly didn't want to be found, that c-could block the magic from seeing her."

Maybe that was it, then. He shouldn't care. He'd told himself – and her in not so many words – it was a decision he could live with, and it had been. He'd left Carrie with a silver bullet and hadn't looked back; had forced himself no to.

But he'd been treated to a double-dose of mate-deaths since then, which had seared his insides like nothing he'd fucking experienced before. Sure, there were stories written about the pain you felt on the death of a mate, but to actually go through it... If Taylor had died that night, too, he was pretty certain he wouldn't have lasted to see the dawn. He thought of Althea, thankful her passing had been peaceful, and sent her a silent prayer. He thought of Richard, and had no idea how the old wolf had coped the past three decades – and with the loss of both his children, too.

And he thought about the position he'd left Carrie in.

"Have you thought about the offer?" he asked, changing the

subject, for his sake more than Adam's. "We'd love to have you and Tiegan back here."

"We h-have. Tiegan n-needs a little more time."

"Take as long as you need – you'll always have a home here."

"Th-Thank you."

"All right. I'm gonna leave you to try and get some sleep."

"Never do sleep on the full m-moons."

"Yeah, I know the feeling." Even if the mating pains had gone extinct with the Trident, all senses were still heightened on every full moon, as was libido, albeit not as savagely as before. "Say hi to Tiegan for me."

"I will. 'Bye."

"'Bye, Adam." Ryan hung up and chucked his phone on the grass next to him, then lay back on the turf with an exhalation of defeat. The stars and moon looked wondrous for exactly five seconds, and then *that* memory invaded as it always did when he looked at the stars: the memory of staring through the open top of a pyramidal structure while lying naked on—

No. With a soft growl, he stood, ignoring the faint echo of Nikolai's voice, forever a part of that pyramid which he, Adam, and a bunch of other males had torn to the ground six months ago. It wasn't a story he was ever going to tell his kids, that's for sure. How would they look at him if they ever knew—

No. He turned on his heel and headed back towards the house – nearly an hour's walk from here, but he didn't mind. He needed the time. If he could just find Carrie, maybe—

Maybe what? You'll say what? Sorry for murdering your mate? Sorry for the knifing pain you felt when I did?

He didn't regret killing him – leaving him alive had not been an option knowing what they knew and with the choices they had faced.

So, why the guilt?

Fuck the guilt.

Blood doesn't wash off hands that easily, does it? Not when you have history with that blood.

It rattled him Taylor had wanted to take his little trip down memory lane, even if Ryan understood it completely. He was more than glad Taylor had decided to be open with them all; include Lawrence in his excursion – no more secrets was what they'd promised each other and no one had held to that promise more so than Taylor. Could he say he was doing the same?

What good would it do to let anyone know you're looking for Carrie? What good would it do to let them know that every now and then you still think you see Nikolai standing in the shadows out of the corner of your eye?

An hour passed quickly when deep in thought. He was glad the atmosphere felt peaceful and silent when he finally stepped into the house. It sounded like everyone was asleep.

The first stream of light broke across the horizon, heralding dawn, as he quietly closed the front door.

He stilled and had to mentally compose himself as Lydia and Taylor's *marked* scent reached him at the bottom of the stairs. *Fuck me.* It didn't surprise him Lydia had hit possessive mode – he'd thought of taking that male and doing the exact same thing the minute he'd come back from 'eighteen months ago'. And he still bloody might do just that.

The thought of that turned him on and thankfully lifted him out of his own dark thoughts of the past – at least until he remembered how Nikolai had laid his hands on Taylor. He had to temper a growl at that as he ascended the stairs towards his two beloved mates. He sensed Lawrence was sleeping in his own bedroom.

Silently, he approached the door to Taylor's room, where their joint musk was coming from. It was shut. He wondered if he should make his way to his own room, but Lydia had asked him to come see her on his return.

Holding his breath, he homed in with his ears and heard steady breathing from both Taylor and Lydia on the other side of the door. They sounded asleep. As gently as he could manage it, he opened the door, glad the turn of the handle was barely audible. He swung it halfway open and spied them both sleeping on their sides, on the bed. Taylor looked like a smooth, marble sculpture, carved by nymphs or something, and Lydia looked nothing less than a goddess about to give birth.

To a whole new era.

He took a step back, uncertain. He didn't want to ruin that scene. And the bed was barely big enough for him to spoon up behind Taylor – especially with Lydia being the size she was.

His phone vibrated in his back pocket, and he bit back a curse, switching the vibration off completely as quickly as possible. His gaze snapped back to the almost-mythical scene in front of him: neither of his mates had stirred. He let out the breath he was holding and looked back at his phone. The message was from Samuel, the Beta of the Wiltshire pack: **No news on Carrie, sorry. I tried all my sources.**

Ryan switched the phone off. He'd reply later. That she-wolf had either taken her life in some secret place no one could find, or... Could she still be alive and successfully hiding – even from Adam's magic – after five months? With the mating pains gone, it might be possible she survived. The truth was, no one knew. No one knew the rules of this new era upon them.

He pocketed his phone and then stared at his hands in the greying light. These hands had touched females they'd had no right touching; had killed enough Tridents; had spilled blood.

The scent of Nikolai's blood suddenly hit him fast and fiercely; the look on his face that millisecond before the bullet had met his head; that split-second he'd understood his end was upon him.

Ryan shook his head to rid his mind of the past it

stubbornly held onto. He kicked his shoes off, then took his clothes off, and shifted. As a wolf, he settled on the floor by the door, often Taylor's favoured spot, and he took comfort in that. He also took comfort in how the merged aroma of his mates hit him ten times stronger as a wolf. Breathing it deeply, he sank into it, letting it secure him in safety and warmth and love; letting it wash away the sins he couldn't quite manage to himself.

His eyes were already closed, the marking scent like a welcome drug. And he was far more tired than he'd previously thought.

In her asleep state, he heard Lydia call his name. *Ryan?*

Aah – one of the greatest comforts of all: the dream connection he had shared with her for over ten years. It had saved him a hundred times over and it was still going strong. While her heteropaternal superfecundation (at least that was the assumption of the babies' conception) had clouded her thoughts from all her mates, the dream connection appeared to be independent from her pregnancy and had not been broken.

Finally relaxing, he let her in, and every dark thought evaporated. *I'm here, darling. I'm right here.*

I love you, Ryan.

I love you, too.

SINS OF THE FATHER

CHAPTER ONE

He kissed her neck; under her chin; the side of her jaw; her ear lobe. It was divine – she *was divine. Moving inside her was heaven itself, if he believed in such a thing.*

She moaned a long, lustful sound.

He buried his nose in her red hair and breathed her in. "God, Lydia – you're ... what did I do to deserve you?"

He felt her smile against his cheek. "You never stopped looking for me. Thank you for looking."

"I couldn't stop looking. But it was you who found me in the end." He moved his head up to see her.

Violet eyes met his dark brown ones, just as they had a thousand times in dreams – and now in real life, too. They shared a life, and for now at least, it was a peaceful one. A hopeful one.

But this... This was one of those dreams. He knew this because, unlike in their waking reality, no baby stretched her belly – although he couldn't immediately tell if the dream was his alone or one of their shared ones.

"Mmmm," she moaned again, squeezing his length with her insides. Heaven, indeed. "Don't stop moving. I love how you feel. And I love you."

He thrust deeply within her.

She gasped – as did he – as he set a pace and rhythm. "Ooh ... yes. Ryan ... more."

He obliged, driving himself harder; deeper.

She twined her fingers into his hair; grasped it. "Don't stop."

"Can't stop," he mumbled.

"It's so real ... the dreams are so real."

Hell, he was close to coming. She didn't feel like she was quite there yet, though.

"You were my first," she breathed into his ear. "My real first. In every way but physical."

A single ray from the moon beamed onto the bed.

Not a bed, *whispered his mind. He frowned – partly in concentration as he tried to stave off his climax, and partly because a horrid feeling stole over him. It was familiar, and it had a name: dread.*

Lydia clenched around him, matching him thrust for thrust, and he cried out despite the unfurling foreboding; the sensation too much ... too close. "But," she added, "I wasn't your first, was I?"

Unbidden, his 'first' came to mind and along with her, fear, sorrow; lust and disgust in equal measure, although not because of her specifically – she'd been nice enough. Everything was suddenly as confusing as it had been that night twenty-five years ago. "No." It was a protest, but Lydia took it as a direct answer to her question.

"It's all right, Ryan." Her movements beneath him altered, becoming urgent and frantic; pleading and desperately amorous in that way only the moon's monthly pangs could accomplish. But the moon no longer hurt them this way and he needed to wake up from this dream.

Nightmare, *whispered his mind.*

It was not the soft firmness of their bed's mattress that bounced under his hands, but the hard, cold, grey of stone, tinted blue by the concentrated moon ray above him, that chafed his palms as he moved. This was an altar.

It's a prison.

Red hair turned to blonde, back to red, back to blonde. Realities merged and he tried to stop, but he couldn't, the need of ... whoever was beneath him driving everything he had no voice for. He was only fifteen.

Forty.

Fifteen.

Forty.

“It’s okay, James.”

It wasn’t. But his protest was now an inexperienced groan, the peak of his fervour upon him.

“It’s for the pack.”

He looked down, trying to find a way to stop his climax, even as it somewhat chaotically erupted from him, and froze at the large belly under him.

She was pregnant.

“No,” he whimpered. It’s a dream, it’s a dream. *That hadn’t happened – no female had* ever *conceived with him, much to Nikolai’s great disappointment.*

“You love your pack, don’t you, James? You’d do anything for your pack, wouldn’t you?”

Those words coiled around him like a Boa constrictor. Air rushed from his lungs, and he couldn’t take any back in. And he couldn’t stop it – what those words conjured: that fierce need to demonstrate his loyalty, his duty, and his protection of his pack. For all the wrong reasons.

He fought it, aware this wasn’t real. It wasn’t happening.

He pulled himself out of … he blinked. He didn’t know who she was anymore – didn’t trust his senses in this corner of his own mind.

He was sweating, his panic rising. He fixed his stare on her large belly. “I’m sorry,” he said. “I’m sorry.” He was *sorry. For every female he’d ever touched who hadn’t known her own mind. For the sorrowful fact he’d never known his own. He squeezed his eyes shut, willing himself to wake up.*

No such luck.

“Is this what you’re sorry for?” Her voice had changed.

He forced his gaze to travel up to her face once more.

It was Carrie now sat there on the stone slab, face streaked with tears and anger, back straight, the gun he'd given her jammed under her chin.

He glanced back at her belly – still pregnant.

"How many lives, James? With one decision made on a whim."

"Carrie." He choked on her name. "It wasn't a whim."

"Oh, so you planned this? You wanted *this? Do you know how much it hurts?"*

"Carrie—"

"Let me show you." She pulled the trigger.

"NO!" But he wasn't as fast as a bullet. He closed his eyes against the blood that sprayed his face, his body already lunging for her; arms catching her. She was like lead in his embrace – she felt heavy; much heavier than she should. With trepidation he opened his eyes, blinking away the red that clung to his lashes.

It was Lawrence he held, his lifeless eyes staring upwards towards the massive hole at the back of his head.

Ryan screamed, both at the sight of him and at the agony that lanced his heart, his abdomen – his whole being – shredding him from the inside out.

He dropped his mate. Both his arms were painted red, coated in his blood. Last time Lawrence's blood had coated him this way he'd been saving *his life. He let out another defeated, enraged scream, but it was someone else's scream of similar torment that caught his attention. He swivelled towards the sound, straining his eyes against the night-infused gloom of the pyramid's walls ... and there he was.*

"Taylor!" He sped towards him.

He was kneeling, doubled over on the floor, naked, sobbing, his hands clutching at his torso for dear life.

"Taylor!" Finally reaching him, he dropped a hand on his shoulder and Taylor swung around, fury contorting every curve of

his face, pure hatred in his eyes. Ryan recoiled, his mate's tangible loathing nothing short of a punch in his gut, only it was his face that felt the punch when Taylor's fist came up and pounded his jaw.

The attack threw him backwards. He landed on his spine with a winded cry, and there was no time to catch his breath because Taylor was on him, thighs gripping his waist like iron, pinning him to the ground as he thumped him again.

Through his cry, his nose cracked. Blood gushed down his lips. "Stop."

He didn't stop.

His mate's balled fist came down again, and then again, cracking his cheek, splitting his lip... "You did this!!" he screamed, and it was as painful as Lawrence's death tearing through him – he'd never *seen Taylor like this. He tried to speak again – calm him down – but he managed barely a sound before the next punch, and the next.*

"You think I wanted you like this?! I NEVER wanted you like this!"

The following blow felt near fatal. His head spun to the right and stayed there. But he wasn't alone in his pain. Nikolai lay to his right looking as bruised as he felt. Blood seeped from the older male's head – pooled around it. But he was still alive. Their eyes met, Nikolai's eerie ones – knowing ones – reaching parts of his soul he had no right seeing; no right being inside.

He barely felt the next punch, but he didn't have to. The words hit him harder than a punch ever could.

"I NEVER wanted you this way!"

To say Ryan startled awake was something of an understatement. He *bolted* awake, the door he was lying against banging into the wall behind it, although he wasn't sure why it would. Horror-filled sleep clung to every recess of his mind, and it took him a good few seconds to realise he'd cried out loud and that his hand was smarting.

A gentle murmur came from the bed.

Lydia. Last night's walk came back to him, as did how he'd curled up to sleep in the doorway to Taylor's room on his return. Which was where he was now. *Oh, god...* He prayed Lydia had not borne witness to any part of that dream. They'd connected, hadn't they? Just before he'd fallen asleep, in that way they so often did in dreams.

She yawned, stirring, but still mostly asleep, even though he was becoming aware he'd made a bit of a clatter on waking.

He moved his focus to his right hand – the one that stung with pain. "Shit," he whispered. He'd put it through the damn door.

"Ryan?" came Lydia's voice, still thick with sleep.

"It's okay ... everything's fine," he replied, still whispering because for the life of him he could not speak – not without feeling he might crack. The nightmare was too present; too alive inside him. He hurt everywhere. And all he could see were the usually kind green eyes he loved aflame with rage.

With a grimace, he wriggled his hand and gingerly pulled his fist back through from the other side of the door. Wood splintered as he did, and the smell of fresh blood hit his sinuses – his own blood. *Great.*

Lydia must have caught the scent. He sensed, rather than saw, her eyes fly open.

"It's all right," he said again, trying to speak the words properly and not whisper them, though he was mostly still whispering. "I just ... nicked myself on something. It's nothing."

Sitting up with some difficulty, Lydia rubbed sleep out of her eyes. "You're okay?"

"Right as rain, sweetheart." His system still in shock, he forgot to try and hide that lie from his voice. Luckily, the whispering tone he couldn't shake off seemed to cover it enough. Maybe she wouldn't see the great big hole at the bottom of the door either.

"Is Taylor here?"

His gut churned as he thought of Taylor. *Get yourself together – Jesus Christ – it was just a fucking dream.* "I heard the shower running – it's just gone off. I'm guessing that's him."

He saw Lydia look at the clock on her bedside. "It's nine in the morning already." She flung the corner of her duvet to one side. "I'd better— Oh, god... Oh, no."

"What is it?" He forced himself to get up and fucking failed. His thighs were trembling, every scene from his nightmare still tumbling through his mind like a horror movie on repeat. He made it to his knees.

"Shit – this is sooo embarrassing." Her hushed voice broke, and he really had to get himself up. "I've wet the bed. I can't believe I did that."

Okay ... just get up and go to her like the goddamned Alpha you are, you useless piece of—

"Lydia, you okay?" Taylor waltzed into the room, running a towel through his washed hair, still naked, water beading off skin, Lydia's scented mark on him still noticeable; although his own masculine aroma was back now, too. Presumably he'd seen Ryan futilely kneeling on the floor by the door, but his full focus was on their female and Ryan assumed he'd heard her cry of dismay.

Your focus should also be on Lydia. And he was trying, he really was. He finally brought himself to standing, grabbing his clothes as he went. His chest was tight with lodged panic. He hadn't had a nightmare like that in forever – it was even worse than the string of dreams he'd had when Nikolai had been here six months ago. But not quite as bad as the flashbacks. They'd started about two weeks ago coming out of goddamned-no-fucking-where, and when they came they were like pieces of a *living* dream he didn't know he was dreaming. Only for a few seconds at a time, but enough to ruin him for hours. In silence. Because he hadn't told anyone about the bursts of cold terror that caught him unawares at any given time. He'd been waiting for them to pass... *Just a phase; they'll disappear.* And he hadn't been able to form words for them, anyway. Any time he tried to explain them, even to himself, he just sounded mad. And weak.

He forced air into his lungs and let his diaphragm expand fully as he pulled his jeans and T-shirt on. *Clear your head.*

Lydia's eyes were wet. She looked from Taylor to the mattress. "I peed in my sleep." She was clearly mortified.

"Honey, no ... here." Taylor offered her his hand. "I think your water broke."

Now her eyes widened. "What? Are you sure? I didn't feel it."

"You were asleep. Let me help you up."

She stood with Taylor's help and then let out a gasp as more liquid – a *lot* more – surged down her legs.

"Definitely your water breaking. Let's get you downstairs and I'll call the doctor."

"Oh, god. My dress..."

Taylor grabbed it from the back of the chair beside the bed. "I've got it. You're gonna be fine." He guided her towards the door and now his gaze met Ryan's own ... travelled down to his cut fist ... the hole in the door ... and back up to his face. His green eyes lit with concern, and Ryan looked away. Couldn't actually meet his stare without seeing those same eyes lashing at him in—

"It's nothing," he said, curtly, interrupting his own thoughts because he damn well needed to. "An accident. I'm fine."

He ignored the way Taylor's gaze stayed on him as he steered Lydia out of the room, and was thankful Lydia didn't seem to have noticed his hand or the door. If she had, she was clearly ignoring it for her more pressing issue.

Lawrence's bedroom door sounded open, then shut, one floor above them. "Did I hear that right?" he called out from the top of the stairs, already making his way down.

"You did," called back Taylor.

"I'm dialling Dr Matheson now."

"Can you take her down, Lawrence? I need to get changed." He passed Lydia her dress and then they were on the other side of the door, shielded from Ryan's sight.

Ryan zoned them out. His head was fucked. Lydia was about to go into labour and his head was *fucked*. Visions of Carrie, pregnant and suicidal, swam in and out of his mind. Automatically, he reached for the phone in his back pocket and looked at the messages. The battery was low: 18%. There was another text from Samuel, now confirming that the Somerset pack had heard nothing about Carrie's whereabouts either. He pocketed the phone and staved off the slight feeling of suffocation. He needed to go downstairs with Lydia. He also needed to find Carrie.

"You need something for that?"

He started, not even aware Taylor had made his way back in and was standing right in front of him. He followed his gaze to his hand. "Just scratches."

"What happened?"

"Bad dream."

"Did the door try to eat you?"

God, that was so Taylor – that nonchalant, diffusing, careful, yet *caring* reply; humorous and serious all at the same time. A part of him sagged inside wanting nothing more than to fall into his arms, but he couldn't quite bring himself into those arms with his mate's crazed fury imprinted in his memory, even if it wasn't real. It had felt fucking real. So had Nikolai's very much *alive* stare.

"Hey..." Taylor's tone and whole demeanour softened. He reached out to take his grazed hand, and Ryan backed up. Right against the wall behind him.

Taylor froze.

"I'm sorry," mumbled Ryan, and he was. Truly. He couldn't look up to meet his eyes – didn't want to see the worry there and didn't want to talk about his nightmare anyway. But Taylor's voice remained steady, still soft, and he knew. Ryan *knew* he knew because he'd let him inside once – just once – into the dark of his mind; to that place; to the pyramid and every wretched secret kept in its walls. He'd let him see it and feel it because it was the only way he could get him to understand – very quickly – the complexity of it all so he could stay the hell away from Nikolai and keep safe.

Taylor pulled his hand back and took a step away, all without a hurry in the world, his movements easy. "I'm going to put some clothes on. And then I think Lydia needs us." He went on to do just that as he chatted away about a variety of menial things, and Ryan tried to listen – tried to take it in – but it was Carrie who filled his mind, pregnant, even though she'd never been pregnant in reality. He shook his head to shake her away, but she was a persistent ghost... *"Is this what you're sorry for?"*

"Ryan."

Taylor calling him just about broke through the echo of a gunshot in his head. Somewhere in there, Lawrence – dead – flashed through his mind, *that* memory all too real, and he was glad the wall was holding him up when the phantom pain of the death raced through his body – *not* a fucking nightmare at all. He wasn't sure which took the trophy for the worst night of his life: the one where he'd lost everything he'd known at eighteen, or the one in which he'd watched and felt Lydia and Lawrence die as a horde of deranged beasts invaded their home; Taylor nearly dying too – the wolf with nine fucking lives. He *had* held him dying once, choking and convulsing on silver.

Perturbed, Ryan did look up at him this time, needing a semblance of whatever 'reality' actually was amid the screams and gunfire in his periphery. *That's not real – not anymore.*

Taylor smiled.

That was real.

Fuck. He welled up as he bent at the waist and exhaled the dream out. And the memories; the real bits and the false bits somewhat merging, trying to create a new version of darkness that didn't happen. But *Taylor* was real, wasn't he? This version, right here.

Taylor stepped into his space again, carefully, still not touching him, but open to contact, arms hanging loose by his side. His body heat made the hairs on his arms prickle, and it was wonderfully familiar.

Closing his eyes, still bent double, Ryan let himself fall into the scent and feel of him. *This is real.* This was Taylor. Not the distorted copy his mind had corrupted.

He stopped an inch from him.

The inch was enough. Ryan leaned forward and couldn't help the soft groan of relief that left him when his forehead met Taylor's abdomen, the T-shirt he wore doing nothing to hide the definition of the smooth muscles under there.

Arms came up around him; hands found the back of his neck and shoulders; said nothing as they held him, pressing him into his embrace.

"I'm sorry," said Ryan for the second time. He *was* sorry. For having lost himself enough so that for a handful of minutes he'd allowed his nightmare to dictate his living world.

Taylor's caresses against the nape of his neck were the sweetest absolution. "You know"—his tone was so hushed, so peaceful, so the opposite to everything cascading through Ryan

—"I've missed you. We've each spent a lot of time with Lydia recently – which was needed and is bliss in itself – and we've spent a lot of time together, generally, as the three or four of us, but it's not been just you and me for a while."

God, yeah. He'd missed that too. Although he hadn't realised the depth of that need until this second.

"I've noticed you've seemed agitated recently..." That statement hung there, obviously waiting for some kind of reply.

A grunt was all Ryan managed, scared his words might ruin the sanctuary of the moment. And he didn't want to think about it.

A pause stretched out before them, and then, a soft sigh from his mate.

"Must have been a hell of a dream," Taylor said, his tone hushed. He ran his fingers through his hair in a nurturing fashion, gently tugging as they stroked. "Have you been having a lot of those?"

He shook his head against his torso. "First bad dream for maybe half a year, but it was ... too real. It felt too real."

"Not one of your visions, though."

"No. Not the same, but just as real in some ways."

"It's big, what we went through – and what we're about to go through."

"Been through big stuff before," he mumbled.

A pause ... Taylor's next words were very quiet. "We railroaded ourselves into a suicide pact. And you saw it play out, Ryan—"

And *he'd* railroaded Carrie into the same.

"—along with a whole world of events we don't even have words for."

Taylor's stark analysis of what they went through was a reality check he didn't need. He didn't want to get into it. With a shake of his head, he pulled himself away from Taylor's safety, slightly annoyed at the damp patches he'd left on his T-shirt – hadn't realised he'd been bloody crying.

He pushed away the now dimming image of Lawrence's skull exploding. The nightmare, too, had finally faded, and he didn't want it creeping back. He straightened, standing tall. "We'd better go down to Lydia."

Taylor frowned slightly. "Lawrence is with her – we have a bit of time."

"I don't want to talk about it."

"You don't have to."

He met Taylor's eyes, warm and caring, and no longer part of that god-awful dream script.

"But you also don't have to do this alone."

He forced out a smile. "I know." Every damn day he was grateful Taylor had seen none of it: Lawrence making Richard shoot him and the look on both their faces; Bab's infiltration of their house; that fucking Trident almost walking off with Taylor; the way Bab had taken Lawrence's blood... Even that goddess (or whatever the hell she was) wearing Lydia's body had scared the freaking life out of him. The possession of *all* their bodies... He remembered every mind-shattering second of that night. And then, hours later, finding Hendrickson and Amelia. They'd trusted his instruction. They'd *trusted* him.

Taylor stood there, contemplating him. And then, he nodded. "Okay. Let's go downstairs."

"Wait." Ryan caught his arm as he turned. Even though it had only been a dream, it was too painful to contemplate that the words pounded into him with fists might have any significance in Taylor's waking existence. Ryan's fretting mind needed some assurance, even though he felt stupid asking. "Last night, in the woods, with Sarah..." That had come out wrong – it wasn't exactly what he meant.

Taylor let out a sharp breath, his expression apologetic as he stepped back into his frame. "Lydia told me." He brought his hand up to his chest. "I had no idea you'd feel me being with her through a bloody memory, I'm so sorry."

"No, that's not..." He rested his hand on Taylor's, unsure how to ask what he needed to and annoyed the dream had rocked him enough to feel even a sliver of insecurity about what they shared – they'd shared so fucking much. Asking felt almost detrimental. But the demand for cold, hard certainty – anything to stop the crippling flashbacks that had somehow now made it into his sleep time – outweighed his reason. "You were married and in love, and I'm a big, forceful, sometimes overexcitable, ugly fucker."

Taylor's eyebrows hit his hairline, his look of apology giving way to incredulous amusement.

"At least compared to Sarah. I just want to make sure you ... you do and *did* want ... 'this' – right?" *'This'? As if you're holding mouldy lettuce? Can't think of a better word for one of the relationships that give your heart a reason to beat?*

Taylor went from confused to ... still. He stood very still. He brought his hand back down. "'This'?"

"Er..." Ryan gulped, pushing his rising sweat and constant jitteriness back down through his pores. That's what it bloody felt like, anyway. "Being ... with me the way you're with me. I mean like"—Nikolai's fucking smile darted through his mind and if his insides could shrivel in disgust, they did—"touching." *What?* Damn, *no*. Damn his head! What he felt inside was colouring his words and that had come out sounding—

Taylor's face looked pinched.

Anger at his own total incompetency rose. He had to put this right. "I just mean you never felt ... I never pushed you or ... forced you into anything, did I?"

Nope. Still wrong. But he suddenly felt exhausted. Thinking of the right words while trying to stave off all the unwanted thoughts and feelings and images was *exhausting*.

Taylor might as well have been frozen in place, his look one of … ugh, Ryan wasn't sure what that look was, but he felt shit he'd just put it there.

After what felt like an age, his mate finally took a step back. Whether that was hurt or anger that showed through his countenance, Ryan instantly regretted his poor choice of words – should have explained it better; should have let him in on the details of the dream. *Should have, could have, would have.*

Jaw clenching, Taylor glanced at the open door and then back again, his voice low and tight. "I'm sorry – you seem to have bypassed the hundred or so times I shouted your name in pleasure as I came in your hand, your mouth, over your chest, inside you—"

"Taylor, I'm—"

"The many times I *told* you I wanted you – wanted *this* – and the several times I initiated that intimacy so you'd have *no* doubt of my intentions."

Yeah, he was pissed. "Tay—"

"Do you honestly think I compare you to my ex-wife? She was her and you're you and I've laid myself bare for you in a way I never did for her."

Really pissed.

Shit.

He was *shit* at doing the 'deep feelings' thing when it came to his own crap. "Taylor—"

"You're not the first male I've found attractive."

Not the first…

Stupid, really, that that had never occurred to him, and he'd never asked him, either. Equally stupid was the jealousy that unexpected statement ignited, and right on its tail, possessiveness.

"You're just the first male I found attractive at a time when I could actually examine what that meant and *do* something about it. So I did. Do you think I went into 'us' blind, without thinking about it or questioning my past, or knowing myself? When you were away for those three weeks – after our kiss – *all* I did was question everything I knew. I decided to trust it – what I felt. You. Us. I've been *open* with you – completely – even though you shut me out all the fucking time—"

What? "I don't sh—"

"Even though you went half-cocked to Nikolai's, *deliberately* not telling me, after *everything* he did; even though for the past five months you *won't* talk to me about *that* night everything went to hell as if I wasn't even fucking there. I *was* there."

If he had no words before, he sure as hell had none now. Taylor never usually got angry. "I didn't mean to—"

"I *told* you – *all* of you – about what I wanted to happen in those woods last night." His cheeks reddened under his sheening eyes. "Do you think it was easy for me to ask of Lawrence what I did? I was honest with you all because we promised we would be. Because of everything we've been through."

"I *am* being—"

"Who have you been texting?"

Now Ryan took a step back, his turn to look bewildered, that question catching him off guard.

"The past few days you've been quiet, irritated, constantly looking at your phone..." Taylor waited for an answer, the look on his face already one of disappointment at knowing he wasn't going to get one.

Guilt surged. So did panic. Ryan searched inside for some answer he could give him. *Just tell him the fucking truth.*

But the truth was stuck in place, lodged under his gut, its rigidity safely plugging in the chaotic mess behind it. He opened his mouth, wanting nothing more than to ease the wound he hadn't meant to cause. Nothing came out. Taylor was right.

Ryan *did* shut him out – when it came to the wreckage of his life, anyway – although he really didn't mean to.

Taylor shook his head just a little, sighed almost tenderly, but when he looked back at Ryan his features had hardened. "Being with you, body and soul – '*this*' way, as you so eloquently put it – is like an epiphany for me. But you've been so distant recently... I let it go – thought Lydia and the pregnancy was on your mind; thought I'd pissed you off by wanting to explore the memories of the night I was turned – only you've barely touched me for going on two weeks. And you get even more distant when I try to get close, like right now. So perhaps the question you should be asking is do *you* want *me*. *This* way."

He turned and left.

CHAPTER TWO

Dr Matheson pulled up on the gravel driveway just as he was turning the mattress over against the open window.

Ryan had stripped the sheets off Taylor's bed, sponged the mattress down with soapy water, and now stood it up to let the fresh air dry it. It did little to get his mind off that fuck up of a conversation and the way he'd hurt Taylor with his *excellent* vocabulary skills, but it kept his hands busy, his body moving, and he'd needed the time to collect himself before Lydia gave birth.

He'd wanted to run after his mate down those stairs, grovel an apology, and make him listen. But he also didn't want to talk because he was – in part – terrified that talking about the things that pushed his panic button would trigger the new, chaotic flashbacks. He couldn't give Taylor what he wanted to hear because it meant he'd have to *think* about it.

On another level, he didn't want him ruined by the events of that night of the storm. Nor by the events of Ryan's childhood; his history. Selfishly, he wanted Taylor untouched by all that; his kindness was something good and untainted. Even after Selena had messed with him, that kindness had proved incorruptible. *He* was incorruptible. It was a certainty Ryan could come back to time and again, and by god, he needed it because he sure as hell couldn't find it in himself sometimes.

And that *was* selfish. Because Taylor wasn't a pretty canary in a cage waiting to relieve him of all his woes at the end of every day. He was his partner and his equal, just as all four of them were to each other. He had been there that night, too, as he'd rightly pointed out. He'd suffered Lydia's death before he'd passed out, already ill because his human DNA had been rejecting his wolf. He'd suffered, too.

The doctor rang the doorbell, and Ryan swore under his breath. Time was up. He had to go down now, and he needed to be bright and strong for Lydia's sake.

Gritting his teeth, he took another look at his phone as he left the room. No messages and 15% battery. *No time to charge it now.* Probably just as well. He was aware his search for Carrie was becoming something of an obsession. His focus needed to be on Lydia and the babies now. An absent father wasn't a father – he knew that from experience – and he sure as hell didn't want to be like his father. What kind of father he was going to be, though, was a question he didn't know the answer to. Cradling a baby with the same hands that had put a bullet through his—

"Fuck," he mumbled, and then he did his best to empty his brain of anything that wasn't Lydia as he headed out of the room and down the stairs.

Lydia was in the front lounge, pacing as she breathed in and out slowly, rubbing her bump gently; Lawrence was at the front door letting the doctor in, and Taylor was nowhere to be seen.

"Ryan?"

Blue-violet eyes met his dark brown ones. "How are you doing?" he asked, softly, as he approached her.

She reached for him and he relished the feel of her hand in his. But she frowned as she looked down at it. "What happened to your hand?"

"Already healing. Just a cut. Already washed it." It *was* mostly healed now. He wondered if she had caught sight of it earlier after all.

"Are you and Taylor fighting?"

"What? No."

"You never fight."

"There's no fight."

"I can *feel* it."

He did his best to suppress his sigh and kept his voice calm and steady for her. "It was just a misunderstanding, nothing more. You know I'm shit with words sometimes. I said the wrong thing; didn't mean it; I'll make it up to him. You don't need to worry about it."

"Now."

"What?"

"Make it up to him now, Ryan. Before the babies come."

"Er—"

"I mean it. No tension around the babies." She squeezed his hand and gave him a shove towards the kitchen. "He's getting hot water and towels – go speak to him."

This time, he didn't bother suppressing the breath that left him. "I'm here for *you*. What about you?"

She stilled, stuck her chin out, her gaze went steely, and that was that.

He wasn't about to argue with Lydia on the brink of labour.

"I want *both* of you sorted out and back in here when I start screaming and pushing, got it?"

The doctor's voice reached them from just outside the door.

"Now," she whispered, more urgency in her tone, and then she headed for the doorway, smiling a greeting at Dr Matheson as he and Lawrence entered.

With a silent grunt, Ryan turned and made for the kitchen before Lawrence could catch his eye. Bad enough he had to try and explain things to Taylor, he didn't want to explain things to Lawrence, too. He didn't want to make a fuss over this at all – not now of all times – but it was too late because he knew Lydia wouldn't rest until she felt the harmony she needed, and he wasn't sure he could fake it. Not with the way they were so in tune with each other, and not with the way all wolves could read lies.

The kitchen tap was on, running hot water into a bowl and billowing steam. He heard Taylor's movements, although he couldn't see him, right in that broom cupboard that led to the cold room.

That faint sense of dread that was starting to feel too familiar stole over him, and before he was fully aware of it, spiralled towards his brain and seemed to freeze it. And him. He stilled, all his senses primed for danger. It was as if ice ran through his veins.

That's how they died: veins turned to ice.

Unbidden, Amelia's terrified face filled his mind, Hendrickson's eyes wide with panic and blinking away the blood that streamed down his face as they both fled into the space Taylor now occupied. Every sound from that moment shrieked in his ears: gnashing teeth, screams, Amelia's sobs...

"The freezer! Go!"

Right in front of him a Trident loomed. His fist closed around the shard of glass he'd grabbed from the broken window.

Ryan...

Hendrickson called his name through the cacophony.

Should he drive the glass into the monster's gut or his throat? No time to decide – it was lunging for Taylor.

"Ryan."

He growled, baring his fangs.

A door slammed. Hard.

The oddness of the slam pushed him out of his body for a second – he hadn't heard that slam that night ... had he?

"Ryan." Taylor's voice.

Ryan blinked. And he blinked again because something clouded his vision. He became aware of his breathing – laboured

– his canines still emerged. The smell of the kitchen came back to him – his home – the sound of running water sloshing over the side of the bowl it had filled.

"Breathe in."

He did, not quite registering straight away it was Taylor's instruction he was following. *Taylor...* Standing right in front of him. Not dying. Not in danger. He was blurred, though. Ryan blinked away—

"You're sweating." Taylor's voice was as soft as it had been previously in the bedroom. If he was angry at him from their earlier conversation, he wasn't showing it.

Ryan finally managed to blink the sweat out of his eyes – could feel it dripping off his chin. He looked down. His T-shirt was half-soaked across his chest and under his arms. *Jesus Christ.* How long had he been standing here? No more than a few seconds, surely?

Taylor, still a few feet away, took a step forward. He held clean towels in his arms. The broom cupboard was now closed behind him.

Another step and he held out a towel for Ryan who suddenly came to his senses. He shook his head and took a step back. "They're for Lydia," he rasped.

After a beat, Taylor nodded, but he still held it out. "I have eight here. We can spare one. Lydia would say the same."

And she'd worry more if she saw the state of him. More shakily than he'd like, he took the towel from Taylor and did his best to mop up the sweat dripping off him and blot the sheen to his skin. He felt cold though – not hot. And clammy.

"You didn't hear me calling you."

"I didn't?"

"You weren't really here at all until I slammed the door shut."

Ryan met his gaze. It was knowing. He'd slammed it on

purpose.

"I, um..." He heard Lydia say something from the other room across the hall. Time wasn't on his side today. "I came to find you. I wanted to apologise."

Taylor raised an eyebrow. "Lydia made you apologise?"

He attempted a laugh and mostly failed. "She had words with me, but I wanted to apologise anyway."

Taylor gave a half-smile. "She had words with me, too."

"Our timing kind of sucks."

"It does."

"Everything came out wrong earlier – I'm sorry. I couldn't find the right words for what I wanted to say."

Taylor turned, headed to the bench on his left, placed the stack of towels there, then went to the sink and turned the tap off. When he faced Ryan again, he was a couple of feet closer than before. "And what did you want to say?"

About a hundred things he had no words for. He allowed himself a minute to take this male in – his posture at ease, even though he probably wasn't at ease; his naturally trim build somewhat hardened by eighteen months of outdoor living and working and running. "The dream I had this morning clouded ... everything for a good while. Nikolai was in it." He had to force that fact out. "You were in it, too, but it wasn't you. You were ... furious with me. No – more than that – you ... hated me. You were hitting me; punching me in the face over and over again, and screaming stuff. It left me feeling a certain way when I woke, and I couldn't shake it. That's why I asked what I did. I couldn't shake it."

"You could've said." He was just a foot away now. "I'd have understood. It makes much more sense now."

"I should've said, I know. It still felt too real, though. I couldn't pull it apart enough to find the words."

"Is that also what happened just now?"

"What do you mean?"

"About it being too real."

His reply stuck in his throat.

Taylor seemed to hesitate – studied him – and then he said, "I thought you were going to attack me a minute ago."

Ryan looked up, startled, shocked at his words.

Taylor maintained his nearness, stopping just short of touching him. "You *didn't* attack me. But the look on your face ... I'm not sure you were even here. I don't know what you were seeing."

"I would *never* attack you."

"I know. That's why I'm still standing here."

God. If Taylor had *thought* that, though – if he'd seemed *capable* of it... Was he? He hadn't exactly had control over what he was seeing; the things he was hearing. And if he couldn't tell illusion from reality... How could he be near Lydia? The babies? What if one of those flashbacks consumed him while he was holding a newborn?

"Stop. I know what you're thinking and don't. You *didn't* hurt me. You won't hurt anyone. I wasn't sure whether to say anything about it, but you put your fist through a door earlier, and your fangs are still showing – a little."

They were? He ran his tongue over them and willed them to retract.

Taylor's pupils dilated at the action, and despite all his present insecurities, his own body responded to his mate's heating gaze. It felt fucking good. Better than every crushing doubt over his ability to function.

A mischievous glint lit Taylor's irises and damn if that didn't drive all the cold from his veins. "You didn't have to put them away just for me."

Ryan's stare fell to the way the corner of his mouth curved deliciously when he was in teasing mode. When had he first noticed that? About six or seven months after they'd found him near dead, he recalled. He hadn't smiled at all at first – not for weeks and weeks – his life all but ruined. The first day Ryan had caught a smile on him, he remembered *really* well, although he hadn't at the time analysed exactly why he'd felt so lightened by it. His smile had felt like a breakthrough; like an acceptance of the pack and life as a wolf – *Ryan's* life. A life Taylor had brutally awoken to one crisp, sunny, autumn afternoon, his peaceful surroundings belying the emotional and mental torment that had followed for him.

Ryan had taken him under his wing knowing how important he was owing to the vision he'd had of him all those years ago, even if he hadn't understood the full complexity of the three visions of his mates at the time.

And had he kissed him this morning yet? Had he even kissed him last night? The day before?

Ryan lowered his head towards his lips, but Taylor straightened and pulled back a few inches – *too many inches* – his eyes holding more than one question despite the desire also evident.

God knows what Ryan must have looked like – if the disappointment in that tiny action showed through with as much force as his heart had dropped over it – but in the next second the back of his neck was grasped in Taylor's hand, hauling him forwards until Ryan's lips were under his. *Under* was right. Taylor took full charge, and in spite of Ryan's bigger stature, something in him submitted – completely released himself and every damn shadow that clawed at him – at the subtle command of this beautiful man and his open care; his open soul.

How the fuck his mouth moulded with his so goddamned *perfectly* was something he couldn't fathom. A small moan of need left him, and Taylor lapped it up; enticed another accompanied by a trail of hoarse words. "Taylor..." It had been days –

days – since they'd shared a kiss, surely, and maybe longer since one like this. "I'm an idiot." His mind had been filled with trepidation over unannounced bursts of panic, and he'd happily let Lydia's pregnancy needs flood him in trepidation's place, insisting on being there for her every waking moment so he wouldn't have to feel *anything* else.

Taylor made him feel.

As did Lydia, of course. But Lydia had always represented unconditional strength to him, a decade in dreams holding him up whenever he stumbled, that strength only made more solid when he'd discovered she was real. Lydia made him feel strong and sure of himself in clear, immediate ways. Taylor, though, sensitised his vulnerabilities. Maybe it was a 'men know men' thing, but Taylor *saw* every crack he tried to hide and recently, with the flashbacks, Ryan hadn't wanted him to, and without really meaning to, he'd kept him at a distance – emotionally and physically.

By god, what had been the cost? *This*. This earth-trembling kiss that wasn't just a kiss and rendered everything inconsequential. "I need you," he let slip, the words there before he even heard them escape his lips, and he didn't mean it physically – although very little matched the feel of Taylor against him – he meant it literally and exactly. "I—"

"You have me." The reply was whispered and laden with a conviction that was wholly echoed in his gaze.

A deliberate and not-too-quiet cough sounded from the kitchen doorway.

Both males whipped their heads around to find Lawrence standing there, arms across his chest, his face carrying a somewhat appreciative look at the scene before him. "When you're ready, you're both wanted next door. Contractions are mild at the moment but starting to come fairly regularly."

"We'll be right there," Taylor replied.

Lawrence nodded and left.

"Come on – we're not going to want to miss *this* first." Taylor grabbed the towels and passed them to Ryan who took them.

"Am I forgiven, then? For being a clumsy oaf this morning."

That teasing half-smile was back, curving Taylor's lips upwards in that delicious way once more. He dipped his hand in the water bowl, feeling for its temperature. "Your tongue just made up for its lingual ineptitude."

Ryan couldn't help his grin.

"I'd already forgiven you. I was just pissed off."

"Sorry."

"I know. Hey"—he turned the tap to cold and released more water into the bowl—"tell me next time, okay?"

"About any nightmares?"

"Yeah, but also"—the tap went off, and Ryan sensed he was picking his words carefully—"if you feel the panic coming on; if you start to zone out, like earlier."

He had to catch himself. His breath stuck in his throat. Had he let that slip earlier? Had he accidentally let on about his panic? No matter how much he trusted Taylor, that sense of vulnerability washed over him and threatened to drown him.

Taylor worried his lip with his teeth, not bothering to hide his attentive assessment of him. And then, he let out a slow breath. "I don't suppose 'post-traumatic stress' is a term werewolves pay much mind to."

He squeezed the towels in his hands tighter and frowned. "Stress? Everything's great now."

"But it wasn't for a long time, and six months ago it was literally hell. You watched us *die*."

He shuffled on his feet, itching to leave this room and this conversation.

Taylor ignored his unease, though Ryan could tell he was

wary of pushing. Nevertheless, he went that little bit further, even as he spoke gently. "You killed someone important to you."

Ryan flinched. Those wretched words fell heavily. Anger churned his gut. So did loathing.

"It's *because* everything's great now the stress comes on. It's like your mind finally has the time to deal with it all, so you get it all at once – every detail you shut out to cope comes at once. Maybe..." He paused. "Maybe speak to Dr Matheson about it."

He could feel his cheeks grow hot and pinched. "I *had* to do it. There's nothing wrong with me."

"I *know* you had to, and I didn't say there was anything wrong with you. What you're feeling is *normal* after everything we've been through."

"No need to speak to the doctor, then, is there. No need for this pep talk, either."

"Ryan—"

"Been through worse."

"You said that earlier. Ryan, it's not about the past year – it's about the past *thirty* years catching up with you." He waited and stared. To let his words sink in or something?

Annoyed, Ryan pushed them away. "I'm *fine*."

A wail from Lydia reached them through the doorway.

Taylor and Ryan both sighed – Taylor in defeat; Ryan's sigh was one of relief. "Let's go," he said, and he didn't look at Taylor or wait for any confirmation before walking out of the kitchen.

CHAPTER THREE

Whenever he felt restless, or angry, or anxious, he sought a mission. Historically, that was his modus operandi. Through a mission, he could work everything off. Five months of peace – bar those few hours last month when Lydia had ventured into a snowstorm – had him not knowing what to do with himself. Decades of being taught to sense danger – to fight; to protect – had come to a grinding halt with no Tridents in existence. Never in a million years would he have thought he'd have to get *used* to peace, but he did. And he was still trying.

Ryan suspected that was why his brain had homed in on Carrie: it had automatically sought a mission – something to find; something to fix. And as much as he despised himself for thinking of her now, he felt next to useless hearing Lydia cry out in this much pain and not being able to do a damn thing about it. Dr Matheson had it sorted, and nature had to take its course.

As she stood, half crouched, gritting her teeth against another contraction, Lawrence supported her under her right arm, Taylor under her left, and Ryan silently cursed himself for sneaking a quick glance at his phone before slipping it back into his pocket.

No news about Carrie. 8% battery left.

"Perfect!" said the doctor on the back of another cry. He was on his knees by her feet having just carried out an examination. Sofa cushions eased the hardness of the wooden floor against his joints. A couple of towels lay flat under Lydia, catching any bodily fluids. "I suspect this will be an easy birth."

"Are you *serious*?" Lydia exclaimed, her skin shiny with a

sheen of sweat.

"Absolutely. Unlike humans, werewolves are biologically primed for multiple births of up to three. Your fluidity and flexibility – the very reason you can shift – allows the babies to go full term in the uterus without damage to anyone, and natural births are no problem. You're fully dilated already and from what I can tell, the babies are in position. I can see the top of a head already. I'm uncertain where the placentas are, but we'll take that as it comes. All right ... I want you to push this time – bear all that weight downwards on the next contraction."

"Oh, god," Lydia panted, "so this is it? What if ... what if—"

"No 'what ifs', My Lady. These babies aren't hanging around for what ifs."

"You're doing great," he heard Lawrence whisper. "Richard sends his love, by the way. I let him know to take my calls for the rest of the day and until he hears from me."

Lydia's head fell back onto Lawrence's shoulder. "Didn't he leave early this morning for Devon?"

"Yes – only for a couple of days."

"He lost her, Lawrence. Evelyn." Richard's mate had died giving birth to Selena. "We have no hospitals or—"

"That was an anomaly and there was no Hendrickson here back then; and no Dr Matheson. You're going to be fi—"

The end of his sentence got lost on the wave of another contraction. Lydia grimaced in pain, and then yelled.

"I need you to push *down*," pressed the doctor.

"I'm trying," she heaved on a gasp before another wave hit her.

"Down."

She bent her knees fully, although it looked more instinctual than by thought, and used Lawrence's and Taylor's supporting arms as crutches so she could bear down harder, crouched as she was near the floor.

"Good! That's good – first baby's wanting out, no hesitation. Strong leader this one," grinned the doctor. "Push again. Towel!"

Towel... Shit! That was his cue. He strode to the pile he'd brought in and grabbed one.

Dr Matheson took it from his outstretched hand, opened it, and draped it across the seat of the chair to his right. "Push!"

Lydia's cry was a big one, this time. Her face, flamed red, contorted in both agony and determination. He thought he saw Taylor grimace slightly at the way she clutched his wrist and—

"Again!"

"*Fuck.*" But she complied. Not that she looked like she had a choice in the matter.

"Good! Once more – last time... and—" He laughed in victory as a newborn stretched its vocal cords for the first time.

Wow.

An awed silence filled the room around Lydia's relieved panting. Sure, they'd all been preparing for this, but ... *nothing* had prepared them for this. It was suddenly *real*. Lawrence's face was a picture, and hell, Ryan never thought he'd see it: that look. This day.

His mind catapulted him back nearly twenty-one years ago now, when he'd found the blond wolf bloody and mutilated; all but dead under the furred bodies of his kin, including his sister. *That* had been his first mission and the first time he'd found purpose after two years roaming rogue: save the royal line.

A gurgle ... then a cry. "Ten fingers and toes – so far, so good. You have a beautiful, healthy boy." Wrapped in the towel, the doctor brought him up to Lydia whose 100-watt smile outshone pretty much all else in the room – except maybe Lawrence's tears.

"Hey, little guy," she whispered, her finger coming up to stroke his cheek, her own tear falling.

Ryan found himself blinking his back. A quick glance at Taylor told him he was equally affected.

The moment was, unfortunately, transient. Lydia tensed, growled, then clutched at both her mates again.

"Ryan!" Lawrence calling his name brought him out of his awed state. "Take my place."

"And put the next towel on the chair," instructed the doctor.

He gladly did both, grateful to have something to do.

Lawrence took their son – *their son* – from Dr Matheson.

"Stay close – the cord should stay on until all three are out."

Lawrence nodded.

"Ryan…" Lydia strained, then gasped.

"I'm here. I've got you."

Her hand found his arm.

"First placenta's out," stated the doctor. "Okay, I suspect baby number two will be just as eager to emerge."

"Ugh, I've got to do this twice more," was her reply.

"But what a reward," Taylor interjected.

She threw him an attempt at a smile, and then another contraction hit.

"Here we go." Dr Matheson was back on his knees, on the cushions. The older man was agile for a human of his age. "I see another head, so baby's the right way round. You can go ahead and push, just like before."

Ryan had no idea how he was supposed to feel. His emotions were like a churning sea – warm and inviting near the surface, just like his tears were near the surface – but underneath there was a clasping cold and dangerous distance. He couldn't figure out if it was due to the wonder of the moment, or every other thing he'd tried to battle the past two weeks.

As Lydia wailed and bore down on his arm, he snuck a look at Lawrence. *He* seemed to have no problems at all. Go figure.

The king – known well by everyone for his sharp frostiness and uncompromising steel – who had spent all of his adult life in self-imposed solitary confinement, was clearly done with that. His grin elevated him as solidly as his new legs as he gently rocked the little blighter in his arms; the baby's cries had become occasional gurgles of contentment. It was plain to see both baby and father had found a home in each other.

Lydia's tightened grip and anguish brought him back to the female that dominated his heart as fully as his dreams.

"I can't ... I can't..." Her head lolled back onto Ryan's shoulder.

"You can, sweetheart. You took on 90,000 Tridents."

"They weren't in my fucking uterus," she growled.

"Thank Christ, sweetheart."

Taylor stifled his amusement, but Lydia's next growl told him she'd regained some of her fight.

"You're already doing it, My Lady," said Dr Matheson. "The head's almost clear – you need to push hard now for the shoulders."

Lydia gritted her teeth against what seemed like a swell of pain. "*Don't* call me 'My Lady' when you're between my legs." That was very definitely a command with no room for argument.

Taylor couldn't hold back his laugh this time.

The doctor smiled. "Understood – Lydia."

She bit her lip and pushed. And screamed.

Ryan's chest tightened at the sound – far too high-pitched – and it was Amelia's scream that suddenly deafened him; terror-fuelled; heralding death. "A-Are you all right? Is she all right?" He wasn't sure who he was asking.

Lydia let out a heavy moan and let her head drop back onto his shoulder again.

"Lydia?" He didn't mean to sound as shit-scared as he felt.

"Ow, Ryan, my arm..."

"Sorry." He released his hold, though not without effort, as if his fingers had ossified around her. God, he hoped he hadn't just bruised her.

Another baby wailed its greeting to the world. "We have another boy." Dr Matheson held the tiny thing triumphantly for Lydia to see. "Could be identical – I think they shared a placenta. That would mean the same biological father for these two, at least." The finest wisps of white-blond hair coated his cranium.

"It really doesn't matter – makes no difference to us." Lydia smiled, clearly happy, although Ryan could feel her sag against him; could *feel* her waning energy.

"Oh, I know," said the doctor. "I'm just very excited to write the case notes for a phenomenon so rare as a storm wielder giving birth with her three mates as the fathers. No one really knows what happens. The only account we have is four hundred years old." Excitement was evident in his speech and Lydia let out a tired laugh.

Ryan knew she was thinking of Hendrickson and how equally excited he would have been to see this. He gave her a squeeze and then he rubbed her arm where he'd gripped her, in what he hoped was a helpful gesture. The labour, birthing, pain, and screaming was all very much out of his comfort zone. Strange given he'd been in so many battles over the years.

And now he was thinking of Hendrickson.

Wrapped in the other towel, the doctor handed the baby to Taylor.

Taylor dropped a kiss on Lydia's cheek, then left his place by her side. He'd never seen *that* smile on Taylor before: soft – very soft. Even maternal as he looked down at the still wailing life in his arms.

For some reason he couldn't grasp, the sense of panic

knotted harder in his chest.

"Ryan, if you could support Lydia from behind now," came the doctor's voice.

His feet followed the instructions as Dr Matheson went to get the towels and something from his medical bag.

Lawrence huddled next to Taylor, neither of them able to go far because of the umbilical cords, and the nearness of the older sibling seemed to calm the baby down.

"Ryan?" Lydia uttered, softly.

"Yes?"

"Are you all right? You're trembling."

He was?

Ah, fuck – he was. He didn't know why. Couldn't really stop it, the same way you couldn't stop teeth chattering with cold. "I'm ... it's just a bit overwhelming, but I'm good. And I can hold you just fine."

"You and Taylor made up?"

"Yeah – all sorted."

"We were dreaming together last night – do you remember?"

She knocked the wind out of him with those words. He could feel his heart pound in his ears, all but deafening him.

She dropped her voice so human hearing wouldn't pick up the words that feathered his cheek. "We were making love. It reminded me so much of my teenage dreams with you." She smiled. "They warmed my heart; made me feel so safe. But last night, you left. Halfway through our making love, you disappeared. It felt different to you waking up. I was worried about you."

He didn't know what to say. It seemed she hadn't been present for the horrific mess his mind had conjured, and he was relieved. "I'm fine." He'd said that a lot today. It wasn't even lunch time.

"Wrist tags." Dr Matheson handed them to Lawrence and Taylor with a pen. "Just write 'baby one and two' on them if you're not sure on names yet. And how is mother doing?" He glanced at Lydia over his glasses.

Lydia's withdrew her attention from Ryan – thankfully – bringing it back to the more pressing matter at hand. "Can I just rest a bit before baby three?" She yawned.

The doctor chuckled. "Not for me to decide, I'm afraid. But I'm guessing the answer is going to be no." He got back on his knees before her. "I'm going to have a look and a feel, all right?"

"Mmm," she nodded, using this opportunity, no matter how fleeting, to close her eyes and lean right into Ryan's frame.

Ryan closed his eyes with her and focused on her breathing to calm his own. Lawrence and Taylor's hushed words of reverence over the bundles they cradled also calmed him.

"Okay, Lydia." Dr Matheson shifted his position on his knees. "Baby three is feet down, so this is going to take a bit more effort."

She lifted her head, though she seemed half-asleep. "Is it all right?"

"Heartbeat is steady and strong, but I only want you to push when I say. I'm going to guide baby out supporting its head and I need to make sure the cord isn't around the neck. I'm going to ease my arm further inside you, okay?"

"Okay." She pushed herself forward and upright.

Ryan felt the loss of her warmth.

"I don't feel any contractions," Lydia added.

"That may change in a minute as I encourage the baby down a bit ... hang on..."

"Have you done this a lot?" she asked.

"Werewolf births? About fifteen over my many years as a Human Hand – nearly forty years. Singles and twins. You're only my second triplet."

"Only fifteen in forty years?"

"Fertility has dwindled in werewolves greatly over the decades – although I wonder if you haven't just broken that mould." He smiled while frowning in concentration at his movements. "It might not feel like it, but this *is* an easy birth."

"Was that triplet birth you did an easy one? Oh-oh ... *Ow*. That's a contraction!"

"Not yet – don't push yet."

She sucked in a breath.

"Not yet."

"I want to."

"I know – wait. Shallow breaths only."

Lydia groaned and clenched her jaw, trying to keep her breathing light until she couldn't anymore. "OW!"

"I've got the back of his head – it feels clear. Okay, *push*."

He didn't need to tell her twice. She clutched Ryan's forearms as she bore down, and he bent his knees to take her weight.

Her cry ended on a wail which broke on a sob. "It really hurts this time."

"I know, Lydia. It's the position of the baby. But it will be out soon." Dr Matheson's tone was steady, giving no worry away. It calmed Ryan, anyway, after hearing Lydia sob like that.

"We're all here for you, honey," Taylor encouraged. "And these two can't wait to become older brothers." Lawrence and Taylor didn't look like they were putting those boys down any time soon.

Another contraction hit, and Lydia gritted her teeth and pushed, but Ryan could feel her flagging. She gave up halfway and sagged against him, gasping for air, the sobbing threatening to return.

He pressed his cheek to her temple and kissed her there. "I've got you, sweetheart."

"I can't," she whimpered, her words breaking. "I can't get

the baby out."

Dr Matheson, looking *far* more comfortable than he surely was given where he was positioned, glanced up at her over his glasses. "He's halfway out already. It's just the shoulders and head left. It's harder because he's feet first, but I have a good hold of his head. I need to keep it straight as he comes out. Try one more time for me."

"Come on, Lydia," coaxed Ryan. "Take a deep breath in." Ironic that those words had been directed at him little more than an hour ago. "We can do this together."

"Ryan." Lydia nuzzled her head against his neck. "Join with me."

He contemplated her request. "You mean, in your mind?"

"Yes – like we do in dreams. Please. I always feel strong when you do."

Did she know the feeling was mutual? His fear wanted to rise. Like a tempest it warned of tossing her and drowning her in his darkness if she accessed the wrong part of his mind.

He felt her gaze on him. Ryan looked down to find loving eyes – a very deep, almost indigo-blue from her straining – taking him in. "I know you, James."

His heart leapt in his chest.

"There's nowhere you could take me that changes that."

Whether she'd read his thoughts or just his expression, he couldn't decipher. But he tamped down his fear and closed his eyes against the tears that had sprung at her words. She needed him. He focused on the feel of her – her need; her love – and joined with her. It was so easy. It had *always* been easy.

He heard her sigh with contentment as he travelled her depths; felt her hold him in her arms as they connected in a way no words could ever describe. In that connection, he felt the strength she had mentioned – hers and his. They wrapped themselves around each other and became *more* than they were alone.

And then...

Ryan stilled; let out a small sound, not sure he was feeling what he was really feeling at first. "Lydia, can you—"

"Yes."

The *baby's* mind joined with them. "My god..." It was—

Lydia moaned and he *felt* the contraction coming – the force of it; the *life* of it. On its wave, she bore down and pushed, and he pushed with her from his place within their psychic nook as he stayed with the baby, consoling it, telling it – no, *him*; the baby was a *boy* – that he was safe. He was loved. He was wanted.

"Good! One more time!" Dr Matheson's voice was faint, coming from some other universe.

They complied, riding the final ripples of the birth like surfers on waves, carrying the most wondrous prize home.

Lydia's cry of relief was met with a glorious, high-pitched cry of arrival from the newest soul on the planet.

"Another boy!" came the doctor's confirmation.

Lydia was streaming tears as their third son was bundled into her arms, Ryan still taking her weight. He could still feel the boy in his mind – the *innocence*. It was astounding; like a far-distant memory of everything he had known once upon a time. With effort, he disconnected from the baby's mind – and Lydia's – wanting him to have his own sense of the world he'd just come into.

Lawrence and Taylor crowded in from the left, and suddenly, all three newborn faces were in view.

Lydia let out a muffled laugh filled with delight.

His grin was so wide, he could feel his cheeks ache.

"You did it, My Lady." Dr Matheson made quick work of snipping the cords in order of eldest to youngest.

Lydia looked up to find Ryan's eyes. "*We* did it. Thank you."

Hell, yeah. He squeezed her shoulder. That was an

experience like nothing else, and it was only when he felt his mobile phone vibrating in the back pocket of his jeans that he realised that experience had topped all others. *All* others. Joining with the baby's mind, even if accidentally, had wiped a slate clean. Purity was an actual, tangible thing.

Ryan frowned and ignored the buzzing of the phone.

"You may want to try feeding them in a short while. But they seem pretty content at the moment." Ryan noted the satisfaction in the doctor's tone. *Now* the old man looked a bit haggard, and he could finally see how much the birth had taken out of him. Still, he looked as happy as the rest of them. "I'll check your vitals in a few minutes, Lydia, and that of the babies – their height and weight and so on, too. I'll be here for a few days just in case anything is needed. We'll do the prick tests tomorrow if that suits everyone, to check for any lupine diseases or abnormalities. But for today, you've earned your rest."

Ryan's phone went off again – that irritating buzz. Trying to ignore it was getting frustrating.

"Dr Matheson," Lydia started.

"Ernest, my dear. If I can call you Lydia, you can call me Ernest."

She smiled. "Thank you so much. I don't know *how* to thank you."

He shook his head. "Seeing this – the start of a new era – being part of it, is thanks enough."

Ryan dropped a kiss on the top of Lydia's head. "I'm going to get you a chair."

She nodded.

He did just that and sat her on it with the baby now cooing in her arms. "I'm going to get you a drink of water, sweetheart."

"Yes, please – thank you."

He nodded and left the lounge, not really wanting to, but needing to put an end to the buzz in his back pocket, on its third attempt to reach him now. What was so bloody urgent? Lawrence had told Richard of Lydia's labour, so he was sure those closest to the pack would all know of it by now. He should have forwarded his own calls to Richard, too – hadn't even thought of doing so amidst the craziness of the morning's events. The digital clock on the oven read 13:13 – not much more than four hours since Lydia's water broke. It seemed like four days ago!

He pulled the now quiet phone from his pocket. 3% battery – he grimaced – and *shit*loads of texts and two calls from Adam. Dismissing the calls, he scrolled down the texts, making quick work of them before the battery gave in. There were attached images, too. *What the hell...?* His skimming stopped at words that clenched his insides.

> **Bettie Blueprint went down after Bab's magic. No one hurried to fix her as there was no pressing danger and so much more to see to. But I didn't realise the cameras were still rolling all this time – was just the servers that were ruined. I worked on them remotely after we spoke last night and pulled up some images: attached. Carrie's there. She's on your land. Camera picks her up near the lake ten days ago and then nothing. But she might still be there – water and mud will hide her scent.**

"Fuck, no." But the images didn't lie. He zoomed in on the three slightly fuzzy pictures Adam had sent and felt himself turn cold. That was Carrie all right. At the bottom of them, Bettie's deduction read: **Body heat: werewolf. Movements: suspicious, scared, erratic.** And in her right hand was a gun – *the* gun. The one he'd left for her with the single silver bullet inside. And he'd bet anything that bullet was still in there.

Ten days? She'd been here ten *days*?

And then a chilling thought set in: did she know Lydia had just given birth?

The blood drained from his face as he looked back towards the large room across the hallway. They'd made a helluva noise. Any wolf within about three miles might have heard Lydia's birthing cries depending on the wind's direction.

He could hear the chatter now from in that room, coloured with euphoria and the still-present sense of happy, dazed bewilderment. He heard one of the babies let out a sound of what could have been delight – *might* be delight one day – and the stark realisation they might *not grow* to know delight set Ryan in motion. Lydia wasn't going to get her water.

He whipped his top off and made quick work of the rest of his clothes, opened the back door to the kitchen, then halted. Carrie and her history currently stirred his erratic emotions and, lord knew, virtually *anything* could trigger his flashbacks. He was an idiot to do this alone.

He closed his eyes and breathed in deeply. Carrie *was* his responsibility for the impossible position he'd left her in, no matter the apocalyptic circumstances. And so was his past. He was the one who needed to deal with this. Lawrence wholly deserved this once-in-a-lifetime moment with the children he never thought he'd have.

But he couldn't completely trust himself right now. As much as he loathed to admit it, the last two weeks had left his nerves fried.

Mind made up, he picked up the phone, swore at the '2% battery' glaring at him – and belted out the fastest text of his life to Adam: **Contact Taylor. Tell him everything.** He was pretty certain Taylor *wouldn't* have forwarded his messages since

Richard and himself were usually the first ports of call after Lawrence. He pressed send.

1% battery.

He waited for the 'Delivered' note under the text, felt almost dizzy with relief when he saw it, then shifted and high-tailed it out of there.

CHAPTER FOUR

Scent was such a powerful thing. So powerful that no one was allowed near newborn pups for days – some wolf clans insisted on weeks – unless they were immediate family (doctors and midwives notwithstanding). It gave the newborns the needed chance to familiarise themselves with who would feed them, clothe them, and nurture them. It gave them the chance to learn love and safety, and who to turn to should they need anything. Scent and sound were the first languages they knew, existing even before they opened their eyes. But *scent* was strongest for a wolf.

His grandfather had once told him, when he was around twelve, that although humans didn't have the heightened smell of a wolf, they still reacted strongly to scent-memory. A whiff of something strongly imprinted during childhood could conjure up memories and feelings forgotten, with the force of a gale, often bringing a sense of nostalgia and the tears or joy that came with it. He'd brought it up with Taylor once, and he'd confirmed what his grandfather had recounted.

While a wolf's ability to decipher pretty much anything through smell was virtually unrivalled, wolves were *also* just as affected by scent-memory, and right now, Ryan was battling a blast of mental conjurings he hadn't fully prepared for. It was a *far* cry from the beautiful innocence he'd been privileged to connect with less than an hour ago, and he held onto *that* memory like a lifeline.

Carrie's scent had not been hard to come by once he'd found the right spot – not quite by the lake, but near the yew trees before it. Around the same area The Trident had attacked Lydia and ended up taking Selena, as if the damned spot was a hotbed for badness.

There was also a strong enough hint of mud, chalk, and aquatic vegetation in the air here. Adam was right: she was using the lake to hide her scent.

Her scent, of course, still carried the bonded musk of her mate despite his departure from this world, and Ryan hadn't quite been ready for that – was still adjusting and trying to shut down every ugly, visceral feeling that came with Nikolai's aroma. Feelings that spanned a lifetime, almost to the point where he had no memory without *that* smell. *His* smell.

At the cottage in the New Forest, when he'd put a bullet through Nikolai's skull, he'd been prepared. He'd gone there with his barriers up and his childhood-self primed for what he had to do, and he never thought he'd have to revisit that moment. Mostly, he thought he might not survive long after that, even if he were to fight death like he'd never fought before. And if he were to survive, he'd just assumed he'd deal with his bouts of guilt, or whatever, in his own time and far, far away from Nikolai's corpse and everything the male represented.

But Carrie was here, bringing the dead back to life. Only now did he realise he hadn't expected to find her. All those times he'd contacted Adam and Samuel for information – it had been to keep his mind busy and his emotions in check; it had been to give himself something to do so he wouldn't go off the deep end. In actuality – secretly – he'd thought she was dead. And that's why she'd been a safe mission.

He slowed down his pace, knowing he was close. She was very near – probably knew he was here. He had no idea what to expect, so he stayed in his wolf's form, prepared for both defence and attack if needs be.

Coming to a near halt, he lowered his snout, and then his whole body, stalking the scent that had forever held him hostage.

She was in the yews – the thickest cluster of them – and probably behind a trunk since these trees didn't grow that close together. His nose zeroed in on the *exact* trunk he was sure protected her.

But it could be a trick. It could just be her clothing.

She *must* know he was here, though, if her own nose was doing its job properly. *Or she's swimming in the lake*.

He wasn't sure he was close enough to detect sloshing water, but his ears picked up no sound. He decided to shift. While he favoured his wolf's senses, speed, and agility, Carrie liked to talk from what he remembered – liked to use words for power and leverage. And if Nikolai's influence had settled deeply, she was probably still more enamoured by the human form.

"Carrie," he called out, scanning the trees for any movement at all. "I know you're here. You've been here for days – over a week." His voice sounded echoey and a little eerie under the chamber of the yews' canopy. "We need to talk."

Silence.

"I came alone. I wanted to give you a chance to say your piece before Lawrence ... well, I don't think he'll be too happy to see you."

Finally ... a rustle. And a head – a wolf's head – emerged from behind the trunk Ryan had correctly homed in on. She had a dead rabbit in her mouth. She placed it on the ground and then shifted, still half obscured by the trunk like she was using it as a safety net.

Ryan made no attempt to move with her motives unknown.

"Very noble of you, James." Her voice was high; strung tight. The rabbit's blood smeared her mouth and cheeks, and some of her right hand and wrist.

"You've been living on the wildlife?"

He'd expected perhaps a snarky comeback – he got nothing. She just stared at him, a bit jittery, her eyes wide and framed with shadows. Her short hair looked unkempt. She wasn't looking after herself.

"Why are you here?" he asked.

"And where else would I go?" she whispered. "Where do rogue wolves go to die?"

Guilt was a fucker. He brushed it aside, but not before the next words left his lips. "I'm sorry I did that to you. I did it because I thought it was the end of everything."

She emerged from the trunk's safety, the gun in her left hand. "It was."

Fuck.

She held the thing up; looked at it with both confusion and longing. "I've had nightmares about doing it"—she waved the metal weapon in front of her like it was a rag doll—"and other times they're the sweetest dreams. But when I'm awake"— her face crumpled—"I can't do it."

He gulped. Her fingers looked white where she gripped the handle – and the trigger. When she placed the muzzle under her chin, he wondered if his heart had actually stopped. "Carrie!"

"See?" Frustration flitted across her features, and then she was waving that damned thing around again. "I can't *do* it."

He really fucking wished it wasn't Lawrence he saw dead all of the sudden, just like he had in his own nightmare after Carrie *had* shot herself. No – just like he'd seen in reality. Fuck it, that had happened. And he was finding it hard to breathe, that prickling sensation of panic and sweat announcing its sweet arrival. Now was the worst time to lose the plot.

"I need you to help me do it." Her tone was pleading and desperate.

"I—"

"It's what you wanted. You need to help me do it."

"No ... look, you don't have to do it."

"I do."

"You don't."

"He's gone. I almost did it then – in the beginning – the hurt was so bad. It was like being sawn apart inside. But"—the gun went back under her chin; tears streaked a trail through the rabbit's blood on her cheeks—"this felt bad. Wrong. I couldn't. And then, the pain got better. After a day or two the sawn up feeling went away."

"That's because The Trident all died."

"But it didn't matter because ... I ... I..."

"What, Carrie?"

"I didn't know what to do. And I didn't know where to go. And everyone I knew was dead. And that hurt just as bad. Different, but bad."

"You know me." He slowly raised his hand in a gesture of peace, hoping to calm her jerking hand. "Is that why you came here? Because you know me?"

"I can hunt. My wolf knows what to do – she hunts. But I ... the human ... I don't know what to do. There's no pack. There's no..."

She didn't finish that sentence, her eyes glazing over instead and focusing on some distant image Ryan couldn't see. But he could guess at it because he knew – he *knew* the desolation she was feeling now Nikolai and his instruction were gone. His leadership might have been the dirtiest, most repulsive kind, but it was still leadership. And more than that, it was the only path he'd ever laid out for any child he'd praised and groomed.

"Carrie, we can talk about how to fix this if you put the gun down."

She regained her focus, then suddenly snapped her gaze back to him. "How did you do it?" She bit the question out in a desperate and bitter fashion. "How did you live? When you left Wiltshire you were young – eighteen? How did you know what to do?"

"I *didn't* know what to do." That was no lie. He'd been fucking terrified that day and for weeks after that day – for months. The only thing that had kept him sane was that one vision he'd had of Lydia that fateful night his grandfather had thrown him out of the pack for his own safety. The way she'd told him she'd loved him; the way she'd called him by his middle name, Ryan... He'd replayed it in his mind over and over again, and he'd *become* the Ryan he felt deserved that love. She had been his saviour – quite literally. The leadership he'd craved and sought to replace Nikolai's, he had ended up finding in himself because of Lydia. It hadn't mattered she'd been nothing but a vision – she'd been *real* enough that he could muster a clear head on waking and could begin to make plans; could begin to think for himself; could begin to trust *her* trust in him, no matter how ethereal.

He wasn't about to tell Carrie any of that. "I didn't know, but I *fought* to know. I made mistakes and had to try over and over again, and some days, all I wanted to do was give up. But I didn't. And I can help you find your way again, Carrie ... just put the gun down."

She didn't budge on the damned gun. "I can smell the new life on you. And I heard the cries. You're a father now."

He said nothing. She wasn't going anywhere near his family in her state, even if it meant she shot herself and he had flashbacks of her death forever.

"Nikolai wanted me to conceive so badly... Five moons..." Her face crumpled and she started to sob.

Nothing he was bloody saying seemed to be making a scrap of difference. He cursed under his breath. It didn't help she was churning old wounds he thought he'd mastered. His insecurity over his own capabilities these past two weeks seemed to shriek in response to – in *concurrence* with – her anguish.

"It's b-b-been five moons and I ... I don't know what I'm

for. I ... I have no purpose."

"You do."

"I have no reason to exist now."

It was a fucking tragedy and all the more so because he knew the depraved depths of it. Carrie had been 'bred' every full moon; offered to human-blooded wolves – like himself – who had obeyed Nikolai's every demand because they'd all been schooled, for decades, into believing it was the only *right* way that existed for the salvation and evolution of every wolf. The human-blooded females, like Carrie, had been 'willing' to give of themselves, believing the same. It seemed ludicrous now he was well outside of that wreckage, but it had been his whole world until it had ended.

Carrie was right: it *was* the end of everything.

"Yes, you do." But his own voice was shaking because Nikolai's stare blasted through his mind just as it had in last night's nightmare – all seeing, all knowing – made much more real with his musk on Carrie's scent. And how wrong – how *unfair* – the bastard could still command such leverage over his very being after so long. *After dead.* "You are *more* than what Nikolai taught you to be."

The change in her features was so sudden, he didn't see it coming at all when she swung the gun at him.

Christ.

"*You* don't say his name!" she spat, hatred and reproach in her words. He knew half of it was directed at herself, even if she didn't. "I had to carry him inside after you ... his *blood* was on my arms and chest. You *took* him from me! From *everyone*!"

He swayed on the spot as he battled the memory of rolling onto Lawrence's blood as he'd tried to save Taylor that night of the storm, the smell of the king's blood – his mate's blood – suddenly *right there* in the wood and right up his nasal passages. "I'm ... I'm sorry." *Not Lawrence – not dead. This is about*

Nikolai. "But he hurt us, Carrie. He hurt everyone, and you know it, even if it's hard to admit it."

"He didn't. We *consented*," she hissed, repeating Nikolai's own words – many times stated and often on the billow of drugged smoke that blinded the mind from all discernment.

"We had no idea what we were doing; what we were agreeing to. That isn't consent – not the way we were brought into it at our age. But..." He hesitated, not knowing if what he was about to say would make anything better. He really fucking wanted to see his new sons grow up. "The parts we played in his world – really ugly parts; the hurt *we* caused others – we need to forgive ourselves that."

Everything went quiet. She looked horrified for a couple of long seconds, and then, a strange clarity took over her. Her gaze grew lucid. She straightened her stance and the gun – aimed it directly at his chest, all her jerky movements gone.

Oh, god.

"Forgive? I'm *never* going to conceive now. I'll be alone forever. But you won't. Is that fair? Are my sins worse than yours? I never *murdered* any person or wolf. Do you think your children will forgive you once they know what you did? Will their forgiveness cleanse all your sins? *Who's going to forgive me*?" The sad waver in her tone did not reach the hand which held the gun far too steadily. Her voice dropped. "Have you forgiven yourself, James?"

God help him, he was going to take the bullet he'd given her five months ago.

Still ... if there was still just *one* bullet in there, as he suspected there was, it meant no one else would get shot before she was caught. There was a strange poetic justice in it, he supposed, because for the life of him he didn't know how to make up for all the females he'd violated under Nikolai's 'guidance'; all the mated couples he'd ruined – no matter that they *thought* they'd consented; no matter that he'd known no better. He knew better *now,* and while he'd worked hard for his mates' sakes to forgive the part of him that had been innocent, he'd found it impossible to forgive the part that had been the pernicious perpetrator of wrongdoings, enabled by that same innocence.

"No." He shook his head, and a tear he hadn't realised he'd blinked loose slipped down his cheek. "No, Carrie, I haven't forgiven myself."

All at once, she looked defeated, and he bloody well felt it in his bones. "Well ... if you haven't managed it in all this time, there's really no hope for me." She cocked the gun, then placed it in her mouth, and he should be lunging at her; stopping her; doing anything to save them both, but he was out of words – all out of place in the future he'd found himself in, even if he'd fought for it. He was here: stuck in the same historic mire as she, joined by one silver bullet they'd both feel, no matter who took it.

Her hopeless eyes met his and he poised for the gunshot he knew would come.

CHAPTER FIVE

A bird shrieked and took flight.

No shot rang out.

What came in its place was scent. One very specific scent.

He wasn't sure if Carrie's shock matched his trepidation, but her eyes widened in disbelief as she slowly let the gun fall from her mouth.

Scent was *such* a powerful thing.

He saw it pull Carrie out of herself ... *out of herself...* as he clamoured to keep himself in. He growled with effort to keep it out of his head – that *smell—*

Don't breathe it in!

—as he simultaneously wrestled with the impossibility of what was happening. "No..."

Carrie's gun fell out of her hand and onto the ground. She whimpered in need, half-sobbing, following the faint wisps of herbal smoke that floated towards her like incense – a seductive spectre from beyond the goddamned grave.

It's not happening.

Except it was.

The woodland teetered and Ryan sank to his knees, unable to keep the world in balance, that fucking *scent* in his head, kick-starting old programming – he couldn't keep it out. His vision blurred, and ... shit. He was *reacting* to it – bodily – his penis hardening, just like he'd been primed to do since he was fifteen. *His bloody incense!*

"Carrie, my love."

Holy fuck.

Carrie audibly gasped and Ryan might just throw up.

That was Nikolai's *voice* bouncing off the trees.

Ryan did his best to clear his eyes so he could see what was happening. Carrie was spinning around – she was looking for Nikolai. "No, Carrie..." He had to warn her. That *couldn't* be Nikolai. He'd put a bullet between his eyes.

Although that was all starting to seem hazy now. God ... if Lydia and Lawrence could come back from the dead, maybe Nikolai could, too – maybe he *had*.

"Nikolai?" she called out, her need for him unmistakable.

"Have you forgotten everything I taught you?" came his voice.

"No ... Nikolai, no, I remember."

"The teachings of the Inner Circle."

Shit. Ryan groaned and sagged against the ground in his crouched position. Whatever the fuck was happening, he couldn't do it. Was this a flashback? Was this the drug in the smoke? Another nightmare? (Was he asleep?) Was it Nikolai's fucking corpse? It was too much to figure it out and keep himself intact. That despicable pyramid loomed before him in his mind's eye, and he turned away from it. He'd destroyed it with Adam and a few others, hadn't he? Yes, he *had*, he *had*. He wouldn't put himself back there again, not for anything. And Nikolai ... was dead ... right?

"Nikolai, I didn't forget," she implored.

"You would damage your sacred body, my love; your human lineage."

"I'm sorry," she cried – pleaded. "Please forgive me. I'm so lost without you."

Ryan attempted one more time to reach her, although his voice sounded hoarse to his own ears. "Carrie, no, you're stronger than this."

"I need you, too, my love. We need to finish the important work we started."

A hand appeared from behind a tree, adorned with a white-robed sleeve.

No... Bile rose in Ryan's throat. His flashbacks always seemed real, but this was on another fucking level. He tried again to fight through the fogginess clouding his mind. He needed something to put that bloody smoke out.

Nikolai's hand beckoned Carrie to him, and even in his affected state Ryan could see things weren't right here, but Carrie really was lost it seemed, because she smiled so happily, tears flowing as she stumbled towards the wide trunk of the yew that shielded Nikolai.

"Nikolai?" She reached for him with her own hand.

"For the pack, my love. We would do anything for the pack, wouldn't we?"

"Yes."

Her hand fell into his and she was ... gone. Behind the tree? *What the...?* He'd taken her behind the tree – must have done.

Ryan blinked to clear the blur away from his vision and tried to get himself together. Because there was no fucking way *he* was going behind that tree – he had to get the hell out of here.

Silence reigned heavy, and he wondered why it had gone so quiet. Why had Nikolai not gone for him, too? *It's a trick. His ghost is waiting for you to make the first move.*

He growled and shook his head. *Not a ghost.*

Why not? A whole load of supernatural shit wrecked your home five months ago, so why not ghosts?

Yeah, he wasn't going to give that musing an answer. And whatever the fuck had just happened he wasn't staying. He forced himself to his feet, relieved he could without falling, although he did stumble. He stumbled *forwards* at least, *away* from the trees – he needed the clearing. He needed things to be *clear*.

Time evaded him. He had no idea how much had passed, but that had always been the way with Nikolai's smoke. The smell of it was less now, but his mind was still jumbled. He needed fresh air ... he needed—

Another scent caught his attention. A *far* more agreeable one. It came from ... *there.* Just a bit further away and in the opposite direction of the zombie-yew. *Zombies. Right. Fuck that shit for a game of laughs.*

Marshmallows.

He could smell beautiful, glorious marshmallows melting over fire, and that meant... "Taylor?" But he only whispered the name, frightened of what – or who – he might find.

If Taylor's a zombie, you'll know at some point you fell asleep and had the worst bloody nightmare of your life.

He was thinking stupid thoughts.

What if it's Nikolai tricking you, just like he did with the incense?

Ryan stopped in his tracks. That hadn't occurred to him. Carrie hadn't been a dream, right? That *had* just happened.

Christ. He was breathing at a rate of knots, his heart going just as fast. He was losing his goddamned mind.

"Ryan."

He zeroed in on the one who had called his name, and sure enough there was Taylor holding a marshmallow on a stick over ... not a fire, but a lighter. He looked like he had tears in his eyes, but other than that, he couldn't figure out the expression on his face. There was a steeliness to it, though. "Taylor?"

"Yeah, it's me. I promise. Come here. Come to me."

But he stalled. His gaze dropped to Taylor's hands now lowering the stick and marshmallow. His hands were caked in mud. Ryan frowned, unable to figure out why that would be. He was naked, too, like himself. He guessed he had run here as his wolf.

"Ryan, please."

"It's a ... you could be a trick." He didn't know who to trust – what to trust. He pressed the heel of his hand against his forehead in frustration.

"I'm not a trick. You can trust me, and you're *not* going mad. Adam called me and then he sent me the same information he sent you about Carrie. He said you asked him to – do you remember that?"

He nodded. Yes. That seemed like a really long time ago now.

"That was nearly two hours ago. I could tell from Bettie's images Carrie was unstable – I *wrote* Bettie. I input all her instructions and commands. I felt I needed to get to you quickly, given your own state of mind earlier, which we talked about. Do you remember?"

"Yeah." He gulped. "In the kitchen."

"Okay, good. Shall I carry on talking?"

Ryan nodded, slowly, while he took in his mate's appearance. It was normal to have some mud on feet and hands when running as a wolf, but not caked on like that. It bothered him. But then, he was still reeling from everything that had happened, some of it fuzzy now the drugged smoke had faded. Carrie had been real, though – Taylor was confirming it. And Nikolai? His frown deepened.

"I took Lawrence to one side and told him everything, and that I would deal with Carrie and also find you and bring you back, whole and unharmed. He didn't argue with me – we didn't have a lot of time and, well, the babies are kind of a big deal. He's needed at home."

"The babies..."

"They're good. Doing really well. Ryan ... come closer. Please."

He did take a step closer – wanted to. Couldn't quite release his control yet, though, to collapse into Taylor's embrace. It *looked* and *sounded* like him...

"It was easy to track your scent here. I arrived when you and Carrie were talking – it was before she turned the gun on you. I decided to stay out of sight and assess the situation." He flicked the lighter once more, then placed the marshmallow on top of the flame, toasting it all over again. "I got a pretty good handle on where she was at – in her mind, I mean. It was sort of what I suspected. I'd come prepared – as much as I could running as a wolf, anyway. There's a limit to what I can carry."

The sweet aroma of the pink goo hit him and relaxed his tense muscles. Ryan sighed, softly, at the release of his tension.

Taylor studied him, a sadness to his features. "The smell of something can be so moving, can't it? It can transport you. You asked me about it once – how I experienced it as a human."

"Yeah, I did. Because of what my granddad told me."

Taylor looked very carefully at him. "And you showed me once – let me in your mind for a few seconds and helped me understand how Nikolai used his smoke on you, Carrie, and others."

He stopped; shrivelled inside. That uncomfortable feeling

pressed on him – the one where everyone got the joke except him.

"Ryan—"

"No." He stepped back, the pressing feeling growing into a slow horror which filled him.

"Carrie's fine, just out for the count – I pierced her skin with a tranquiliser dart. She's still by the tree."

"You." Nausea churned. "It was you."

"I thought everything out very carefully."

It wasn't a violation, but it *felt* like one. "You said words he—"

"Ryan—"

"You—"

"It was the only way I could see to stop it all without bloodshed."

"You *played* with my *mind*."

"No. Jesus, no. I played with *Carrie's* mind – I admit that – to stop her killing herself and hurting you further. You were just there and there was no way around that."

"The smoke..."

"I had to. It was the perfect trigger to get her attention, and you will never know how sorry I am it got yours too."

"But ... how?"

"Remember the trial six months ago? How Lawrence swiped a cigarette from Nikolai's pocket? We still had it. I brought it with me and used it. Lit it with this lighter. Wasn't sure it would work, to be honest, without me sucking on it, which I didn't – I didn't take any of it into me. But it lit fine, and it didn't go out. It worked. I washed my hands in mud after 'cause I don't ever want to smell like him to you."

Like him... His chest felt tight. He closed his eyes.

"I'm *not* him. And he's dead. Do you understand?"

"He's dead."

"He is."

"But you ... it was like ... he was inside you."

"No. Not once. Not ever. He's *dead*. It was *all* my idea and it was just me speaking to Carrie. To protect you. Breathe, Ryan."

He did. And then he did again because he needed to. The air was sweetness and trust. "The marshmallow," he croaked.

Taylor nodded. "Another trigger. A good one. To bring you back to me." His voice cracked.

Ryan nodded. He let his tears fall.

"I carried all these things, and the tranquiliser, in a white shirt I had which was the best I could do to mirror the white robe he wore. I hoped, because of the smoke, Carrie's own mind would obscure any inaccuracies with her own memories."

"Mine did, too."

"I'm sorry." He placed the lighter and marshmallow on the ground. "But I'm *not* sorry I saved you both from a bullet, and I'd do it again. Because I *know* you can get through this and out the other side."

"The words you used..."

"It wasn't hard to remember the way he talked; the specific phrases he said. I remembered a lot of it from the memory you shared with me, and Carrie was too far gone to notice any differences. But I'm *not* him. And those were not my words. Ryan – this is *me*."

He shook his head, gulping down the lump in his throat. "Don't you see? *I* was too far gone to notice. I thought *you* were *him*. He's everywhere. He's in my head." He tried to stop going to pieces and couldn't, his face contorting with his effort to keep from openly weeping. "He'll always be in my head."

"Then he's got some competition, 'cause I'm in there too. Ryan, look at me."

He did. Shit. It *was* Taylor. Of course it fucking was – eyes green and just as wet as his – and he *wanted* to fall into his arms and never leave, if only his past wasn't hosting a fucking parade in his mind.

"I'm that clueless, nearly dead guy you picked up at one in the morning after a Halloween party. You taught me *everything* I know about being a wolf. But Nikolai taught you nothing. He never had anything on you – *anything*." Taylor stepped towards him. "How old were you when you had that vision of me after I'd been bitten?"

"What?"

"How old – tell me."

"Um..." He sniffed. "Seven, I think. Maybe eight."

Taylor took another step forward. "And how old were you when Nikolai began grooming you for his purposes?"

He shook his head, not wanting to think about it.

"Tell me," Taylor pressed.

"Ten."

"Yeah ... ten." He was right in front of him now, and he smelled like *Taylor*. Not Nikolai, or anyone or anything else. Just Taylor. Taylor who held his gaze like he had his own gravity. "I was there first."

Ryan caught his breath and stilled at the possessiveness of those words and, more so, their simple truth.

"Three years before he got inside your head, I was already there promising you a future worth having, and I wasn't lying. So tell him to get the fuck out of your head, 'cause you're taken. You're mine." Taylor brought his forehead to his. It was like a warm blanket on the coldest night. "Can you show me that day you saw me in your head? Where were you?"

"Walking through a field with Gramps and Nanna, on our way back home."

"Show me."

He just about managed it – brought up that memory like it

was yesterday, and in a way it wasn't hard because, hell, he'd *loved* time spent with his grandparents. To feel their warmth and hear their laughter again was wonderful. And safe. He projected as much as he could into the telepathic line they all shared as mated wolves – sent it to Taylor's mind, and he felt him smile.

"I see it."

He let it play out, not really wanting to leave the warming nurture of his grandparents anyway, and he let the rest of it play out, too. Didn't push the oncoming vision away, but let it ensue, allowing Taylor into his memory to feel that small boy experience a startling moment of clairvoyance for the very first time – one he'd had a starring role in.

Taylor's hands came up to his arms as he let out a sharp breath. "There I am. There." He pulled back a little and Ryan opened his eyes to see his mate staring right back. "There I am in your head."

Ryan managed a smile, and nodded, as he welled up again.

"I was there first. And I'll always be there, as quietly or as loudly as you need me to be."

And what could he say to that? Overwhelm at this male crashed over him and he took him in a kiss, hoping it said everything he couldn't. And when the kiss ended, Ryan hugged him tight – felt Taylor's relief as he returned his hug for like; relief he'd brought him back. Taylor always brought him back.

"I love you," Ryan whispered, and Taylor's embrace tightened further.

When he replied, his voice was thick with tears. "I love you, too."

CHAPTER SIX

A month ago, after learning of Lydia's pregnancy, he and Lawrence had sat here, facing the rubble of the outbuilding and its cursed legacy, and talked about clearing it away and starting over. Building something new here.

Ryan had felt uneasy about the notion given the horrific slaughter that had taken place here, and Lawrence hadn't pushed, despite the fact he had finally seemed ready to let it go.

Now, as the blond 'king of wolves' strode up the side of the rubble towards him – bundle in arms – Ryan couldn't help but notice he really had conquered his past, and perhaps the reward for all his efforts were those legs that now moved his body with the strength and grace that had always been his.

Lawrence met his eyes and they shared a silent greeting as he found purchase next to him on the large, oak log that had lain here on its side for two years.

Ryan glanced at the baby in his arms. All he could see were closed eyes and a tiny button nose, but it was enough to turn him to putty inside. "You brought the little tyke here?"

"Taylor said this is where you were."

"Yeah, but ... *here*."

Lawrence looked down at the sleeping form in his arms and smiled. "What better place to show him how heroic his dad was when he saved the royal line, allowing his birth to even be possible? That's *you*, by the way." Lawrence glanced at Ryan. "You're the hero. It does no good to let the bright and good side of the story get lost in the bad, just because bad often screams louder than good."

Ryan smiled, but said nothing, looking back at the

dereliction.

"Carrie's still unconscious. She's in the caravan near Richard's house. She's secured – tied up – that can't be helped, I'm afraid. I've called Samuel – he's coming down as soon as he can to speak with her. There's a chance Wiltshire might take her back; after all, many were in the same boat as her – as yourself – even if some despise her for her role as Nikolai's mate. She needs mental and emotional support; there's a chance some of them will be willing to give it."

"I'm sorry my actions brought her here."

"*Her* actions brought her here."

"I shot her mate."

"You did."

Ryan looked at the beautiful boy swaddled in the blanket. "Not the most heroic thing I've ever done."

"Given the circumstances at the time, many might disagree. We can only do what we can, with the information we're given."

Ryan let out a long sigh. "After you and Lydia died ... the pain was so ... I don't even have words for it. I thought it was bad when I was unmated at forty. I thought it couldn't get worse when Taylor was poisoned with silver. But even then, he hadn't died. *You* died though." He moved past the lump that had risen in his throat. "Lydia died. Every vision I had of the future died with you both, and I found myself thinking in the weeks after, I should have killed Carrie, too. Because I had no idea it would feel like that.

"That's when I started to properly think about what I'd done. Shooting Nikolai. Not just thinking about it, but ... feeling it – the guilt; seeing it happen all over again. I've been getting flashbacks – all happening like it's real. And then other times, I'd replay the moment on purpose, even though I didn't want to. I'd see the look in his eyes as the bullet hit home, and... It's kinda fucked up I felt so ... like I'd killed someone I..." He couldn't say it.

Lawrence could though. "Like you killed someone you loved."

"Hmmn," he mumbled. His jaw clenched.

"Nikolai saw that your father was never around, and he stepped into that role deliberately, knowing his power, and knowing his influence. He made himself available in a way your father wasn't, and you looked to him as one. You loved him, even if just a little, like a parent. There's no shame in that."

"I tell myself that, but—"

"Saying and believing are two different things. I know. But you're going to be fine, and we all know that. We're here for you. The flashbacks will fade over time – mine did. But it does help if you share your stresses – the same way you pushed and pushed me to express mine all those years ago, remember?"

"Took you bloody long enough."

"I was hoping you'd be less stubborn."

That coaxed another smile out of him.

"You know we won't judge you – we were all there. Let us help you."

"Yeah." Ryan nodded his thanks, still finding it too hard to talk about, but knowing Lawrence was right and knowing he could now – it was better than it had been two hours ago. And it would be better tomorrow, and the day after that, and the day after that. "I can't believe you let Taylor come find me on his own."

"Why not? He got that phone call from Adam..." Lawrence laughed. "Poor Adam with his stammer – he was trying to explain, but was in a bit of a panic. He finally said he was going to text the info over. Taylor received it and I'd never seen him look the way he did when he read it."

"Like he wanted to tear me a new one?"

Lawrence shook his head. "Hard. Poised. And like he kinda

wasn't totally surprised. And he just knew what to do, Ryan. It was that simple. He didn't *ask* if it was all right he go and find you – he *told* me point blank that's what was happening. He took command of it all like he was me. I let him go because it was obvious he knew what he was doing and because I trusted him. And where you're concerned, I especially trust him. Lydia felt the same way."

"I've been pushing him away."

"We know – you think we don't have eyes? And we all knew you were struggling, but no one more than him. After Adam texted him, he had it all clocked. Carrie, you, the lot. So ... my unwarranted advice is stop pushing him away."

"I plan to. I already have."

"Good. Now..." Lawrence shifted around until he was facing him and held the baby out. "Take your son, Ryan."

His mouth felt dry. He was *so* tiny. "Are you su—"

"Don't even dare ask me that."

He huffed out a semi-laugh, and then tentatively reached out and took the boy. He was *so warm*. "Look at him ... he's smaller than my forearm." His eyes welled up again – it seemed to be the day for it.

"And he's going to grow to be as big as us. And here..." Lawrence retrieved a wrist band and a pen from his pocket. "We'd like you to name him."

"Me?"

"Well, he is your son."

"Our son."

"Semantics."

"Are the other two named?"

"Yeah. Axel and Christopher. Lydia and I agreed on Axel – it's an old family name on my side I've always liked, and luckily for me, Lydia loved it, and I'll just pretend I never heard her say Guns 'n' Roses was her favourite teenage band."

Ryan laughed.

"She couldn't settle on a name for the second one, and she decided she wanted Taylor to choose, so he chose Christopher. It was the name of one of his favourite uncles. He died when Taylor was about twelve, but he had a hundred and one stories to tell about his time in the army and all the years he'd spent abroad; the different cultures he'd experienced. Taylor loved to listen to them. He was quite high up in the ranks, apparently, but suffered badly, in the end, with post-traumatic stress from the wars he'd fought in. Although, it was a heart attack that killed him – I think that's what he said."

Post-traumatic stress? *That's* how he'd clocked him so well – and why he'd brought it up in the kitchen. And if he'd spent any bloody time with his mate, he'd probably have told him all about his uncle. Ryan vowed to change that starting tonight, annoyed he'd missed out on learning about someone that meant so much to Taylor. He hadn't even known he'd *had* a favourite uncle.

"And Lydia and I would very much like you to pick the third name. Lydia told me you helped to birth him, after all."

"I wouldn't go that bloody far."

"Still," he smiled, "she's very taken about whatever you did."

He looked down at baby number three. He was still sleeping fast. "I joined with Lydia like we do in dreams, and I ended up joining with the baby, too – his mind. It was unintended, but amazing. It was so ... perfect. It reminded me a bit of a boy I knew – a wolf – called Elias. We were very young – about three or four – and we played together a lot. He was the only other person I could do the dream-connection thing with. We shared dreams, but they were different from Lydia's, obviously, in that we were only three and he wasn't my mate. We played in dreams sometimes, and because we were so young, we talked about it the next day not knowing it was strange or rare to be doing such things.

"His family left the pack just before my fifth birthday – I'm not sure I knew why. I don't even think Elias knew why. But I heard two years later from some of the other adults that his whole family had been killed by Tridents. Elias, too. I cried so hard for days after hearing that. And then much, much later, I remember being grateful he was never around when Nikolai started showing up – he would never become victim to Nikolai's ways and that was a blessing. But I never forgot him. Used to think about him a lot. If you like the name, I'd like to call him Elias."

Lawrence's grin was wide. "It's perfect." He wrote it on the tag and then managed to fasten it on an arm that had slipped out of its blanket.

"Thank you. How long are we keeping these tags on for?"

"Until we can bloody well tell which baby's which. They all even smell the same at the moment."

Ryan chuckled. "Is Dr Matheson gone?"

"He's in Adam and Tiegan's barn until the babies make their first shift. He'll be able to check all their wolf functions then. After that, he'll be off. But he says they're all strong and healthy. Lydia made him *swear* to her, for the hundredth time, they won't be able to run when they shift until they can walk on human legs."

"I'm with Lydia – just imagine! It's a clever physiological safety mechanism, that one."

"Indeed. He told her she's safe for about a year and then she'll be pulling her hair out trying to find them all the time."

"We were just as bad," smirked Ryan.

"All boy pups are."

Lawrence's phone sang a familiar note.

Ryan raised an eyebrow. "Is that Bettie Blueprint?"

"Ah! Yes," he said, fumbling to get his phone out of his back pocket. "Adam is working remotely to try and get the servers back up; Taylor will be helping him tomorrow if he can. Mine's the first phone Bettie's reconnected with." Lawrence looked at the screen, then sighed. "And it seems not a moment too soon – look." He turned the screen his way.

Ryan's mood darkened a fraction. "Is that Bella?"

"Yes. Can't say I've been chomping at the bit to see one of the Human Hands again."

"Want me to come with you to the entrance?"

"No. Take Elias back home – we've agreed no one except us should be around the babies for at least two weeks, and he'll be needing a feed soon. I'll see to Bella."

Ryan nodded and they both stood. "Be careful."

"I will be. And I'll check in on Carrie after I've spoken to Bella. Let Lydia know, and text Richard when you get back – keep him informed."

"I will."

"And Ryan..."

He turned back before setting off.

Lawrence's gaze dropped to Elias, and then back to Ryan. This new smile on him was both loving and warm, and in that moment, Ryan felt as welcomed into the world as the three newborns. "You're going to be everything our sons need in a father. And more."

EPILOGUE

Was a king still the same king once he was a father? Could he oversee all packs in the country with as much devotion as he protected his new family? Dying for what was left of his species, and for the safety of humankind, had been a tall order, but one he had ultimately accepted as a course of duty, although perhaps not with as much conviction as Lydia had. She been brought up as human, and propelling humans into a future in which they would be enslaved and tortured had been a hard 'no', no matter the consequences.

Holding his sons in his arms brought him the clarity of her conviction. He'd thought he'd given all his heart to Lydia only to find his children – through her – had given it back to him with theirs, completing a circle that would ripple through the generations to come.

So, seeing Bella standing there, poised, a slight smile on her face in greeting, had his back up, even though Bella herself was an ally and perfectly likeable. But Human Hands never turned up just to say hello.

"Bella," he nodded.

"Your Majesty."

"It's good to see you alive."

"Some of us made it, although not my sisters."

"I'm sorry."

"And I'm sorry I have not been to see you sooner – we needed to lie low and make sure The Trident truly were dead. All of them. I came, in part, to inform you officially that they are. Our research and conclusions on this are now final."

Lawrence contemplated her. "Have you been keeping tabs

on Sarah's daughter, Jasmine?"

"We have insofar as we can. Our 'workings', shall we say, show us she is not a Trident, and I do feel we have been thorough where she is concerned because she *was* a concern of ours."

"But you don't fear her anymore?"

"On the contrary, we believe she is something rather special, and potentially ... good."

"Good?"

"A force for good is perhaps a better way to put it. Of course, these things are not up to us."

"Do you think she's human?"

Bella hesitated. "It is not known to me or any of my kin what she is, but we believe... How to say this... We believe the gods will protect her."

"The gods?" He couldn't help the cynicism in his tone. Nor the way his legs tingled. Gods had never exactly felt like his 'friends', yet, they had made him physically whole once more, so he had no particular grudge against them. Well ... if you didn't count the entire 'curse' his species had lived with for thousands of years – now lifted. "Speaking of gods protecting children, are you familiar with what this land was before my grandparents bought it? What it was used for?"

"Before wolves lived here? Should we be?"

"We found a disused mine and cottage up on the other side of the lake, as well as human remains. They're not on the title deeds of the land. I wondered if my family ever discussed with your ancestors anything *they* might have known about this land."

"Not that I know of. I could attempt to find out for you, but if the information is not on the deeds in the first place—"

"It's all right. I already have someone looking into it, but he's found nothing. We think perhaps this location might have been a base during the First or Second World War – that would explain the exclusion from the deeds. The human remains, though, were that of children, and the carbon-dating my contact has acquired puts them at a century old."

"I see. If the dealings that take place are not that of wolves, we, as Human Hands, tend not to get involved. Our commitment, since the beginning, has been only to your kind. And the gods that look after you, of course."

"Of course."

"I will not keep you, Your Majesty. I understand you have a new family to return to and I wish you my most heartfelt congratulations." She took a step forward. "But I wanted to give you this – this is the other reason I came to see you."

He took the round, metal thing she offered him, and then stiffened when he realised why it looked so familiar. He'd seen this before ... through Taylor's eyes. The copper had been cleaned and looked almost brand new; the lion's head on top of the snake's body shone under the setting sun. Himet and Yemet's symbol could clearly be seen carved into the sun disc behind the lion's head. "This is Sarah's bracelet." He snapped his gaze back to her. "You were *there* in the woods with us last night?"

She sucked in a breath and nodded. "I saw you and your mate – how you helped him search his memories."

"I made a *choice* to walk away from this," he ground out as he clutched the bracelet, annoyed his attempt to leave the past behind had been somewhat thwarted.

"I know, but I feel it will be important to you in the future."

"Why?"

"I cannot explain it."

"Try, Bella. Because the three little boys my wife gave birth to today come before *anything* you bring to my door."

She stared at him, let out a breath, and then nodded. "All right ... have you heard of deific births?"

"Deific? As in—"

"As in children borne of gods – at least in part."

He shook his head. "What are you—"

"We know next to nothing about the mechanisms of how such births take place, but there must be both human *and* deific interference. I suggest before he leaves, you speak to Dr Matheson – unless I am mistaken, he is not unfamiliar with such births for he has not only worked with wolves, but with other beings, also, for many decades."

"What does any of this have to do with Jasmine? Amil – a *Trident,* not a human – was her father, and Sarah was her mother."

"And last night, did your mate not recount seeing a girl hidden amongst his memories, who called him Dad?"

He went cold.

"Magic has no scent to wolves, Mr Gunvald – at least not to most. That is how I was able to be there last night, undetected by your keen senses. But there *are* traces of magic that can be hunted by other beings. The magic of gods comes with even more obscurity, but once the pattern is known, it becomes easier to see. In the case of deific births, one mother, two fathers. Please speak to Ernest Matheson – he will explain it to you in a way I cannot."

"Two fathers? If Sarah had been pregnant that night, we would have smelled it on her."

"Magic has no scent to wolves," she repeated.

He stared at her, his stomach falling. His next words were forced. And hushed. He scanned his surroundings before speaking. "Are you telling me, Taylor is Jasmine's father?"

"One of. At least, we think so. At the will of the gods."

"I can't ... Jesus, he's *just* become a father today. Do you have proof? He's come *so far* after Sarah's death, and we have a family now. I cannot tell him—"

"It is your choice what you tell him, and the proof is your legs, Mr Gunvald – I am not sure what other proof I can give on the capabilities of the gods. But please, speak to Dr Matheson. I will take my leave now."

Bloody Human Hands and their timing! "Wait ... you drop this on me and now what? What am I supposed to do with this?"

"We tell you the information so you have it and can be prepared should anything arise. That is all. When it comes to the greater plans of deities, we know nothing, I'm afraid. But there are other beings who have a better connection with the gods. Speak to Ernest Matheson. Goodbye, Mr Gunvald, and congratulations again. Those children of yours will be the jewels of your crown." She smiled with sincerity.

And then, she left.

He let her, stumped as to what else he could ask. He turned back towards the house, and as if on cue, saw Dr Matheson in the distance getting into his car on the gravel driveway.

He ran to catch him before he drove away.

The doctor looked up and saw him, and waited. "Your Majesty," he called out when he was closer. "Your wife and your sons are doing even better than I could have hoped. You have a very strong family."

"Thank you, doctor. I've er ... I've just been speaking to Bella. She dropped by."

"Aah – I assume you mean the Traveller." Another name for the Human Hands: the Travellers.

"Yes. She wanted me to ask you about deific births." *Might as well jump straight in and get this conversation over and done with.*

Ernest Matheson's eyebrows hit his hairline. "Goodness, I'm not sure I've ever been asked about that before. Nevertheless, it was only two or three years ago I heard about one."

"You heard about one?"

"Yes, yes ... through an old colleague of mine – he was murdered in quite a gruesome way, god rest his soul. It was a paranormal attack, but these are the risks we take in our field. Ivan Jefferson was his name – a good doctor. Not involved with werewolves, but more so with demons."

"*Demons?*" He was already sorry he'd asked.

"Mmm, anyway, our paths crossed a few times over the decades and he and I were always good sounding boards for each other's cases. He sent me some files before he died about a birth he was dealing with. He called that one a deific birth."

"Bella said there was a pattern to them. Something about two fathers – I didn't really understand it."

"Well, it is hard to understand," he chuckled. "Not really the science we're used to, and not even anything like superfecundation. There's not really any research on it, I'm afraid, just ancient texts which are a bugger to decipher, but the pattern seems to be one human woman who is the mother, two males who appear to create some kind of joint genetic blueprint as the father, and the deity or deities themselves, who manipulate the seed from which the child grows."

Lawrence was about to ask how that was even possible, then felt the reality of his legs in his trousers and shut the fuck up. "Do the males have to be human?"

"No, I don't think so. The mother does as far as I'm aware, but in the files Ivan sent me, one of the fathers was a demon if I remember correctly – or half-demon. Something about shapeshifters and a dragon, too. Yes – now that I think on it, it was just before those big quakes happened – remember those?"

"Yes. They didn't really affect wolves."

"No, the human world was much more affected – it altered their perceptions and beliefs on things, too. It was an interesting time. They had a fable or a myth about a dragon rising and bringing an apocalypse, or something like that. That was connected to this birth."

"Was the child born?"

"I believe so. I was abroad at the time and more involved with wolves in North America. I didn't keep in touch so much with human happenings. Or demonic ones. I could look for you. Is it important?"

Lawrence sighed. "I have no idea, to be honest. No – there's no need to look." He needed to check in on Carrie, and he wanted nothing more than to take his sons in his arms again. "There's just one more question, if you don't mind me taking up your time."

"Ask away."

"The way these births work – would it be possible for a conception or a child to be ... I don't know, maybe kept or held in the womb for a longer period of time? Nine months longer than usual? A year?"

"Hmmn." He frowned in thought. "The usual pattern is the sheer *speed* of the pregnancy – sometimes the child is born within a month or two of conception as was the case with Ivan's patients."

And with Sarah. Shit. So, it could be true.

"But I suppose the opposite could also occur if gods have anything to do with it. Time doesn't really exist for them in the same way it does for us, so I'm sure they could bend it at will."

He was clutching the damned bracelet too tightly. This was all information he didn't want. "All right. Thank you, doctor. I really appreciate your input."

"You're welcome." He opened his car door and got in. "You know where I am if you need anything."

"Yes. Thank you."

Lawrence watched him drive away and found himself a bit lost. Before seeing Carrie, he needed to put this bracelet away.

He made for the house and walked through the front door, intending to go to his study, but he stopped at the bottom of the stairs when he heard everyone in the kitchen. Taylor's laugh floated toward him, followed by Lydia's, and then Ryan's. Unable to resist a glance at his family, he stuffed the bracelet into his front pocket as best as he could and made his way there, quietly.

The smell of sausages cooking was a welcoming one and obscured his own scent from his mates. Probably just as well since he really couldn't avoid seeing Carrie and then speaking to Samuel about her when he arrived, which would be soon. So, he stood at the open doorway and avoided saying hello instead. It would be too hard to leave if he went in there. *All* he wanted was to be in there.

Before he could stop himself, he turned away and left with a sigh on his lips. Duty called at his doorstep, even though he'd tried so hard to avert it anywhere else. So much for fielding his calls.

The image he held in his mind as he got himself on his bike to see Carrie, was of Taylor holding one of their boys, the grin on his face one reserved just for those newborns. And he sure as hell knew that feeling. They all did.

How could he keep this information about Jasmine from Taylor? But, equally, how could he tell him when he had nothing to go on at all? What he had was someone's guess based on obscure patterns of otherworldly origins. It wasn't enough – not enough to break up the happiness of today or any day. *Not enough to break up my family.*

And it would, wouldn't it? In some way, it would, if Taylor knew he might be Jasmine's father. Would he leave? Go look for her?

Today he'd become a father. He was a father to *their* boys and he was needed here. And they'd gone through so much;

overcome so much; even just this afternoon with Ryan. And last night, Taylor had said goodbye in those woods. He'd let Sarah and the past go, and all his doubts about fatherhood – Lawrence had felt the change; had helped him through it.

Mind made up, he resolved to sit on this news he'd been given – at least until he had something tangible and solid. Then, he'd tell him – he'd have to. He couldn't keep something so big from his mate if it turned out to be true.

He started the engine and took off down the driveway towards the trail that led to Richard's cottage and Carrie's temporary lock-up.

But *until* he knew it was true, his family came first. Kingship or not, and whatever a 'deific' birth might mean for the world at large, those he loved came first. He was the king. But his heart wasn't for bargaining – it belonged to too many others, three of them reliant on him for the very air they breathed. From now, he would always be a father first.

JEWELS OF THE CROWN

CHAPTER ONE

About a quarter of a million pounds in turnover a year – profit.

Lawrence let out a distracted sigh, his annual tax documents finally in place and ready to be handed over to his accountant. Not for the first time, he wondered why on earth they bothered with the work they did when they had more than enough from investments in stocks and shares to not need to, but it was all more for practicality's sake than any other. Maintaining solid purpose in the human world meant no one blinked an eye at them or went poking into their affairs. Their existence needed to be above board, so to speak. No werewolf liked to be outed by the human world; it could be dangerous to say the least. His parents and grandparents before him had been diligent in maintaining the outward appearance necessary for their integration into mainstream society. And, ultimately, Lawrence didn't mind. Out of all their financial avenues, it was the dance and their work in the arts – his and Lydia's – he loved and valued the most. Anything that kept them dancing, even in smaller circles, was akin to gold.

Ryan much preferred throwing himself into the land they owned – the export of its timber, its meat...

Taylor worked anywhere and everywhere, being something of a thorough and detailed manager of all their projects and operations, but he'd very much established himself as the IT systems and network guru whenever they needed anything created, fixed, or updated, which between the theatre, its restaurant, and the land, was often enough. Much to Taylor's satisfaction, he had a very happy and competent right-hand man in Adam.

And work kept them from isolation. As much as a wolf or its pack might claim they craved their solitude – which they did – to be cut off entirely from every person and resource (human or otherwise) that made the world turn, was devastatingly destructive. Lydia careening into their lives over half a decade ago had held up an unintentional and stark mirror to the sitting corpse Lawrence was on his way to becoming. Isolation was not a place he'd ever go to, willingly, again.

A scraping sound against the wooden floorboards outside his office, followed by a small gasp, had his hand frozen, mid-air, pen in hand, for the briefest of seconds before he carried on writing the address on his envelope – feigning ignorance of his intruder – lip twitching at the scent he'd just caught. One that warmed him from the inside out and turned him to puddle. Little over five years ago, he'd never thought that talent could be attributed to anyone but Lydia.

Out of the corner of his eye, he caught a glimpse of flaxen blond hair flash around the corner of his ajar door, betraying his trespasser's attempted stealth. A scurry of hushed whispers had him biting his lip to keep the wide grin from forming on his face – it would do no good to let the little snoopers know they'd won him over before they'd even begun whatever they intended to do.

He dropped his pen, waited, and was finally rewarded with a tentative rap upon the door.

Schooling his face into a neutral expression, he put on his best 'stern' voice and said, "Come in."

Axel was literally shoved into the room, more whispers and a giggle rushing in after him, followed by a pattering of feet that stayed well behind their appointed leader – Christopher and Elias took up his rear. From the age of about two, without word or argument, it had been clear Axel – the first born of the triplets – was this little trio's commander, taking the flak for any trouble they landed in, but also stepping up whenever any of them wanted to brave something new.

And it was going to be really fucking hard not to break, Lawrence's smile already threatening to burst forth. But first thing was first: these three were as naked as they day they were born with dark smears on their hands and feet, and he was pretty sure, whatever they were up to, this wasn't Lydia's plan for them at quarter to ten in the morning.

"Daddy," began Axel, his voice trembling as he took in a deep breath, "we have something very important to say."

Chris and Elias nodded in earnest behind him.

Lawrence steepled his hands, brought them up to his mouth, and *pushed* the impending grin from his face. How the fuck did they manage to look so *cute*? "And what might that be?"

Axel and Christopher were identical; same hair and the lightest blue eyes, just like his – Gunvald through and through.

Elias, the most sensitive of the three – which certainly didn't make him less courageous – had darker blond hair; bore a more serious expression, even at the tender age of five; and his blue irises were just a shade darker. Faint freckles that became more prominent in the summer, sprinkled the bridge of his nose. Lawrence thought he sometimes saw his mother in Elias, but Lydia had also said she saw *her* mum in him even if his eyes were not violet. Taylor had thrown a spanner in the works and stated Elias reminded him of his own dad fairly often.

The boy may also have picked up Ryan's prophetic skills since he had the spooky ability to predict where he should and shouldn't be in a way most five-year-olds could not.

None of them minded the uncertainty one bit – Elias was a son to *all* of them – save to say the third-born was the anomaly no one could quite pin down.

Encouraged by his dad's question, Axel puffed his chest out a bit with his next breath. "We're really big now – we're also bigger pups than we were – and...” He hesitated.

They *all* stared at him: their dad and the keeper of whatever permission they sought.

Axel took the tiniest of steps forward, his eyes widening as he looked upon him with total sincerity. “We think it would be good to go into the woods without a grown-up watching us.”

“Hmmn.” Lawrence leaned back on his chair and made a show of contemplating their words. “So, you think you’re responsible enough?”

Three heads bobbed up and down like they were in a race.

“And you can, of course, tell the time well enough to always come back when you’re supposed to.”

A pause. And then slower, more uncertain nods with wider eyes as they thought that last point through.

Shit. He couldn’t do this to them. His heart swelled whenever they got fearless enough to ask anything, and their confidence meant everything to him. But Lydia was going to flay him alive if he didn’t deal with the obvious. “All right, boys, I’m going to think about what you’ve just said, but if you want more responsibility, you have to *first* show Mummy and me and *all* your dads how responsible you can really be.”

More nods. “Okay,” breathed out Axel.

“Mm-hmmn – where are your clothes?”

He didn’t think it was possible for their eyes to get bigger, but they somehow managed it as a few guilty looks were exchanged.

“And what’s the *one* thing you should never do when you shift?”

Christopher sucked on his bottom lip while Axel’s came out in a semi-pout. Elias just looked like he knew this was coming. “Run away from Mummy.”

“Right. And what were you *supposed* to be doing instead of shifting and speeding your way into my office?”

A shadow fell across the gap of the door and Taylor poked his head through, saw the display in front of him, then sighed. "There you are, you three! Mummy is not impressed at your disappearing act, or the trail of clothes you left down the stairs and in the hallway, and guess who just got an earful?" Taylor glanced at Lawrence and poked himself in the chest with a finger, mouthing, "me".

Lawrence forced back a snort and turned his attention back to their sons. "Boys, when you live in a house with Mummy, her rules come first, no matter how old you are and even when you're great big Alphas, got it?"

Sulky nods this time, followed by a chorus of "Sorry, Daddy."

"So, what did Mummy ask you to do?"

"Help get Brendan and Layla changed and wash their hands and faces," replied Elias.

"And she explained why, right?" chipped in Taylor.

"Because Dr Ernie's coming over."

Christopher sighed. "And because Ethan's a baby and she has to carry him all the time, so she can't look after us anymore."

"And Layla and Brendan are too little to put all their clothes on properly," added Axel.

"She *still* looks after you, Chris," said Lawrence, "all of you. She just needs help with *some* things, but you also know why she asked *you* three, right? Not me or your dads, but you, specifically?"

Blank stares met his.

"Because you're old enough to be *responsible*. And once you show Mummy you can be, we can see about you going outside, nearby, alone."

Christopher's mouth dropped open, Elias' eyes got large, Axel's grin pretty much filled the room, and Taylor's left eyebrow went up in question.

"Really?" Axel all but shouted in excitement.

"You three want to be Alphas, right?"

"Yes!" was the reply, pretty much unanimously blurted.

"Well, what do you think is the most important thing to an Alpha – the one thing beyond all others an Alpha must learn to do and *still* do even when he's really, really old?"

They looked at each other; lips quivered, but no answer was forthcoming.

"The best Alphas know how to look after their family. They put the ones they love first because family makes the strongest foundation for your pack, no matter how large your pack grows."

They soaked in his words for exactly three seconds before a commotion sounded outside: Layla crying, Brendan whining, and Lydia's rushed footsteps at the bottom of the stairs, already making their way to the small gathering in his office. Before long, she'd flung the door all the way open with her foot and five pairs of eyes took in her harried face – baby in right arm, Layla's hand in her left hand, Brendan hanging off her casual, three-quarter-length dress with an angry, bunched fist... "My god, look at the *state* of you three!" she started.

But it was Layla – violet eyes aflame with nothing short of hurt betrayal – who got her piece in first. With an angry scowl, she threw the article of clothing in her small, chubby hand – a pair of trousers (presumably Elias' trousers) – at Elias. "You're naughty!" she yelled.

And Lawrence thought poor Elias was in for it, but Layla's enragement quickly became a trembling lip before her face scrunched up and more tears streaked her already stained cheeks. "You r-ran a-away from m-meeee." And then came the sobbing.

Axel and Christopher ran up to their mum, apologising endlessly, words about family and responsibility tumbling from Axel's lips as Christopher tugged on Brendan to lead him back upstairs and get him changed – a look of haggard bemusement was starting to overtake the look of annoyance on Lydia's face – but it was Elias and Layla that had Lawrence's attention.

The two were ... unique. They shared a bond he didn't fully understand. The triplets had loved Brendan instantaneously the moment he was born, and it had been no different when Layla had arrived nearly a year later. Being the first and only female of the siblings made her quite the centre of attention at times – but Elias...

Twelve hours after her birth, Layla had been wailing the place down, and no amount of feeding, burping, belly strokes, or anything had calmed her, until Elias – half-asleep and just under three years old at the time – had sneaked past Lawrence and Lydia arguing about what to do in the far corner of the bedroom, and climbed into her large cot. He'd lain down beside her, put his hand on hers, and sweet silence had reigned once more.

Stunned, they'd asked a bleary-eyed Elias how he made her stop crying.

He hadn't really seemed to understand the question. He'd replied, "She was just scared."

"Scared?"

"The air was biting her, Mummy."

Biting? "Erm ... okay ... but she's not crying anymore."

Elias had mumbled, "Stopped now," as he'd drifted back to sleep, still holding her hand.

Those two could argue as much with each other as they did with their brothers, but from that moment, Elias had stepped into some unspoken role of protector and guardian to Layla, though to be fair, she was just as good at verbally flaying alive anyone that put down, picked on, or otherwise hurt Elias, even with her limited vocabulary.

That one time in the cot had not been an isolated incident over the past three years, as proven right now by what Lawrence saw in front of him. No words were said, and Elias didn't hurry. He walked slowly towards Layla. She looked up, their eyes locked, and her heaving breaths faded into a quivering pout. "Sorry, Eli," she whispered, barely audible.

"Sorry, too," came his reply. "I didn't run away."

"But I can't be a wolf like you and run like that."

And Lawrence swore more words were exchanged. Silently. Telepathically. He had to sit down with Ryan and Lydia and talk about it properly. They'd skirted around the 'isn't it interesting' part of it all, but had so far avoided an in-depth discussion.

"All right, that's *enough*!" Lydia's tone cut through everything, and everyone fell quiet. "I forgive you – for now – but I'll be talking to your dads about it. Dr Ernie will be here in one hour, and we must always be dressed for visitors. Go upstairs, clean yourselves up, and get changed *quietly* and *quickly*. Elias, help Layla; Christopher, help Brendan; Axel, pick up *all* the clothes off the floor and the stairs, and make sure you three clean your hands and feet – yuck! Look at them! No more shifting until *after* Dr Ernie is gone. Understood?"

Yeses all round.

"Mummy, we *are* responsible." Axel had taken the lead again in both tone and action. He rushed ahead picking up socks and shirts as they went.

Amused, Lydia cocked her head at Lawrence. "This is your doing, isn't it?" she asked, softly. And perhaps a little suspiciously.

"We negotiated a deal."

She smirked. "Negotiations – at the age of five. How ... *kingly* of you." He swore a flicker of lust darted across her violet irises, never mind that she rocked a baby in her arms.

He couldn't resist returning her smirk with a smug smile of his own. Even under the strain of the cacophony surrounding them, he responded to her, his body hardening – she was fucking sensational. She would be until forever.

"Come on," pressed Axel to the others from the hallway, not that they needed telling. The deal had been agreed: time outside with no grown-ups.

Good thing they had no clue of all the places in and around the house Lawrence could see, hear, and smell *everything* going on outside within about a two-hundred-metre radius. Years spent hiding here in secret, like a hermit, avoiding everyone, had made him quite the clandestine voyeur.

"Here," said Taylor as he approached Lydia. "Let me take him for you."

"Yes, please." She sighed with gratitude and handed Ethan over.

"I can't believe he slept through all that."

"He finished feeding just ten minutes ago, but he is, without a doubt, the most laid back of them all – at two months old, anyway. Not sure how he'll be when *he's* five."

The front door opened and closed, bringing a waft of 'Ryan' in on the breeze before the male himself appeared with an update on practical matters. "The mini substation is sorted; it's tested safe – no electrical hazards. Seems to be up and running fine. I've just seen the engineer off." They were building two more cottages on the grounds as well as an extension to the main house – the substation was now completely necessary with a growing family, *and* with Adam and Tiegan now living on the land with two toddlers and a newborn. "Heya, little tyke," grinned Ryan as he swooped down to stroke Ethan's cheek. He then gave Taylor a kiss on the way up. "I heard a lot of shrieking from down the drive – it wasn't this tiny one, then."

"Nope, it was all the others."

"What did I miss?"

"A business meeting, apparently, complete with negotiation strategies for preschoolers," answered Lydia.

Lawrence grinned.

Taylor chuckled as he adjusted the blanket around the baby. "I'll go upstairs and keep an eye on them. Are you happy for me to take Ethan up?" he directed at Lydia.

"Absolutely."

As Taylor sidled out, Lydia sidled up to Ryan. The placement of her arms around his neck was met with a gentle groan from him and a pull into his chest. She sniffed his hair and neck before dropping a kiss on his lips with a sigh. "You smell of outside. I *miss* outside."

"You go out every day."

"I miss *child-free* outside."

"Aah." He returned her kiss with a deeper one. "We'll have to remedy that, won't we? I have all of Wednesday off – why don't you spend the whole day outdoors, anywhere you want, while I look after the brood."

"Oh, are you going to breast-feed Ethan, too?"

"Can't you express into a bottle just this once?"

"I've tried. That boy knows, before the rubber teat even *touches* him, that it's not my boob, and he starts screaming – he refuses to drink from it."

Lawrence watched in amusement as Ryan's gaze landed on her chest – snugly fit into her dress – just before his hands did the same.

"So wise at such a young age," the large male mumbled.

Lydia snorted, grabbed one of Ryan's hands, turned, and led him to ... well, it turned out she was heading straight to Lawrence's lap where he sat on his chair, and she didn't stop there.

Intrigued, Lawrence watched her – she wore the most alluring half-smile – climb onto his lap, balancing herself on her shins while she guided Ryan's hand to her arse; an arse she angled with not the slightest pretence as to what she wanted.

"Um, Lydia..." King or not, he was already losing his poise, his voice giving way to huskiness in his growing fervour.

Ryan seemed to have lost his altogether, completely mesmerised by her backside. "Jeez, sweetheart, did you know this gorgeous asset of yours becomes more sexy every year?" He flicked her dress over her back.

She moaned, grabbed Lawrence's hand, and shoved it between her legs and inside her underwear, her face now flushed; her eyes, glazed. "Okay, master negotiator – one of you's going to give it to me hard and fast the way I like, right now, and I'm not going to choose who."

Ryan's negotiating skills were suddenly better than Lawrence's. "Two of us, two points of entry – I'm not seeing a problem."

"Except you've left the office door open," whispered Lawrence, her delightful wetness all over his fingers.

She tugged ferociously at the belt around his trousers, nothing but want in her eyes. *Clearly* he was going to have to do fatherly negotiating things more often – in front of her. "You'd better hurry up and fuck me then, hadn't you." A command – not a question.

Ryan's pants fell to the ground.

The doorbell rang.

They all froze.

Lydia growled, then cursed. "That *cannot* be Dr Matheson – he's never this early!"

She scrambled off him with a second, more ferocious growl.

Ryan looked like he'd just lost a million dollars as he pulled his pants back up.

Lawrence stood and made himself presentable as Lydia marched towards the office door, smoothing her dress down; frustration in every stride.

She turned back to him just before she left the room. "Can

you *please* speak to the doctor about living here again? Please? It's ridiculous the number of times I have to call him over."

"I'll try. He very much likes his independence."

She muttered something he didn't quite catch as she exited the office.

"Gawd, that actually hurts," grumbled Ryan, adjusting his nutsack as he refastened his trousers.

Lawrence snickered. "Still worth a shot. There's no telling when the next chance will be with the way our six are. Ethan doesn't sleep through and Brendan has a habit of wanting to slide into bed with us at random times in the night."

"And with us sometimes," added Ryan. "At least he's not picky with his sources of comfort."

A gasp and squeal sounded from Lydia, and then familiar voices filled the air. And two familiar scents.

Lawrence stilled.

Ryan looked just as surprised as he met his eyes, then he shot him a lopsided grin as he made his way to Lydia and their unexpected visitors.

An unwelcome, long-forgotten realisation unfurled within him, and a shadow of guilt had Lawrence glancing towards the stairs Taylor had disappeared up – a shadow that fast solidified and threatened to engulf him whole.

He'd forgotten.

After all this time – after the craziness of parenting their now six children and growing this land into something warm and familial ... he'd forgotten. *How* could he have forgotten?

Cautiously, he made his way to the edge of the office doorway and angled himself enough so he could see the heartfelt hugs Lydia was giving them all. He could see Pete and Beth – no, she was *Claire* now. And by god, they looked like they'd just walked away from the apocalypse barely alive.

He could see a young girl he assumed was Jasmine. All she

wore was an adult's coat as far as he could tell, and she was covered in smudges of soot from head to toe. At least, it looked and smelled like soot.

As he wondered what the hell had taken place, pieces of an uncomfortable conversation from five years ago surfaced and disturbed his conscience: "*...last night, did your mate not recount seeing a girl hidden amongst his memories, who called him Dad? Magic has no scent to wolves, Mr Gunvald – at least not to most... but once the pattern is known, it becomes easier to see. In the case of deific births, one mother, two fathers.*"

Bloody gods and their meddling.

"*Two fathers? Are you telling me, Taylor is Jasmine's father?*"

Fuck it.

He'd sat on the somewhat unreliable knowledge Bella had forced upon him, not wanting to give false hope with no evidence and no tangible future for her claim; not wanting to break Taylor's heart on the day their first three sons had been born, but vowing to tell Taylor when the time was right. If it was ever right.

Almost imperceptibly, Jasmine – she would be five now, like their eldest three – flicked her eyes towards him, spying him spying on her. He had no idea when it had happened or if she'd been born that way, but one brown eye and one green eye stared at him. The exact same shade of green as Taylor's eyes.

Fuck it to hell.

CHAPTER TWO

Lawrence didn't want to play the stone-hearted bastard. He'd long since come out the other side of that torture. But he wasn't about to – *couldn't* – give free permission to let anyone live on his land without categorically knowing his family wouldn't be endangered by it.

This trio brought high-level risk to his door. He knew there was more to this story than had been spilled on his porch. Why come out of hiding? Why risk Jasmine's life by doing that? Presumably, they'd been forced to.

Lydia wanted him to be lenient on their old friends – he knew that. After all, Beth (damn it, *Claire*) and Pete had saved Jasmine's life after her birth. Claire had nearly died just beforehand, right here on his property, because of an angered rogue wolf. And Jasmine was Sarah's daughter by birth – not that the little girl knew that. No way in hell was it going to be easy to say no to Taylor if he wanted them to stay, too, and that was before even knowing his own parentage of her. *That* was a conversation Lawrence was already bracing for.

But not just yet. Right now, Pete had the floor as Ryan, Taylor, and himself sat around him, the office door shut once more.

Lawrence risked a glance at Taylor. His mate looked a little shell-shocked, Jasmine's return knocking him sideways, no doubt. The girl *smelled* like Sarah had just before she'd given birth. He'd said nothing so far, apart from the same welcome greeting they'd all given.

Claire was upstairs, with Lydia, helping Jasmine to settle in. He knew Claire had wanted to sit in on the meeting, but Pete had finally persuaded her Jasmine needed some TLC – he wasn't wrong.

Lawrence had taken Lydia to one side and asked her to get Ernest – Dr Matheson – to check Jasmine over when he was done with Ethan; he had been party to her birth. Hendrickson had told him everything they had known and Ernest had helped with Jasmine's escape from the hospital.

Ernest had also been the one to school Lawrence in the little information he had about deific births. He wondered if the doctor should sit in on the pending chat with Taylor – his input might help to make it all less *personal* to Taylor's ears.

Yeah, right – you're just too chickenshit to face the backlash you know you're going to get.

Pete had had his hard edges ... not exactly softened, but *deepened* with emotions – no doubt the ones that came from loving his child. And his mate – the way he and Claire moved, talked, and looked at each other, they were as good as mated, even if a human and wolf couldn't biologically quite manage it where breeding was concerned. Clearly, a lot had changed since their scramble from here five years ago.

"There are things I won't tell you because it will risk lives," Pete began, "and that's the last thing I want. I won't tell you where we've been the past five years or who we were with, just like no one can possibly know who we are and that we came back here."

Lawrence sighed, internally. This was going to be one massive problem. But at least he was being upfront about it.

"Holly's dead," he stated, quietly.

Taylor let out a quiet breath and closed his eyes.

"Murdered."

Which was exactly the kind of thing Lawrence didn't want at his door.

"Not sure how well Claire's processed it yet – everything

happened so fast."

"All right, Pete." Lawrence hoped he at least sounded soothing if not immediately warm. "Start from the beginning and tell us what you can – the changes have been vast in both our lives the last five years." He would know by the nuances of his narrative where Pete was omitting the truth, so keen were Lawrence's senses where his family's safety was concerned.

And he knew Pete knew that. The scarred older wolf nodded, stilled in thought for a moment, took in a deep breath, and began.

Forty-five minutes later and Taylor looked a shade paler. Lawrence wasn't feeling any better. Ryan seemed the most together out of everyone in the room, and it was he who broke the silence. "Burnt ... a town? A whole town?"

"A ghost town. Little over two hours ago, and no one knows we were there. Then, we were teleported here."

"By the ... demon? After a whole grand finale with a dragon? You did say *dragon*, right?"

"I know – not our usual type of social circle, is it?" Pete's attempt at a joke fell flat. He sucked in a breath. "You are our last resort – believe me, I did not want to come here and throw all this at your feet, but I don't know who else might be after us with the shaman and his two sidekicks dead. The shaman guy was insinuating things about Jasmine's power ... something about gods..."

Lawrence hid his chagrin. *Oh, here we are with the fucking gods again.*

"No bloody idea what he meant. But I swear to you, no one can follow the trail of our teleportation. I trust the demon's words in that regard. No one knows what Jasmine can do – what she did – and no one knows we're here now."

Lawrence hid his discomfort. "Talk to me about Jasmine's pyrotechnics."

Pete sighed. "She has little control over it."

"Evidently."

"But she can learn and will. I wasn't sure if Lydia—" He cut that verbal train of thought off, perhaps somewhat wisely realising that bringing Lawrence's mate and wife into the equation would not endear him to their hopeful plan of staying.

"Peter, she set fire to a whole town."

"She was pushed and frightened. Jasmine's a good girl, Lawrence – intelligent, kind... I'm not sure she fully realises what she did – she hasn't mentioned it once, and I'm not sure she's put it all together. She might still be in shock. In some ways, I don't want her to put it together – I'd rather we had the chance to start over. I don't think we can or should suppress her ... abilities, and I don't say that lightly given my history with fire. But she does need direction and training and ... Lydia's *been* there."

Lawrence exhaled sharply. "That's for Lydia to decide – did you know she no longer wields?"

Pete's face fell. "Oh ... I didn't know that."

"She hasn't missed it. My concern is for the safety of our kids given what Jasmine did, even if unintentional. There's a lot of space on this land, but there are also hazards. We've just installed an electrical substation, for fuck's sake."

"She's *never* usually like that. Like I said, she's *kind*. But without the proper guidance, I don't know what she'll become. You have resources, and you know people..."

All conversation faded as they each churned over the last hour.

"Lawrence." Taylor's hushed tone reached him and poked his guilt anew. "We should take some time out and talk this over – with Lydia."

"I second that," threw in Ryan.

"All right. Pete, I suggest you, Claire, and Jasmine spend the next few hours winding down and resting. I'll get the large caravan around the back of the house ready for you all, if that's okay – all the cottages are either occupied or in a bit of a state at the moment. Adam and Tiegan are living here, by the way – you might run into them."

"That's more than generous, thank you. Claire and I ... we were hoping maybe Hendrickson could look over our cuts and bruises. We haven't had much of a chance to sort ourselves out physically yet."

The silence fell heavy around them all.

Ryan dropped his head where he sat.

Pete let out a soft curse, catching onto the truth behind the silence. "Sorry ... fuck. I should have—"

"It's all right," said Lawrence, quietly. "There's quite a bit we need to catch you up on, too. Dr Matheson will be here shortly – do you remember him?"

"Of course. That's not a night I'll ever forget."

"You and me, both. He'll be more than willing to look you all over, I'm sure. Why don't you and Claire have dinner with us. The kids usually eat around six – we eat at eight."

He nodded with gratitude. "We'll be there. Thank you."

Lawrence stood, and everyone followed suit. "I'll go see how Lydia and Claire are doing, and then we'll have a better idea of how Jasmine might spend the day."

"How did she seem?" Lawrence snaked his arms around Lydia's waist from behind as she sorted through a number of Layla's clothes on their bed. She'd given Jasmine the largest ones she could find for her to wear after her bath.

"Very sweet – like any other child. A bit quiet and sullen,

but that's hardly surprising given everything she's been through."

"Did Claire fill you in on everything?"

"She said a lot about shamans, demons, and a *dragon* of all things, but not much about anything else. I have no idea where they've been or *how* they've been for half a decade. What did you make of the whole dragon thing?"

He let out an exasperated groan. "Dragons, shamans, magic ... it's all beyond me, Lydia. I detest magic at the best of times. Werewolves – we're very much of the *physical* world. Pete mentioned shapeshifters and that the shaman said Jasmine was one – shapeshifters are always human, and the way they alter their form is different to us. We're not human, we're *animals*, despite our appearance. Unlike shapeshifters, we physically change – crunching bones and the lot – and everything about us is because of our biology and genetics, which make us quite easy to understand for anyone who cares to read the science. The storm-wielding is the one aspect of wolves that steps into the supernatural and it's the aspect I've always been the least comfortable with. Honestly, if a dragon landed in front of this house, I have no idea what I'd do with that. I dread to think about it and I hope it never happens."

"So, you consider dragons to be supernatural creatures rather than animals?"

"They live in another dimension as far as I know, and whether you consider dimensions to be part of quantum physics or the supernatural, they're nothing I can understand or smell – they're not of this tangible world. If dragons ever resided in this dimension, I certainly wasn't around at the time. I know nothing about them."

"Hmmn..." She seemed to give what he said some thought as she piled up the clothes. "Maybe they're a species of dinosaur that escaped extinction by flying into an alternate reality." She sighed. "After Layla took Jasmine downstairs to play, Claire told me a bit more about her fire-conjuring – she set a whole *town* ablaze, Lawrence – and also how the dragon saved her life by *eating* the shaman. Christ, the poor little girl must have *seen* that."

Lawrence tightened his hold of her and pressed the back of her shoulders into his chest. "I don't know if Jasmine should play with our kids unsupervised."

Lydia dropped the last T-shirt she'd just folded and then swivelled in his arms to face him. "I understand the worry, but—"

"There's something Pete's holding back. He admitted he wouldn't divulge everything for everyone's safety, but I feel like there's something big we don't know – possibly to do with Jasmine and her fire. It's no small feat to ignite a whole damn town. Thank god it was deserted."

"She was being *abducted* at the time – by someone she trusted, no less. What you saw was a reaction to her hurt and terror, and *that* I understand. The wielding was the same for me at first – my emotions had free rein and I only got a handle on how to direct the lightning after *forcing* myself to not immediately react to every strong feeling that surged up inside me when my buttons were pushed. We can't turn our backs on Jasmine. Imagine what I'd have become if you'd all just left me in that warehouse as soon as you saw my lightning."

He took in her fiery hair and bright, violet eyes. "I kind of miss the wild you. *And* pushing your buttons."

She raised her eyebrows as a sly smile took over her features. "Oh, you do, do you?"

"It certainly awoke something in me. Something I very much needed."

Her arms went around his neck. "I'll remember you said that, Your Majesty, and I will not hesitate to throw it right back at you next time you're griping at my impetuousness."

His lips gently brushed hers. "Am I that much of a grumpy arse?"

She mumbled into his mouth, possessively, "You're *my* grumpy arse." And the kiss then became a tidal wave of almost desperate intimacy. The back of Lydia's legs hit the bed and they tumbled onto it, lost in a fast-growing hunger for the secret depths they unlocked in each other. She ground her hips against his and moaned around his tongue. "I think I've awakened that 'something' in you again."

"Feral minx," came his hoarse reply, although he was far too distracted trying to tear her underwear off from under her dress to say more.

Her deft hands wasted no time on his belt, button, zip...

A baby's wail could cut through anything, and desire was its current victim.

They both froze; Lydia sighed, her head automatically turning to the cot Ethan thrashed in.

Lawrence clamped his lips to her neck and trailed kisses down it. "Let him cry for two minutes."

"I need more than two minutes, and I can't shut out his crying – look." She gestured downwards to where her chest met his. "He makes my boobs leak with that noise. That's another dress I need to wash." She pushed him off her. Or tried.

He slid further down her body instead, taking the straps of her dress off her shoulders as he did so.

"What are you doing?"

He pulled her dress down past her chest. "Baring you to my eyes, Mrs Gunvald. The idea of you leaking milk to feed my children is a fucking turn on and I want to see it."

"I think maybe I know where Ethan gets his demanding nature from," she teased.

"I thought he was the most chilled out baby ever?"

"Until he wants to latch onto my breast."

"You're right. I *do* relate." His tongue found the bottom of the longest trail of spilled milk and he started cleaning her, lapping up every white streak and smear across her waist and chest.

"And now you're eating his lunch."

"Fuck him – I had these breasts first. They're mine."

Her rich laugh buoyed him. He finished operation clean-up and looked at her, adoringly. "Every single inch of you tastes divine, you know that?"

She leaned forward and kissed his forehead. "Hold that thought." Then she pressed her lips to his. "Go get me our son, Lawrence."

He stood and did just that, watching his newest boy with some reverence as he latched onto his mother's life-giving mound.

Lawrence was more than reluctant to leave and find Taylor, but find him he must. Their dreaded conversation needed over with sooner rather than later. He dropped a last kiss on Lydia's head as he watched their son happily gurgle around her enlarged nipple. "I've asked Adam and Tiegan if one or both of them can help Ryan sort the dinner out tonight since we have guests. I'm thinking of asking Ernest to join us, too – he's done a lot more than he intended to this morning already. Can you let Ryan know if you see him?"

"I will. It'll be nice to have something of a full house for a change."

"For a change?" He glanced incredulously at the baby.

Lydia laughed. "I mean a full house of *adults*."

"That remains to be seen. It looks like it might be a more common arrangement going forward depending on what happens with our new arrivals. I hate to leave you, but I've got to find Taylor."

"Everything okay?"

He hesitated, but decided he couldn't say a word without

Taylor knowing first – he deserved that much at the very least. "Yeah, I just need him for something."

Lydia shot him a funny look he couldn't quite decipher, and then smiled almost wistfully. "This is going to be one of those days we'll always remember, isn't it? One of those important turning points we recount to our kids when they're older."

Lawrence returned her smile with a wry one of his own before he walked out the bedroom. She had no idea how right she was.

He didn't find Taylor straight away, but did manage to catch Ernest Matheson around the back of the house after the good doctor had had a chance to speak to Pete and Claire, and look them and Jasmine over.

"Do you have time to stay a while today?" asked Lawrence, aware he'd put some hope into his tone.

Ernest had become more than a doctor over the past five years – he'd become something of a friend and mentor in matters of health and well-being amid their very unusual circumstances, and as such, he noticed the lilt to his question. "I'm getting the feeling I probably should."

"It would certainly be appreciated. It was quite unexpected having Pete, Claire, and Jasmine turn up on my doorstep given what happened last time we saw them. In fact, you were the last to speak to them – not I."

"Yes, I do recall. I'll stay if it's convenient – and dinner wouldn't go amiss if you have some to spare."

"Of course we do – I was going to ask if you'd like to dine with us. Lydia's also asked me to ... well, you can probably guess what she's insisted I ask you again."

The doctor laughed. "And when, pray, would I have time to myself if I moved here? As much as I delight in all your company."

"I reminded her how much you need your independence. You reassure her, though, and she's incredibly fond of you."

"And I'm fond of her, believe me. Your children, too. They are true gems."

"Thank you."

"Don't thank me yet; there's something I need to speak to you about, but it can wait until later. I feel there's something you need me for that's more urgent, yes?"

"Possibly. Awkward, rather than urgent. I need to speak to Taylor about a delicate matter and I'd be very grateful if you could be present for the talk – I'm sure you'll have some valid input, and you may be able to ... help him understand things in a way I can't. But first, how did you find Jasmine? What are your thoughts on her growth and state of mind given what we know she's been through?"

"Mmm, Pete told me some of it: demons and dragons and fire – oh, my."

"Not sure clicking together red shoes is going to get us out of this one."

He laughed, though it was dry. "I should imagine not."

"My concern is for our safety – especially that of the kids."

"That's understandable. It will take more than half an hour to be certain of her state of mind, but her heart rate is steady, her blood pressure is good – she's a healthy young thing and physically, anyway, does not seem to be fazed by anything she went through."

"So, there's no indication she might become irrational and ... maybe..."

"Set everything on fire?" finished Ernest.

Lawrence winced at the blunt way he'd gotten to the brutal truth of his concern.

"It's impossible for me to say, but I think, in this situation, a bit of trust might be the best course of action – at least until we have a better handle on her. Do you really want to send them packing to god knows where after everything they've been through? It's moments like these that really test us; that determine whether we stay true to our principles or become like those we never wanted to be."

Lawrence sighed and nodded. "I hear you."

"Your children have good instincts. Young ones, more often than not, really can see the truth of the matter far better than adults – they simply lack the words to express it. My suggestion is to let things play out for a few days and then review the situation."

"Thank you. That's the conclusion I was coming to, but it helps to hear you say it."

They both turned at the sound of heavy, approaching footsteps. Richard grinned and waved, not caring the stump on his right wrist might give anyone cause to look twice. Indeed, the kids *loved* his enforced amputation, not least because he hammed it right up, delighting in telling them about how he'd lost it to the monsters who tried to kill their parents. Or words to that effect. He dramatised it for five-year-olds while simultaneously dialling down how violent it had really been.

And Richard loved every minute of it. He'd lost his entire family; his daughter, Selena, was missing and presumed dead. The Gunvald brood were his adopted grandchildren – all but on paper – and he'd been nothing short of a father to Lydia the past few years. "Good afternoon!" he called out. "I was accosted by four boisterous pups fifteen minutes ago – I was completely outnumbered, you understand – and now I have an unscheduled play date in the copse at the front of the house."

Lawrence chuckled.

"Just checking in with the parents first – do I have permission to tire them out until their dinner?"

"Hell, yes. You're a godsend, Richard." *Speaking of which...* "And you have a new addition to the bunch: Jasmine. Have you spoken to Pete yet?" Richard and Pete had been good friends for years, though hadn't been in touch since Pete and Claire had been forced to 'disappear'.

"It's why I'm heading this way now. I told the kids I'd holler for them in half an hour."

"Join us at the main house for dinner tonight. I've invited Pete and Claire; Ernest will be there too."

He glanced at the doctor and nodded. "Don't mind if I do."

"Good. I'll try and find you a bit before dinner – there's something I want to talk to you about. But it can wait. I'll leave you to speak with Pete – he's in the caravan. Have you seen Taylor around?"

"He walked into the house through the back about five minutes ago."

"Brilliant. Thanks."

Richard wandered towards the caravan, and Lawrence turned to Ernest. "I'd like us to see Taylor now if that's all right. Please excuse me for being vague with you about this, but you'll catch on quickly once the conversation starts."

"I trust you have good reason." They both walked towards the house.

He wasn't sure about 'good' – he just had no idea how to say any of what he needed to out loud. And he really wanted Taylor to be the first to know.

They found the male in the kitchen slicing cold meats. "Hi," he greeted when he saw them. "I'm just preparing afternoon snacks for the kids – it will keep in the fridge for when they're hungry in two hours."

Yeah, he was a fucking great dad. Lawrence's gut churned at the way he was about to tear it all apart for him. "Forever the boy scout."

His mate chortled. "You know what they say: you can take the wolf out of the human, but you can't take the human out of the wolf."

"Who the fuck says that?"

"No idea. Sounds good, though."

"Well, I'm grateful every day no one could take the wolf out of you, Taylor."

He looked up from his slicing, no doubt surprised at the affection in Lawrence's tone. His gaze flickered from his mate to the doctor, and then back again. "Is everything okay?"

"Actually, no. I need to speak to you in private – now if you don't mind."

Concern lit his eyes. "Of course. This can wait. Give me a sec." He piled all the meat as close together as he could and covered it all with a food net.

When done, they all headed to the office. Lawrence really hoped it was the last time he would set foot in it for the rest of the day. Locking the door behind them, he pulled three chairs out. "Take a seat."

Once everyone was in a chair, he threw himself in the deep end before he lost his nerve. "Taylor, there's something I should have told you five years ago, and I'm very sorry I didn't, but with the children and the maintenance of this place ... I eventually forgot about it, although I had always planned on telling you at the right time."

Taylor said nothing for a second. "The right time?"

"An arbitrary phrase – there never is a right time." Lawrence took in a breath and opened the bottom drawer of his desk, reaching for what he knew was at the very back, in a pouch, where he'd left it all that time ago. "Do you remember the day the triplets were born?"

"Of course – how could I forget? It was eventful for more than one reason."

"Right. And do you remember that Bella came to visit?"

"The Human Hand? I recall you mentioning it ... she came to confirm The Trident were truly all gone – extinguished, as it were."

"She did. But there's something else she told me that day. About you."

Taylor looked astounded. "Me?"

Lawrence handed him the pouch.

After a moment of hesitation, he opened it and pulled out what was inside. It took him quite a few seconds to collect his thoughts. Lawrence saw the instant he clocked on to what he was holding in his hand. "This is Sarah's bracelet – the one she wore to the Halloween party."

"Yes. We thought she'd dropped it in the woods we revisited when we tried to trigger your memories."

"You weren't going to look for this – you were going to leave the past behind."

"I didn't look for it. Bella did. Bella found it and handed it to me for safekeeping."

Taylor was stumped. "Why on earth—"

"She was there that night – spying on us for all intents and purposes; using magic to cover her tracks, I'm sure. I didn't know until she told me. She overheard our conversations that night and she saw what we did. She ... said the bracelet might come in useful one day and then she told me..." Fuck this part. He forced his eyes away from Taylor as he spoke, for the sole reason it was easier to get the words out all in one go. "She told me about 'deific' births – that she believed Jasmine's birth *was* such a birth: manipulated by deities or gods. Apparently, there's a pattern to these kinds of births – Ernest knows a bit about this which is why I asked him to be here: all deific babies are a product of one mother and two fathers. Bella heard what you said about seeing a child and hearing her call you Dad ... and she believes you are Jasmine's father. One of her fathers. The other would be Amil."

The silence had never been so fucking loud, and it went on for far too long. He could hear Taylor's heart beating at the rate of knots.

Ernest held a look of total clarity, as if some huge puzzle piece had just slotted into place for him. All Lawrence felt was apprehension.

Taylor looked suddenly faint. "I'm ... Jas—what? Jasmine's ... mine?"

"I don't know. I don't know, Taylor. Our three sons had *just* been born, you'd *just* brought Ryan back from a very dark place, and Bella dropped this on me with no evidence, no proof, nothing. Absolutely nothing. I ... I should have told you what she said, but I had no idea how to with nothing solid to give you and then our sons were new and *right there* and needed us ... and I eventually forgot about it."

"You *forgot*?" And there it was. The note of incredulity; coupled with the tinge of betrayal. "You ... forgot. Forgot to mention I had a daughter."

"Until..." Shit, he couldn't finish that sentence – it sounded awful.

Taylor finished it for him. "Until Jasmine showed up this morning, right? Backing you into a corner and *forcing* your hand. Jesus Christ—" He stood up.

Lawrence stood with him. "Taylor—"

"You had no *choice* but to tell me. When would you have told me if she'd never come here, huh?"

"I—"

"Never! That's when."

"That's not true."

"When, then?"

"I ... I don't know."

"Fuck!"

"Tay—"

"We agreed no more secrets between us – am I the only one that means *anything* to?"

"It wasn't a secret."

"I think *keeping it from me* makes it a secret."

"I didn't tell anyone else. This conversation is the first anyone's heard about it."

"Ryan and Lydia don't know?"

"No. It was always going to be you I told first, but I wanted something *real* to tell you."

Taylor huffed as he paced; blew air through his teeth and ran both hands through his hair, briefly clutching at it. "What the hell do I do?"

"Nothing, Taylor."

He whirled to face him, pain and anger all over him. "*Nothing*?"

"What would you have done if I'd told you five years ago? We had three newborn sons, and Jasmine was just a baby being taken somewhere we didn't know because we weren't *supposed* to know in order to keep her safe. She *has* parents, Taylor, and she had parents then, too – two wonderful people who sacrificed *everything* to give her what she needed."

"That could have been me!"

"How? No one knew about the possibility of you being her father the night she was born. We asked if you wanted to go be with Sarah and you *chose* to stay here with us."

"I didn't know!"

"Neither did I! But if you did, you'd have gone?"

"I..." He faltered. Some semblance of control over his anger remained, although he turned every last bit of that anger on Lawrence. "*Damn* you, that's the real reason you didn't say anything isn't it? So I wouldn't go running to find Jasmine, away from the pack. You and your fucking control issues!"

A growl escaped Lawrence and he didn't bother holding it in – not after that reckless accusation, and no matter that it held some truth. His own anger rose. *No*, he was never going to let his fucking pack fall apart, not when he had the tatters of a species to piece back together! Guilt be damned. He broke his mate's pacing when he put himself in front of him and barrelled him, chest-to-chest, into the desk. "We lost *everything* that night of the Trident attack with no hope of getting it back. So fucking sue me, because when hope *did* find us and we all *lived* and started a family, like *hell* was I going to let *anything* risk that. When *you* had finally made peace with your past and *you* had finally pulled Ryan back from his, *yes*, I was going to dig in and hold on and not let you follow the trail of a ghost to heartbreak and grief all over again, because we *had joy right here*. You were a father *here*. You're *ours* and you belong *here*. I'll apologise to you endlessly for not finding a way to tell you the day Bella told me – I should have – but I will *not ever* apologise for the claim I have over *my* mates, *our* children, *our* pack, and *your* place in it."

Lawrence had leaned right into Taylor – not that he had budged an inch – in a clear show of acquisitiveness. Never did Lawrence, as a rule, lay his dominance on the table. Ever. Not like that. He hadn't *meant* to let that side of him slip, but Taylor had found the right button to push – on purpose. Lydia was the only one who'd seen that aspect of him in full.

Yet, he'd never opened himself in *this* way – by throwing the Alpha gauntlet and staking his claim over his males – despite their mated status.

And it was quite a thing to witness, that when Lawrence opened up, Taylor shut down.

A completely unreadable expression fell over the slimmer male in the silence that followed; Lawrence heard the metaphorical door slam. It was a devastating role reversal.

A startling fusion of possessiveness, bewilderment, resentment, and passion filled the air between them, the king's forceful words still bouncing off the walls. Also present, unexpectedly, was the pull of those intangible 'bonding threads' that sealed the four of them. It coated every chaotic feeling with a bizarre trace of sensual arousal, while simultaneously fuelling the ache of regret.

None of it helped Lawrence understand what the hell he was supposed to do next.

Taylor's gaze – very cold – cut through his, giving nothing away, until finally, he stood straighter and, remaining chest-to-chest, stepped forward – pushing.

Lawrence stepped back.

Another step to the side, and Taylor was swift to reach the office door, the hallway, the front door, and then outside, heading somewhere only he knew.

On a shuddering exhalation, Lawrence warred with the unfamiliar feelings of dismissal and rejection that came from Taylor's shutdown. And guilt – yeah, who was he kidding, he still felt guilty. It aggrieved him to know he'd caused his mate's gelid reaction. No matter his intentions, he'd taken away the only chance Taylor had to be a father to Jasmine. Picturing his own children, the thought of the same stolen from him tore him asunder now he knew what it meant to love them.

Shit. He was sure he'd have lost the plot way worse than Taylor if he'd been in his shoes, and he had no idea how to put it right. He wanted to chase the male, fall at his feet and beg for forgiveness.

He also wanted to pin him down and make him understand, unequivocally, where he fucking belonged: *here*.

Because they loved him and he was theirs and he had six other children who called him Dad.

A clearing of the throat yanked him right out of this

thoughts.

Oh, Christ... *Ernest.*

"So," said the old man, smiling a genuine smile and not appearing in the least bit disturbed by the display he'd just witnessed, "when would you like my input?"

CHAPTER THREE

It had only been twenty minutes since Taylor belted out the door.

Everything Ernest was saying held meaning and importance, but the longer Lawrence waited to go after Taylor, the more irate he felt.

But he also wanted to give him time to calm down; to *try* and see things his way.

"—and you're not listening to a word I'm saying, are you?"

"Hmmn?" He met the doctor's eyes hoping his wandering mind didn't show on his face (although it clearly had). "No, I am – I am. Er ... you mentioned the possibility of running a paternity test. Is that possible with two fathers?"

Dr Matheson raised his eyebrows and stifled a small sigh. "As I was saying"—*if you had been paying attention* was the unspoken meaning to those four words—"my colleague, Thomas Guiley, is something of a renowned geneticist, and he's a wolf. Perhaps you've heard of him?"

"I feel like I should have, but can't say I have."

"It's not all that surprising – he never exactly 'shunned' the wolf world, but needing to spend so much time in the human one for his education and research, I do believe he identifies more as a human than a wolf in many ways. Over the years, he's slowly extricated himself from werewolf society. He's turning forty-four in December – the extermination of Tridents couldn't have come at a better time for him, allowing him to survive unmated past his fortieth year. And I do think he's worked with Hendrickson in the past – more than once. If I'm not mistaken, they attended the same university. Thomas is extremely knowledgable and a good man, although ... well, his manner can take a bit of getting used to. He can be rather aloof."

Lawrence held back a grunt. He'd been *more* than aloof half a decade ago. "I'm sure I'll manage to find footing with him."

"Good, good. With your permission, I'll make a phone call to him and see if he'd be willing to look at Jasmine's and Taylor's blood samples."

"I really need to find and talk to Taylor first – I have no idea if he'll agree to it and I can't just take blood from Jasmine without informing Pete and Claire."

"No, of course – there's no rush, but the offer is there and it's always good to know there are possibilities open to you. Hopefully Taylor will feel the same way." And now it was the doctor's turn to seem a bit distracted. "But there is another reason I wanted to give Thomas Guiley a call... Er, this is actually the thing I wanted to talk to you about. I'm nearly seventy, Mr Gunvald, and as loathe as I am to admit it, my time in practice is up."

"Ah..." Now he *really* had his attention. He didn't want to lose Ernest – it still felt too soon after losing Hendrickson and Amelia, although that was under very different circumstances. But he was right. And he was human. He couldn't go on forever, and their six children, whom he saw to often enough, were boisterous to say the least.

"Truthfully, I should already have retired, but what can I say – I love my job far too much. I'd like to give myself three more years, god willing, and then I'll be leaving."

"I ... don't know what to say. Losing you feels almost tragic – everything you do for us is above and beyond."

"And I do not want to leave you in the lurch. I was made aware a few weeks ago that Dr Guiley was looking to move back to England in the next couple of years – he's currently living in Switzerland. With your permission, I'd like to approach him with the idea of being your family doctor – your *pack* doctor – when I retire."

It sounded fair, but it felt disheartening. Lawrence should have seen this coming given the man's age. "I'd like to check him out first if that's okay? I completely trust your judgement, it's just—"

"Absolutely – I would expect nothing less. I have a detailed file for you that tells you a great deal about him. I'll bring it over tonight."

"Thank you."

"Do consider him, though. It would not be a bad idea to have a geneticist such as he on board. He's done some good work with various species on the extinction list, whether they're known by the human world or not."

"Extinction..." That word sent his blood cold. The faint echo of a bullet firing, drummed around in his mind, too.

"If I may be blunt, Mr Gunvald..."

He wasn't sure he liked where this conversation was going, but trusted Ernest well enough to know his intentions were honourable. "Please do."

"There are under fifty adult wolves in the country left that we know of, and most of them are not breeding."

His words were a weight on Lawrence's heart.

"There are not even fifteen wolves under the age of six since that night it all ended, and over half of them are on your land." He spoke slowly and deliberately, letting his words sink in. "Fifteen young wolves is a good start post-extinction – not wonderful, but possible for future survival. However ... you have a lot of boys and only one girl, and that one girl is related to all the boys."

He paused.

Lawrence met his warm gaze with his own anxious one.

"It's good that you have Adam and Tiegan here with their

two girls. It would be better if you could also persuade Doug and Marie to move back with *their* two girls."

He sighed, suddenly feeling the world on his shoulders. "I already spoke to them about it last year – they're very happy where they are in Oxford. I can't force them to move here."

"Then have lots of parties going forward, and invite everyone's children around regularly until they reach adulthood. Do you get my meaning?"

"I do, but it's not that simple. Our mating pains might have gone – we didn't even feel the Supermoon two nights ago, and that was supposed to have been a rare Blood Moon eclipse – and I'm under the impression we can now all *choose* our mates as a result, but scent is still a factor. Wolves mate *through* scent and that wasn't different for Lydia, Ryan, Taylor, and myself. It might seem like fate threw us together, but fate also ensured we were at least aroused by each other. In a few years time, I could hold parties for as many adolescent wolves of the opposite sex as I like, but biological compatibility is still a factor here as far as I know. If they don't take to the scent of the other in the right way, nothing's happening."

"Oh, *something* will happen. Nature created the storm-wielder to bed three mates to *ensure* fertilisation at the most crucial times throughout your history, and nature will take any evolutionary leap it sees fit to do the same again."

"I've been under the impression it was gods who created storm-wielders," said Lawrence, sarcastically, not really wanting reminding of Himet and Yemet.

"For our purposes, gods and nature are synonymous with one another. Lawrence, back to me speaking bluntly: extinction is a hard-edged coin – you and your mates are on one side of it, and your children are the new beginning on the other. You and your mates pulled your species through, but the next generation's numbers are shockingly few. I do not know what will happen when your children come of age to mate, but it would not hurt to have a geneticist at hand to help or advise in any way that is needed."

"Christ..." Lawrence stood and paced, mimicking Taylor just over half an hour earlier. He was itching to get out of there. "It sounds so desolate. I never wanted that for our kids."

"There was no other way it was going to be, and it is as it is. But it's not desolate – you're flourishing, and Lydia is, quite simply put, the healthiest, most fertile mother I've ever known, and all your children are healthy too – very much so. You just might need some medical assistance with flourishing in the *future* you don't yet know. These things have been studied, Lawrence. It's not hopeless, and like I said, lots of gatherings with *all* the children in the country – even if there only remain fifteen – would be wise. But you and Lydia – all of you – may have to be accepting of whatever nature decides is necessary to jump start the new era of your species." On that note, the doctor stood.

Lawrence stopped pacing and turned to look at him. "We've faced worse. We'll get through it."

He beamed his smile. "I have no doubt. I'll leave you to seek out Taylor while I go make a few phone calls."

Right ... Taylor. He wasn't sure if part two of the 'sorry I never told you Jasmine might be your daughter' conversation was going to be better or worse than this one.

Running as his wolf was a gift he had no words for; one that brought very real tears to his eyes every time he did it – tears of deep gratitude – and the novelty had not worn off in the half decade his legs were returned to him. Every time he shifted and ran was like the first time all over again. Not that Lawrence could actually remember his first time, but as far as he was concerned, five years ago *was* his first time.

He reasoned it would be quicker to find Taylor as his wolf. He also wanted to sprint off that horrible discussion with Dr Matheson. Yes, it had occurred to him they might not make it as a species, and to put his children through that was a fist to his chest. But what other way was there? To produce offspring was the *only* possible way to sidestep annihilation, and there was no way around the fact *his children* would have to bear the brunt of leading all wolves into whatever new age they'd already initiated.

"Such children are born warriors, ready for the task ahead," had been the doctor's final words to him, just before he'd walked back to his car. Words that had been intended to ease Lawrence's mind. They eased nothing.

Finally catching the familiar aroma he'd been after, he slowed to a trot. From the meandering of Taylor's scent, he appeared to have headed towards the lake – certainly not his usual hangout. Lawrence wondered why he'd chosen that place in particular.

Picking up speed again, he raced through the trails and paths he knew so well, not missing the palpable tang of the anger still present in his mate's spice.

He wanted this sorted now – this afternoon; before tonight. Their tiny pack could not afford fissures. Weak bonds would not help their kids now or in the future. The little pups needed strong roots and foundations for the daunting future they faced, and it was their job as parents and rulers to make sure they had it.

He spotted his mate in the water, swimming as if he were in an Olympic race. At a guess, judging by the steady, almost robotic pace to him, he'd been at it for quite a while.

Lawrence barrelled into the lake as his wolf, only shifting once under the surface, then used the strength of his upper body to propel him towards Taylor. Sometimes, he still forgot to use his legs in the water. Swimming was as freeing as running for him; it had become his substitute for running – his silent, mostly secret sanctuary – when half his body was all he had.

Taylor saw him the moment he broke through the surface of the water. With his face set in stone, he pushed off the rock he'd just reached, flipped over, and headed out for another lap.

Refusing to ignore or indulge him, Lawrence took off beside him, and before they knew it, they were racing aside each other, every stroke fuelling a competitiveness borne more from hurt and rage than sport.

The second rock jutted out about forty metres from the first. Taylor reached it first, blew water out through his nose, then with a low growl, flipped again and headed back to the first rock. Lawrence followed, not stopping for breath, and this time, he put all of himself into the crawl.

He hit the rock a metre before Taylor and that appeared to be the cork off the bottle.

"You came here to make what point, exactly?" spat out Taylor – water as well as words – every syllable coated in ire.

"We need to talk."

"I'm not ready to talk." He took off again.

Lawrence followed.

Taylor halted, furious at his intrusion, and bellowed a curse that let loose around the bowl the lake created. "What were you *thinking*?! Not even twenty-fours earlier that day, I put my fucking *mind* in your hands – all of me, not even conscious of myself – and the first thing you did was *lie* to me!"

"I didn't—"

"Yes, you did! Yes, you fucking did, because when I said things to you like, *How are you feeling, Lawrence? How was Bella, Lawrence?* and *Goodnight, Lawrence*, those moments were your chances to say, *Actually, I need to tell you something Bella told me...* And what did you say instead? Fuck all! You sat on a secret that wasn't yours to keep, and I *knew*. I fucking *knew* that girl I saw during the regression was mine. I *told* you Sarah was pregnant. Is *that* why you lied? You didn't want it to be true? You didn't want me having any more ties to Sarah now she was dead?"

"I can't believe you just asked me that."

"Why not?" They treaded water as he sputtered. "Or did I miss you putting me in my damn place just an hour ago?"

"That wasn't what I did."

"You all but told me I was *yours* and had no say, and it sounded pretty unequivocal to me."

"Because you *are* – ours, not mine – and when I say ours, I include our six children; three of them just hours old the day Bella told me. I didn't tell you because I didn't want you hurt over an 'if' and a 'maybe' – nor our new family – and yes, maybe I was a little possessive about it, but it was *not* because I wanted you out of Sarah's life – or death for that matter."

"You apologised to me when we were in the woods that night – a *real* apology for taking the memories of everyone who knew me, and then you..." He stuttered. "Fuck." His whole face reddened and his eyes shone with a sudden spring of tears. "That's what hurts, you bastard. Not the fact I can't be a father to Jasmine anymore, although somewhere inside that smarts – it's that you ... *you* took it away. You. Again." He choked on his words. "But this time you were my mate, not some stranger." He lunged forward into a stroke, managed three or four, but his heart wasn't in it.

Lawrence reached for his arm and grabbed it.

Taylor threw him off, but it was reactionary, not aggressive.

Lawrence ignored the action and grabbed him again. He had no idea whether he was blinking lake water or tears out of his own eyes. He gripped Taylor either side if his jaw and brought his forehead to his so he couldn't dismiss him. "I fucked up,

Taylor, and I know sorry doesn't cut it. I don't know what to say or do to make this up to you, but I will. I *will*. Tell me what to do."

The male met his gaze, but shook his head.

"There's got to be something."

"All I feel right now is your betrayal."

"That was *never* my intention."

"I believe you, but it doesn't change what I feel – or how I feel about you."

"Hate me if it helps you – I can take it."

"I don't hate you, you son of a bitch. It would be easier if I did."

"You can still be there for Jasmine."

"Lawrence—"

"You can."

"Lawrence"—he pulled his hands from his face—"I'm fucking sinking. I need to—" He looked at the rock, but Lawrence was already pulling him that way.

Taylor wriggled free of his grasp and swam out to the protrusion himself, but he was looking suddenly exhausted and on the wrong side of pale. And flushed with his pent up tears. Pale and flushed at the same time.

He hung off the rock when he got there, his breathing a little ragged.

"Have you been swimming non-stop since you got here?"

"Pretty much."

"How many laps?"

"I lost count."

"How long for? Half an hour?"

"I'm not wearing a watch."

"Taylor—"

"Stop fussing. My heart hurts more than my muscles."

Lawrence sighed.

"And no. I can't be a father to Jasmine. It's too late. It would confuse her at this age with everything she's been through. And it would hurt Pete and Claire. I couldn't do that to them after everything they've done for her."

"You can be there for her in other ways: be her best friend, be her favourite uncle, be the one she actually listens to – *because* you're not her father."

Taylor let out a small sound at that – it wasn't a hopeless one. The corner of his mouth tugged upwards for barely half a second before it fell again. "She waved at me earlier, before I came to the lake. I was sitting on the porch – didn't see her straight away and then she was just there, standing to my right. At first, she looked so sad."

"Maybe she really is your daughter after all."

Taylor threw him the mother of all looks.

"Sorry. Bad timing – too soon."

"Way too soon. You're still a cunt."

He winced. He deserved that.

"She then smiled, though – and waved. It was lovely. Since I can't be her father, I don't mind the idea of being some kind of friend to her. If I can help her be happy…"

"You can. You will. Look, you should know that Ernest said it's possible to try a paternity test if you want to be sure – even with this kind of supernatural birth and two fathers ... he seemed to think there was a way."

Taylor surprised him by shaking his head. "There's no need. I know she's mine. I knew it five years ago and I know it now."

"I really am so sorry. I won't keep anything like this from you again."

"I don't think that's a promise you can keep, so don't make it."

"I mean it. I—"

"You're the king."

Lawrence swallowed the rest of his words and stared at him.

"It hurt so much that you did that to me after everything, but do you think I don't know you? Do you think I'm not aware that every decision you make is weighed against the needs of the pack and species as a whole, and not *just* me or *just* you, or even just us four?"

"I..." He was at a loss for words. Even *he* hadn't truly considered the ingrained pattern he had to every decision he made.

"I know you love us. And me. But I also know you naturally and instinctively put the pack and the species before all – *even* us. I think perhaps, the only person who gets a pass here, is Lydia. So don't say you'll never keep anything from me again, because when something pivotal arises that compromises the whole, you'll do what you have to, including lie."

It twisted him up inside that Taylor was right. And it would be *him* who saw it this clearly, not Ryan or Lydia. He could barely get his voice above whispering. "Taylor, I—"

"You probably shouldn't apologise for it, even though a part of me would like you to. You see, that's what makes you a good king."

A heaviness settled over him. "If this is you forgiving me, it feels kind of shitty."

"I haven't forgiven you yet. But I am going to ask something of you."

He swallowed hard. "Anything."

Taylor held his gaze, his eyes, thankfully, no longer as icy as they had been in the office. "Don't tell anyone else about Jasmine. Don't tell Ryan or Lydia."

Everything inside him shrank. He shook his head. "Fuck it ... Taylor..."

"You said nothing for five years, say nothing for a few more."

"It's different now you know."

"It really isn't. I'm asking you to do this for me, for Jasmine, and for the pack."

"For the pack – how? Why?"

"I'll give you kudos for keeping this secret hidden so well, but in general, we wolves make horrendous liars. If you know, and now I know, and then suddenly Lydia and Ryan know, how long do you think it will be before Pete and Claire catch on? Maybe Jasmine, herself, and then everyone else. Do you really think all four of us can act naturally around Jasmine knowing she's my daughter – no meaningful looks or affection – every single hour of every single day?"

With a deep unease, Lawrence conceded he was probably right.

"I can distance myself from her if it's just us who know. It'll be that much harder to do it once Ryan and Lydia know."

"Jesus ... you wanted no more lies."

"Jasmine blew up a whole town. She needs to learn control over her abilities before anything else destabilises her. For all our sakes, I really don't want to be the reason she goes off the deep end. She can't find out about me. Which means no one can."

Lawrence searched the herbage growing up the chalky walls that capsuled the lake, as if all his answers somehow lay hidden in the crooks and crannies of the earth. Taylor was right about Jasmine; about bloody everything. "Are you really okay keeping this from Ryan?"

"Because he trusts me so much? The way you kept it from me when I trusted *you* so much?"

That stung as much as it was supposed to.

"No, I'm not. But I'll take a leaf out of your book and constantly remind myself it's better this way to keep the pack safe; to keep the equilibrium for everyone, not least Jasmine who likely needs it the most. That's why I came here, Lawrence – to the lake. This was the last place we were all with each other that night of the storm and we were so ... *together*. We were so bonded. I wanted to get a feel for whether I can really keep this from Ryan and Lydia. I don't know if I can, if I'm being honest, but between Jasmine's talent for setting things on fire and needing to keep our children safe, I can't take the risk of them knowing. And I believe in us four. I believe we're strong enough to get through the other end of the lie, whenever that comes."

"Keeping this from Lydia is going to be—"

"This is what I'm asking of you, Lawrence. You've put me in the position where I have to lie to my daughter, so you're going to do what you can to make it easy for me to keep my lie. If you truly want to make it up to me – this is how."

Lawrence looked at his mate. His countenance was set in determination and in the same hard sorrow that was lodged in his own chest. A strange and sudden admiration for this man stole over him; Taylor was never to be underestimated. Anyone who did because they deemed him an easy target, often found themselves outplayed without even knowing how. "All right. I'll follow your lead on this, and I won't say anything until such a time you state I can."

"Even if that's years from now?"

"Yes."

Taylor searched his eyes out, looking for his sincerity.

Lawrence pulled himself a metre along the water, until he was against Taylor, leaned in, and sealed the vow with a kiss to his lips.

In a rush of feeling Lawrence suspected was rooted in the remorse of what they'd just agreed, Taylor seized the back of his neck and held him firm as he deepened that kiss.

He let him; allowed himself a moment to get swept away in it. Sensual intimacy was not something the two of them often shared, and very rarely when they were alone.

Anger still coloured the male's taste and feel, his pressure against his mouth almost harsh; but any enmity was dying, getting swept away, instead, in a tidal wave of laden sadness over what they'd agreed to shroud from the others.

Lawrence broke the kiss first, the emotion just a little too much when just this morning everything had been damn near blissful and perfect. It wasn't just Jasmine's arrival – it was Ernest Matheson's harsh reality check that triggered the shiver running through him. He bowed his head against the crook of Taylor's neck.

He didn't expect consolation, but his mate's hand curled around his nape and stroked him there. "I know you're sorry," he said, quietly. "I'm sorry, too."

He wondered if the doctor's words were another secret he was going to keep. What was the point of having his mates worry about something so uncontrollable? He didn't want anyone else to feel this way about their children and their future when there was nothing to be done about it outside of what had already been suggested – and he could take care of those suggestions on his own. Organising gatherings was not a problem. He was pretty sure Tiegan and Lydia would do most of it. He just didn't need to tell them *why* he was throwing together an array of social occasions ... maybe. "We have almost everyone – all the adults – joining us for dinner tonight. We should probably head back." He looked up and met Taylor's eyes. "Are you going to be all right sitting with Pete and Claire?"

A semblance of calm had returned to his features. A small smile graced them. "I am now."

And Lawrence could feel the truth in that statement. If his silence truly helped Taylor manage himself around Jasmine and find the peace he needed, he could find it in himself to remain so.

Lawrence returned his smile. "Race you to the shore."

He wasn't sure if Taylor would, given his earlier state of exhaustion, but he managed an impressive speed, his stroke still showing that steadiness from earlier. He stumbled, once, climbing out of the water, but no longer seemed cross. "You know," started Taylor, his tone almost back to its playful self, "if I'd been in a different frame of mind, and if the conversation had been about anything else, that rather predatory performance you put on earlier in your office would have been hot as fuck."

Despite himself, Lawrence laughed. "Is that something I should bear in mind for—"

He never finished that question because Taylor shifted and, standing just half a metre from Lawrence, gave himself a good, hard shake.

Water sprayed all over him.

"Hey! That was uncalled for."

Taylor's wolf stared at him with nothing short of triumph, and *there* was his smile – a big one, complete with lolling tongue. *It was totally called for*, he relayed to his mind. *And fun.*

Not bothering to reply, Lawrence also shifted, shook, and then, almost sagging with the utter relief of hearing Taylor laugh again, sprinted beside him, back through the woods, towards the house.

CHAPTER FOUR

They arrived home to the end of the calamity that had evidently taken place. Richard had, just as he'd promised, worn the kids out. The sitting room next to the kitchen – the one they'd all been birthed in – was littered with clothes, dollops of mud, and five sleeping children – mostly naked – huddled together on the two large floor cushions in the far corner of the room. Elias and Brendan were in their wolf forms, Layla curled up between the two; Christopher was splayed out in his boxer shorts, his human limbs demanding as much space as possible; and Axel was trying desperately to keep his eyes open.

Still in canine form, Lawrence rolled his eyes at the scene. They were going to need bathing again. And so much for staying clothed for guests.

Even though he hadn't thought it telepathically, Taylor picked up on his musings. *Can't blame them,* came his voice into his mind. *Clothes are uncomfortable at the best of times.*

In unison, the two wolves shifted into men.

"Daddy," mumbled Axel, barely awake. He could have been speaking to either of them. "I made sure no one got lost going to the woods and back."

The emotion for his son that surged in him had no name. Some mixture of pride and love and ... just more love. "Thank you, Axel."

"I'm responsible. And I can stay awake like an Alpha." His little head lolled.

Taylor couldn't hide his grin.

Lydia walked in from the kitchen, tea towel in hand. "Hey." She smiled in greeting when she saw them. Her gaze travelled down their forms, her nostrils flared, and … there it was: the slight straightening of her back, the puckering of her chest, the widening of her pupils, and the tiniest intake of breath no human would notice, but *they* damn well did. "Lord, help me, you both smell—"

"Mummy…"

"Oh, Axel, baby…" She wandered to him and knelt down where he sat, his head nodding as he fought his tiredness. "Aren't you napping? Sleeping now will help you eat dinner."

"I'm a big wolf."

"I know you are, but I promise you, even big wolves need sleep. Daddy Ryan especially, and he's the biggest of all."

Taylor made an amused sound, and just when Lawrence thought Axel was going to put up a fight, he said, "Okay, then," lay down, and was breathing rhythmically within ten seconds.

"Richard's earnt his gold medal, I think," said Lawrence.

Lydia laughed. "I don't know what we'd do without him. Mind you, he looked pretty worn out himself."

"Do you know where he went? I could do with speaking to him … maybe after I get a shower in."

Her skin flushed slightly as she took them in again with her eyes. "Smells like you've already bathed in the lake."

"It was an impromptu visit."

"Yeah," agreed Taylor. "I also need to get in on that shower, so—"

"Wait, wait, wait … what the hell." She was in front of them in two seconds. "The kids are all asleep, no one else is in the house, and you're both going to leave me alone, like *this*?"

"Like what, exactly?" teased Lawrence.

"Don't you dare make me say it after we got interrupted earlier." She lowered her voice. "Fuck me first, shower second, Richard third. That's an order." And it was *both* of them she stared at, an arousal in her eyes that was just this side of aggressive. Post-natal hormones were … interesting.

Taylor cleared his throat. "Erm … as much as I'd love to join you both, I need to—" A shuffling sounded from behind them.

They turned to find Jasmine looking curiously at them all.

"Whoa!" gasped Taylor as he snatched the tea towel from Lydia's hand and placed it across his hips.

Lawrence swung Lydia in front of him. They never hid their nudity in front of their own kids – nudity just wasn't a factor most wolves even noticed given how often they shifted – but Jasmine was human and he had no idea how much of wolf behaviour she was used to.

She didn't seem overly shy, but it was still a whisper that came out of her. "Can I please sleep in here with Layla?"

The front door sounded – it opened and closed. "Jasmine." The call came from Pete as he hurried in after her. "I asked you to wait for me."

"Sorry, Daddy."

Lawrence *felt* Taylor bristle, but to his credit, he clamped right down on whatever he was feeling before it went anywhere (he was certain Lydia hadn't even noticed) and did what Lawrence had been so bloody good at doing since the age of seventeen: he put a great big fucking wall up and pretended it was the best thing in the world. Then, he smiled at Jasmine. "I don't think that'll be a problem."

"Sorry, everyone," said Pete. "She had so much fun with Rich, she didn't want to leave. Followed him half way to his cottage and then wanted to find Layla."

Lawrence nodded at him. "Like Taylor said, she's more than welcome. Please excuse me – I need to shower up and find Richard myself."

Lydia shot him the most murderous of glares and elbowed him in the stomach to boot, but there was no way in hell he was hauling her upstairs to make love to her – no matter how glorious that might be – with Jasmine downstairs, when he had no idea of the girl's hearing ability, her sleeping patterns, or what might set her off.

"I can stay and watch over them," offered Pete. "Claire's asleep in the caravan – we haven't actually slept since... Anyway, I brought a book." He waved the novel in his hand as if he needed to prove his point.

"That would be appreciated," replied Lawrence. "Thank you." He was just wondering how in god's name he was going to escape upstairs without exposing himself to Jasmine, when the young girl solved the problem for him.

She looked at Taylor's tea towel, then his face, then his tea towel, then his face, then took a step towards him. "Daddy doesn't wear clothes when he becomes his wolf either, so it's okay. You don't need to be embarrassed."

Taylor actually went red. From head to toe.

It would have been hilarious had the last three hours not happened.

For Taylor's sake, Lawrence forced down the laughter that wanted to break. He knew this was cutting him up in more ways than one, and that pain was raw and sore. It might well be for years to come. "Thank you, Jasmine," he said instead. "And on that note, I'll catch you all later for dinner." He removed himself from his Lydia-shaped hiding place and made to exit the room, but before he left, he threw Taylor a last thought. *You holding up okay?*

Taylor blinked and glanced at him, before smiling once more at Jasmine and walking towards the door himself – still clutching the tea towel, fairly ineffectively – and leaving her in Lydia's capable hands. *I suppose I'm still standing*, was his answer. *I'll live.*

When the grizzled, grey wolf opened the door of his cottage, Lawrence hadn't quite expected to see him so happy given Lydia's assessment of how the children had left him. "Richard, sorry to bother you, but I mentioned I wanted to catch you before dinner."

"Oh, aye, I'm free. Come on in."

"Thank you." Lawrence shut the door behind him and almost changed his mind about telling him what he'd found, but given the moral lesson of the day, keeping yet another secret would have him feeling dirty to the core. He was just going to have to accept he'd be the cause of Richard's mood plummeting.

"Wanna drink?" He led him to the dining room.

"No, thanks. I won't beat around the bush – wasn't sure if I should tell you given how long it's been, but I thought you'd like to know..." He placed the three newspapers he'd been carrying on the table.

"What's this, then?" asked Richard.

"Fresh reports, just a day old, about an incident up in the Yorkshire Dales."

"The Dales?"

He understood the male's surprise – the region had been his old haunt in his younger days. "It might be nothing."

"Five men dead," said Richard, reading the headline.

"And the way they were killed is bizarre, to say the least – certainly not anything a werewolf would do, but"—Lawrence stepped in close beside him, peering at the article—"look at the names of the five dead."

Richard sucked in a hissing breath and ended it with a click of his tongue. "God almighty, I've heard of these fuckers – even met one or two when I was young. Their surnames ... three of them are from a long line of werewolf hunters."

"And I'll bet the other two were hunters, too. Also, take a look at where they all live."

He took a moment to skim through the piece. "It says they're all from the same village: Summerbridge. Christ, does nothing change?" He picked up all three papers, turning them over and inspecting them more closely. "These are all local papers to the area."

"Yes. I caught wind of this story yesterday and immediately put a call in to get the papers sent down here on a next day service. That village is a hub, isn't it? Of hunters."

"Aye it is. It has been for a couple of centuries, at least, but only the oldest of us know it. Werewolf hunters have thinned out since wolf numbers started dwindling, and the ones left keep themselves to themselves. You think a werewolf killed them?"

"Read this bit near the bottom." Lawrence pointed at the paragraph.

After a moment, Richard fell deathly quiet. When he spoke, he barely sounded the words out. "You think Selena did this."

"I really can't know, Richard, and like I said, I wasn't sure I should even tell you about this, but the woman spotted fleeing the village, covered in blood – the description matches her."

"It's a very loose description, though. It says she's a suspect called Jennifer Warren."

"We have considered that if Selena survived, she'd likely change her name."

"I didn't think she'd even know how to do that."

"Well, here's the weirder part: I dug around a bit when I read about this, and I heard the TV stations up north all ran the story, so I searched, hoping to find a photo of Jennifer Warren. I can't find any, but that's not the weird part – the weird part is there *were* photos, but they've all been taken down from the internet and any recorded news coverage. Every last one of them. I can see the placeholders – the links – where the photos were hosted, but no photos."

"What does that mean?"

"It means someone high up is involved somehow. This kind of erasure needs someone with special access and fast, too."

"Government level?"

"Possibly. But I don't know to what end. Perhaps it's just to keep the whole 'werewolves exist' thing quiet, but the extermination of The Trident was no small thing – I did my best in the year after to manage and deflect all potential involvement from the likes of 'special services'. If they found out Selena was in the thick of it..."

"*If* it's even her. Maybe someone's just helping out this Jennifer Warren."

"Or wanting to hunt her down themselves. If she's responsible for those men's deaths, I have no idea how she did it. No wolf can make a person bleed internally like that – to such a high pressure all their blood seeps through their orifices."

"So it's likely not her."

Lawrence said nothing to that.

Richard let out a weighted breath and dropped the papers back on the table. "What do I do?"

"That's entirely up to you. Like you said, it might not be her at all. I have someone looking into it for the sake of our own species' safety, considering the men were hunters. If you don't want to go up there yourself, I'll report back to you anything they find."

The older wolf sighed, pulled back a chair, and fell heavily onto it. "I had such a lot of fun this afternoon."

"I'm sorry. I didn't want to—"

"No, I mean life's *good* now. It's really bloody good. I wanted to find Selena so desperately, I still do, but ... god, this sounds bad to say, but the last couple of years, a large part of me made peace with her being dead – or possibly being dead. Doing this now – opening that floodgate again..."

Lawrence pulled out another chair and sat next to him.

"Maybe wait it out. Let's see what my contact comes back with and *then* decide if you want to go up there, hopefully with something more solid."

He turned to him, years of mourning in his grey eyes. "You've got beautiful children, Lawrence. They're my fucking sunlight, you know that?"

Lawrence gulped back a sudden surge of threatening tears.

"I want to find Selena. But it also feels like turning around and walking back into the dark – really fucking dark."

"Then don't," he choked out. "You deserve time out. You deserve peace. And you know how much the kids love you. I heard Jasmine took a shine to you, too."

"Oh, aye." He laughed. "Protective little thing she is. For some reason, she insisted on sitting next to me and making sure I was all right every time I got a little out of breath telling the story – out of breath for effect, you understand."

"Of course. It would be shit storytelling without the dramatics."

"Indeed it would."

They sat there in silence for a minute, each caught in echoes of the past.

Finally, Richard said, very quietly, "Let me know what your contact finds."

Lawrence met his eyes. "I will."

He nodded, still seeming far away.

"And no one knows I've been to see you about this, Richard. If you decide not to follow this lead, no one needs to know. Even if they did, no one would think any less of you, you know that."

The male made a 'harrumph' kind of sound and said nothing more. The mood had definitely altered to a more melancholy state.

Repressing a sigh, Lawrence stood, taking that as his cue to leave. Damn being 'the king'. Being Alpha was sometimes too much, but at least it was localised to the pack. But to have to follow up on these killings as a precaution for all the few wolves still living across the country...

He shut down the pessimistic thought straight away. Gunvalds were honoured to serve because the bloodline had always treated them well – or at least that had been his parents' teachings. Having cheated death and killed The Trident by doing so, he couldn't exactly argue with the sentiment, despite the nightmares that still lingered when he slept.

Nevertheless, he found himself needing a foundation he was estranged from – estranged through no fault of his own. He'd been looking into his bloodline; following their trail into history and the forests of Sweden – looking for anything resembling support he might have the fortune to lean on. Those regal, dense woods had recently stirred a yearning in him he had no name for – like a faint call home. A voyage to the Scandinavian country was something he'd been meaning to speak to Lydia about.

With somewhat doleful goodbyes exchanged, Lawrence left the grey wolf to his thoughts and looked at the darkening sky, streaked with orange – so typical for early October. He guessed it was just gone six o'clock. The kids would be awake and eating, and Ryan, with Tiegan or Adam, would be getting their own dinner ready – a dinner for eight grown wolves and two humans.

Dinner would feel very different to usual with such a congregation. And different again once Ernest Matheson left them, even if that was three years from now – god knew, *five* years had flown by. Three would be over in the blink of an eye. Lydia was going to be so upset about his retirement. This Thomas Guiley had big shoes to fill.

Picking up his stride, he walked back to the house, lost in introspection. With Jasmine's arrival came so many variables. Try as he might, no vision of how the future might turn out came to him. None at all.

CHAPTER FIVE

"My word, that was the best roast beef I've ever had," exclaimed Ernest.

Lawrence wasn't surprised. It was everyone's reaction once they'd tasted Ryan's cooking.

Taylor smiled. "It's Ryan's speciality. No one does it better, whether wolf or human."

Three mostly devoured legs of the meat sat on the table – *one* of the tables. They'd had to bring another into the dining room to ensure everyone could be seated.

Lydia was glowing, clearly enjoying the buzz of the company. She was also like this at after-parties on performance nights. For someone who had cut ballet out of her life for years, she'd swanned right back in with a powerful grace that had even surprised him, enjoying the social aspect of the art as much as the dance itself. The clumsy, capricious, waitress-cum-storm-wielder he'd fallen head over heels for, disappeared the minute the music began and she glided on stage – Queen Lydia arose in her place. He wasn't sure how it was possible he loved her more each year than the last, but he did. "I can't believe in all these years you've never had dinner with us," she said to Dr Matheson.

"Oh, client boundaries – you know how it is. Best to keep business and pleasure separate."

"Is that why you won't come and live on our land?" Her small pout managed to look both forlorn and regal at the same time. Ernest might be immune to it, but Lawrence damn well wasn't. Thoughts of nibbling that bottom lip suddenly took up his full focus.

"One of the reasons."

"So why the change of heart tonight?"

Ernest glanced at Lawrence.

He gave him a nod – might as well get it out there.

"My Lady, it will pain me so, but I should announce that I am due my retirement and will be leaving you in three years."

The room fell silent.

Lydia's eyes welled up. "No!"

"I'm afraid needs must, but god help me, I will miss you all so much."

"Ernest, you can't! Who will take your place?"

"That is something I spoke with your husband about just a few hours ago."

Lydia swung herself around to face him, scraping the chair hard on the wooden floor. "You knew about this?"

Wonderful. "Only for six hours or so. There really hasn't been a proper time to tell you, and I thought the news best coming from the doctor, himself."

He knew her well enough to know she'd just suppressed a huff. He was going to enjoy fucking that huff into an ecstatic moan later in bed.

"I feel like I'm always the last to know everything with all the kids around," she complained.

"You're not." He deliberately avoided her gaze. And he was pretty sure Taylor had taken interest in a spot on the far wall.

"I never know anything about what happens during the day until they're all in bed for the night."

Ryan stood and swooped down to place a kiss on her head. "I can still take them for you on Wednesday, sweetheart – all day."

Lawrence hadn't been completely truthful when he'd told Pete earlier that Lydia didn't miss her storm-wielding. She missed aspects of it, and anything that represented the independence and freedom she used to have *before* their six children, no matter how much she loved them. Nevertheless, she had categorically told them all last week she was happy to keep trying for more, for a couple more years. She cherished being a mother above all – he knew that – but the white, branch-like scars on her wrists were like tattoos that scored the past into the present wherever she went: the constant reminder of her supernaturalness, a reminder of *that* fatal night, and a reminder that he, also, carried the storm-wielder gene.

Storms had been and gone over the past five years – although none of them on a full moon since the night the gods had paid a visit – but they had all been 'normal' storms. None of them had kindled an ounce of wielding from her. No tingles – not even a slight buzz. Nothing. She felt both relieved and confused about that, and slightly apprehensive. The scars, after all, were still there.

Richard rose after Ryan, and then Lawrence did the same. "Shall we settle into the living room?"

"Sounds good," agreed Taylor. "I'll sort out the coffees and teas."

"We'll c-clear all this away," piped up Adam, he and Tiegan already on the job.

Lawrence was lucky as hell and he knew it. There might be only fifty or so adult wolves left in the country, but he'd surely managed to hoard the best of them into his home. *Your pack.*

A swell of pride took him over. He adored his pack. He loved his family.

The doctor had his arm around Lydia as they made their way to the living room – not really by choice as she was the one who had clung to him and not let go. Lawrence heard him mention Thomas Guiley to her. Then, he turned and looked back at him. "I have his file for you, Your Majesty, in my bag." The formality of their titles was completely unnecessary, but he knew Ernest liked to keep up appearances in front of others. "I'll hand it to you before I leave. And I did manage to speak to him earlier, albeit briefly. He's very keen to know more about the position here and was happy for me to pass on his number to you."

"Thank you, I appreciate everything you've done."

"We all do," added Lydia.

"Mummy?"

All heads whipped around to find Layla in the doorway to the living room, rubbing her eyes with one hand while she yawned.

Ryan was the one who strode forward. "I've got it, sweetheart," he said to Lydia as he walked past her. He hoisted his daughter into his arms, perhaps more vigorously than anyone else would, but it got a giggle out of Layla, and she grabbed his face with both hands and planted a wet kiss on his forehead. "Hello, Daddy."

"Hello, munchkin. What's up?"

If Axel and Christopher were Gunvald through and through, Layla was completely Ryan's girl. Her hair was almost black, just like his, and her eyes, although violet rather than his dark brown, contained the same hardiness as his, that didn't always look at ease on a three-year-old. Perhaps it came from having to loudly stake her claim over almost anything when amongst five boisterous brothers.

"The air feels funny, but Eli is too fast asleep and can't make it better," was her reply as Ryan strode out the room with her.

Lawrence stared after them, his hands finding their way into his pockets as he contemplated her words. What on earth she meant by whatever the air did was something they'd never quite figured out. She didn't smell different, or feel different, or look different at those times 'the air' did its thing. Elias seemed to be the only one who ever noticed any difference in her.

"Here – before I forget," said Ernest from behind him, just before a file prodded the side of his arm. "Because I will forget,

I'm afraid, at my age."

Lydia was now engrossed in conversation with Claire, Pete, and Richard.

"Aah, thank you." He took it. "I'll look through it and get back to you as soon as I'm able."

"Take your time. We still have three years."

"Those years will be gone before we know it. If I'm to consider Thomas Guiley, will you at least consider moving here – maybe for the last year before your retirement? The close proximity might even be helpful in showing Guiley the ropes." Did he sound like he was begging? It was daft how the doctor parting could have such an affect on him. Maybe it was the legacy of Hendrickson and Amelia's exit from the world, or maybe it was an odd foreboding brought on by almost every discussion he'd had today, from Jasmine's hazardous fire and her parentage – the fight with Taylor and agreeing to continue the lie – to Selena's possible re-appearance; to whether the lives of his own children hung in the balance of some ungovernable precipice, post-extinction.

"We'll see," replied the doctor, but he was smiling. "We'll see."

EPILOGUE

Elias woke up to the pitch black of night, unsure as to what had woken him, but he felt the same uneasy feeling he always did whenever Layla was upset or hurting.

In the dark, he looked at his two brothers lying in their bunk beds. They sounded asleep and they weren't moving. With care, he reached out with his senses until he thought maybe he was covering the whole house, but couldn't hear anyone awake.

He also couldn't feel Layla in her room where she was supposed to be. *That's what woke me up*, he suddenly realised.

Gingerly, he stepped out of bed as quietly as possible. The clock on the wall, he couldn't understand – there were no numbers – so he looked at the watch on top of the chest of drawers – Axel had gotten it for their birthday, although Daddy preferred them to learn the time by looking at the sun, moon, and stars in the sky.

He could just make out the numbers without turning on the little light on the watch. It said 03:25. He knew the numbers, but wasn't sure how early or late that meant it was, or when anyone would be waking up.

He made his way to the bedroom door which had been left a bit open. He crept through it, silently, then padded out in bare feet, down the hall, towards Layla's room.

Stopping outside it, he didn't have to go in to know she wasn't there.

He then went to Daddy Ryan's room and stood outside it. Sometimes she slept in there if she was feeling cold or sad.

Closing his eyes, he reached out, and could feel both his dads in there, but not Layla.

The uneasy feeling got worse.

He knew he shouldn't go looking for her – not outside where his senses were telling him she went – but he also knew he'd start to feel sick if he didn't find her and help her with whatever was hurting her. So, he went downstairs to Daddy's office and carefully opened the bottom window all the way. It made less noise than when he opened the front door, and the kitchen door had the handle just a bit too high up for him not to be clumsy with it.

He slipped out through the open window, landing on the grass without making too much noise.

It was cold, but clothes rustled, so he would have to be okay in just his pyjamas. He'd feel better, anyway, once he found Layla.

Using his nose, he sniffed the air, and luckily, he could smell her just a little. Her scent was coming from somewhere quite far away from the house. He knew he'd find her better and quicker as a wolf, so he took his pyjamas off, folded them, left them on the ground where he stood, and shifted.

Combining his sense of smell with the way he could feel her inside him, he followed her trail. He was scared. Something about her felt ... not good. And the dark was creepy because everything was so quiet.

He thought about running back inside and waking Daddy up, but that would mean it would take longer for him to get to his sister.

It was good that when he was his wolf, he could run for longer without getting tired, because it felt like a while before he finally found her. She was near the place Daddy Ryan had been inside this morning when he was with the man who came to check if all the strange blocks and wires were working okay.

He couldn't remember what it was called, but Dad had told him it was to help the electricity work in all the cottages they had and were going to build.

The humming sound it made wasn't nice. No wonder it was so far from the house.

Elias shifted back into human form. "*Layla*," he whispered, loudly.

He could see her. She looked so tiny in front of the big humming things. All the wires and lines across everything made it look a bit like a giant metal spider web. And the humming sounded like lots of flies.

"Layla," he called again as he approached her. She felt far away even though she was right there, and he decided he needed to make her see him before he said or did anything else.

He walked around her and stood in front of her. Her eyes were white.

It frightened him, but he also felt angry. Really angry at whatever made her eyes like that.

"Layla."

She didn't hear him, but he could feel she was in there. She was frightened, too.

The hairs on her arms were standing up, and the hairs on her head were also trying to stand up. It felt the same as when the air bit her, but this time, it was much, much worse, and the bites were bigger than ever.

But he knew he could make it stop, although he'd never tried it before when there was ... so much of it. He came up right in front of her and put himself in her mind, trying to get her to hear him. She didn't reply, but he stayed there inside her, anyway, so she wouldn't be as scared. Usually, holding one hand was enough, but this time, he took both her hands in his.

It happened straight away. The biting air jumped around at his touch, like it didn't know what to do, and then he let out a small sound as it tried to bite *him*. It didn't exactly hurt him, but it made him feel like he was inside one of those giant drills that made large holes in the roads. It shook him up more than it usually did, but it couldn't do more than that. And it couldn't find its way back to Layla because he was holding her hands. The only thing it could do was rush down his body and into the ground where it felt like it maybe died or something; like the earth ate it up.

He had to take some big gulps of air when it had all gone.

Layla blinked. And blinked again. Her eyes returned to their normal colour.

"E-Eli?" she stuttered, only just seeing him.

He spoke to her in her head first. *It's okay, I've got you. The bad air's gone now.* He felt a bit dizzy though.

"Eli?" she said again. And then tears filled her eyes and her face crumpled as she cried.

"It's okay." He brought her into his arms and hugged her.

"I c-couldn't s-stop it."

"It's gone now." He didn't let her go. They had to move away from here – if he stopped touching her, it would get her again. "We need to go, Layla – come on."

She stumbled a bit, but let him lead her away, and only when they were far enough from it that the humming didn't fill their heads, did she start to calm down.

"Why did you come outside?" he asked her.

"I don't know. It pulled me, Eli. It wanted me to come."

"You need to stay away from that place. Always stay away from it."

"I couldn't stop it."

"You have to try. It's dangerous to go there. Even grown ups shouldn't go in there without wearing special clothes and gloves."

"I'm sorry."

They finally arrived back to where he'd left his pyjamas. It was safe to let her go now, so he did and put them on.

Layla still felt shaky inside, but she was more herself now. "Thank you for coming to get me, Eli."

"I'll always come get you." He smiled. "We have to climb through the office window. You might have to climb on me a bit to reach it, okay?"

She nodded, and the fire-like light in her eyes was back. Daddy called her bossy when she looked like that – when she wasn't scared of anything or anyone and told all her brothers off, and even her dads sometimes – but it made him feel heaps better and he was glad. He liked it when she was like that. It was way better than her being frightened, sad, or hurt.

They weren't as quiet as he'd have liked climbing back into the house, and closing the window was harder than opening it had been, but after a moment of standing still and not making a sound, he decided everyone else was still asleep. He could here Daddy Ryan snoring.

"I think it's okay," he whispered as quietly as possible. "We just have to be really quiet going upstairs."

"Okay. Eli, sleep in my room tonight. I don't want to be by myself."

He felt the worry in her – that the bad air might pull her away again. "Okay. Let's go." He took her hand and they both sneaked upstairs like burglars afraid of getting caught.

Once they were inside her room, with the door pulled to, they both let out sighs of relief.

With a smile, Layla scrambled onto her bed and held down the covers for him.

He got in beside her, the relief overtaking everything and making him yawn. He was *really* tired now.

And then Layla yawned.

He didn't need to hold her hand now, but he did it anyway. At least this way, if the bad air came again, it couldn't get her with him there.

Layla groggily pulled the covers over them – sort of – eyelids already drooping as they huddled together to warm up from the chill of the air outside.

Her long hair tickled his nose, but he liked the smell of her hair, so it was okay.

That was Elias' last thought before sleep claimed them both.

ALSO AVAILABLE

Blood Shadow

Blood Never Lies, #1
An Eye of the Storm Companion Novel

This is the story of what happened to Selena in the first five years after the storm.

Aftershock

Blood Never Lies, #2
An Eye of the Storm Companion Novel

This is the story of Jasmine's first five years.

~*~

Further details can be found on Dianna's website.

To keep up with all new releases, works in progress, and general writing updates, please join Dianna on:

Facebook.com/AuthorDiannaHardy
X.com/TheWitchingPen
Website: DiannaHardy.com

Acknowledgements / Author's Note

New Reign: Eye of the Storm Legacy will be the new series that follows *After the Storm*. It takes place approximately fifteen years after this book, and the first novel is due out in 2027.

Many thanks to the usual suspects: Amanda Pederick, my editor; to Ninfa Hayes and Elizabeth Morgan for their support and encouragement; to all my readers for loving these characters as much as I do; and thank you to my family who copes with me writing ... and writing ... and writing.

Dianna Hardy
19th November, 2025

Also by Dianna Hardy

The Witching Pen series

Plus the companion novel, *Saving Eve*.
This is a complete, finished series.

Witches, angels, demons, Heaven and Hell all come together in a dizzying story of friendship, love and forgiveness. A titillating mix of paranormal romance and urban fantasy brings you a sensational series you won't forget.

Blood Surge

A Vampiric Urban Fantasy Novel

A beautiful library in a sleepy town in Hampshire is the perfect place for Sophia to escape a fraught childhood and forgotten past until an old lover borrows a book, a woman dies, a ridiculously gorgeous man keeps turning up around every corner, and a stately home party goes awry. It turns out Sophia's life (and past) isn't what she thought it was at all.
Passionate vampiric urban fantasy.

Once Times Thrice

Practical Magic meets *Serendipity* in a beautiful, fun, and magical series about love, family, and second chances, set in Cornwall, England. Follow Merri, Jamie, Pippa, Jimmy and Candy as summer turns to autumn.

Contemporary romance with a touch of magic.

Broken Lights

One gunshot, one scramble for life, one unlikely couple, one very long night ... can one damaged woman and one ordinary man, find the extraordinary in the very last second they're given?

Broken Lights is a standalone short novel of what's really worth fighting for, when one second is all you have left.

And Coming Soon

Fathoms Deep

A Blood Shadow Novel

Amid the white-washed houses of Greece, lies an ancient secret that will pull Laura and Roman fathoms deep into an atrocity obscured by mythology, and buried by aristocracy. Posing as man and wife, and battling their own villainous shadows from a past best left drowned, a she-wolf and a human afflicted with the siren gene, are about to embark on a deadly mission in the hopes of finding a cure.

13 Days

An Eye of the Storm Companion Novel

It was supposed to be a happy family vacation. But werewolf siblings, Hendrickson and Amelia, find themselves battling the lupine distemper virus that grips everyone in their rented cottage. The first fatality strikes. And there's a full moon coming, twisting the path of recovery. Pain heightens; boundaries fray; breaking point is reached. Survival is going to cost the siblings their future.

About The Author

Dianna Hardy is an international bestselling author of (cross-genre) fantasy fiction, most notable for her dark (often explicit) paranormal fantasy and the raw, intense *Eye of the Storm* series. But her heart-warming *Once Times Thrice* series proves she thrives in the light as much as the dark. Whatever your poison, what she loves most is to bring you stories that are action-packed, fast-paced and not short of heat, with the focus on character development, relationship dynamics, and the plot. She writes full-length novels and short fiction.

In December 2012, *Releasing The Wolf* hit the Kindle Paranormal Fantasy charts in both the US and the UK, where it stayed for three months, enjoying a highest ranking of #20. Both books in the *Eye Of The Storm* series have enjoyed success in the top 100 of Fantasy charts on Kindle US, Kindle UK, and iTunes (Australia, top 40). *The Witching Pen* series, *'Til Death Do Us Part* and *A Silver Kiss*, have also hit the top 100 of iBooks (Apple Books) charts in Fantasy, Romance and Horror in ten different countries worldwide.

Although quite active online, Dianna prefers the quiet company of nature and animals to the hustle and bustle of people. She loves anything paranormal (she doesn't really consider it "para"), organic food, walking barefoot, the smell of the woods after rain, and summer days.

However, she is also sustained by coffee, chocolate and the occasional vodka.

Having graduated from Richmond Drama School (London) in '98, she spent the next few years in a multitude of jobs (both acting and non-acting), studying anything that fascinated her, searching her soul, and finally found her passion where it had always been: at the end of a pen.

She currently lives on the south coast in England with her partner and their daughter, where she writes full time.

Official site:
diannahardy.com

Facebook:
facebook.com/authordiannahardy

X:
x.com/thewitchingpen

www.ingramcontent.com/pod-product-compliance
Lightning Source LLC
LaVergne TN
LVHW091114080826
845145LV00008B/1905

* 9 7 8 1 9 1 6 8 4 0 1 4 0 *